PRAISE FOR *THE IMMIGRANT*

"Mr. Petrovsky has written a vivid and moving novel set in the turbulent time of post-1917 revolutionary Russia. He has the gift of making the reader feel that they are actually experiencing that time and place."

—Charles Belfoure, author of *The Paris Architect*

"The oft-told tale of a teen escaping Russian persecution for the promises of America gets a fresh twist via some unique settings, including a traveling circus, an eventful ocean voyage, and the deserts of Arizona in Fred Petrovsky's *The Immigrant*. A story of survival from previous generations to inspire the next."

—Alina Adams, author of *The Nesting Dolls*

"Insightful and compelling. *The Immigrant* captures the resilience of the human spirit and inspires us with a story of courage. If you want to understand the plight faced by Jewish families in Russia during the 1920s, this book is for you."

—J. L. Witterick, author of *My Mother's Secret*

"I never tire of reading about immigrants who fled the pogroms in Russia for a better life in America."

—Gay Courter, author of *The Midwife*

"A young Eastern European immigrant struggles with issue of identity, love, and loss in Petrovsky's novel. In the Bolshevik Russian town of Komenska in Byelorussia, Lev is a seventeen-year-old Jewish boy who's forced to flee the aftermath of a pogrom. Leaving behind a peaceful past and his hopes for a stable future, he seeks refuge with an eclectic group of Roma travelers who call themselves the Aluşta Traveling Circus & Sideshow of Amazing Freaks. Petrovsky showcases the diversity of this troupe of persecuted people, which, in addition to its Roma founders, includes a Hindu snake charmer and a Middle Eastern performer known as the Amazing Exploding Man. Lev's horizons expand during wild nights with bewitching sex workers, conversations on freedom with a performer who sets himself on fire, and encounters with bigoted law enforcement. Unfortunate hostilities and unforeseen friendships lead him to board a ship traveling from Finland to New York City, where he works in a brothel on the Lower East Side and navigates conflicting local Jewish communities; later, he makes a move to the West.

"Throughout his journey, Lev searches for love, tries to hold on to the values of his childhood, and comes to terms with the traumas of his past. This work balances distanced observations about the world with the intense emotions of the immigrant experience. Petrovsky's prose is succinct and simple, reflecting the perspective of a young man thrown headlong into the perilous task of growing up. Lev's observations are carefully crafted to evoke universal themes; for example, he notes, upon arriving in New York, that "America is no better than anyplace else. . . . As an idea, it is genius, a towering light so bright that it blocks all ugliness and intolerance." The author adds depth to the novel's historical context by showing the complex dynamics among different ethnic groups, including conflicts between Southern and Eastern European Jews in New York and, much later, difficulties between Latinx and Native American people in Arizona. A nuanced and poignant coming-of-age historical novel."

—Kirkus Reviews

"Both timely and timeless, Frederic Petrovsky's new novel *The Immigrant* is a coming-of-age story set in a world of turbulence. Young Lev is forced from his homeland in Russia and, following a thin thread of family connection, journeys to New York and ultimately to Arizona in search of home, love and self."

—Eleanor McCallie Cooper, author of *Dragonfly Dreams* and *Grace in China*

The Immigrant

by Frederic Petrovsky

ISBN 978-1-64663-805-5

Published by

◄ köehlerbooks™

3705 Shore Drive
Virginia Beach, VA 23455
800-435-4811
www.koehlerbooks.com

FREDERIC PETROVSKY

THE
IMMIGRANT

A NOVEL

VIRGINIA BEACH
CAPE CHARLES

For Amy, our children, and all who come after

PART ONE

1920, KOMENSKA, BYELORUSSIAN SOVIET SOCIALIST REPUBLIC

1

On his seventeenth birthday, Lev was delivered to the Aluşta Traveling Circus & Sideshow of Amazing Freaks. He was certain he would never see his parents again.

"You mustn't be late," said his mother, hurriedly packing a small bag for Lev. "Your father will be home soon to take you."

At night, through the brittle walls of their small shtetl house, Lev had heard his parents arguing and then agreeing that the only way to keep him safe was to get him out of Komenska.

"I don't want to go!" Lev pleaded.

"You must. There is too much trouble," said his mother. "It's been arranged. We've spoken of this already. Let's not do so again."

Lev watched his mother fold his clothes and kiss each item before placing them gently into the bag. Two shirts. Socks. Scarf. A jacket for when the season changed.

"I don't want to go," said Lev. "It's not fair. I can be a lot of help." He folded his arms and raised his chin. "We can stop the Cossacks if they come. Dad and I can fight them together. I'm strong."

"*If* they come?" she said, mocking his naivete.

Lev swallowed and paused. "I meant when."

His mother shook her head. "You know so much, but so little. You're nearly as tall as your father, and just as handsome. You have his impossible hair and black eyes. And you're just as stubborn. Your father needs convincing about important things, and you've inherited that, too. But I shouldn't have to tell you that we could organize everyone in Komenska and it would not be enough against an army of Jew haters and their venom, their guns, their torches. All the children are being sent to safe places. Do you understand what I'm saying?"

"I'm not a child," said Lev. "God says I'm a man. You can stop packing, because I'm not going anywhere. I mean it. You can't make me."

Slowly, his mother raised a hand. Lev thought she was motioning for him to stop talking, or she was about to caress his face, but instead she slapped him so hard he bit his tongue. He could taste the copper tang of blood.

She looked at her hand, gathered her shawl around her, and went to the window. "Don't you see what's happening? Every day there are new problems out there, more businesses destroyed for the revolution. Lives erased. The temple is next . . . we're certain. You know this is true. Look at the smoke from the fires—you can barely see the sky. Do you think we will turn a deaf ear to arrangements that promise your safety? What kind of parents would we be? Please don't cry. This is hard enough."

She sat on the bed and wept.

"You're my only child," she said. "I know you're old enough to stay, but we found a way to get you out." She looked up at Lev. "I didn't want this for you. This is not the country I used to know. This land was peaceful and beautiful. The wind carried joy. And now—this. And on your birthday, no less."

Lev sat next to his mother and patted her knee. "It's okay."

"I'm sorry I hit you," said his mother, sniffling. "Do you see what this is doing to us?"

Lev hung his head. "I know why you think this is important, but please don't send me away. Why don't we all leave? We can go to America. We've been learning English. *Uncle Tom's Cabin. The Call of the Wild.*"

"We don't have enough money for the crossing."

"Then I'm old enough to stay."

"It's about safety, not whether you are a certain age," she said. "You're not married or betrothed, and you're still in school. It's only for a while. You'll be home when the trouble has passed."

Lev detected uncertainty in her voice. "When?"

She kissed Lev's face where it had turned red from her hand. "When God wills it."

• • •

It was dark when his father, Maxim, came home. Tall and heavily bearded, Lev saw him as neither kind nor stern, simply a hard worker who always left before the sun appeared and didn't return home until the last customer had left the shoe shop, where he cut leather and made dyes. He was mostly absent, except for the Sabbath, when he would come home early and tell Lev stories of his youth in Kiev. Lev did not doubt his father's love, but he did not see it often.

Lev knew he could not negotiate with his father. Instead, he showed his unhappiness by sitting in the corner of his room. Lev did not raise his eyes from the floor when his father appeared in the doorway. He saw his father's large, stained work boots step closer.

"Now," said his father.

Lev stood, lifted his bag off the bed, and followed his father through the house and out the front door. *It's a small house, anyway,* thought Lev.

His mother was standing at the road, crying. She grabbed him as they passed and did not let go until Maxim touched the back of her neck and said, "It's time."

She released her grasp and sank to her knees. "Goodbye for now, my son, my baby, my Lev," she whimpered.

Lev didn't look back. He didn't want to remember her that way.

• • •

Neither spoke as they walked through the village. Lev understood the danger of calling attention to themselves.

These were familiar streets. Here was the butcher. There was the small lending library. That way led to the wheel and wagon shop. As they walked, Lev noticed remnants of recent fires. He thought he saw a body under a tree, but his father turned him away.

Up ahead, the synagogue looked dark and forbidding in the moonless night. Lev saw a small gathering of people in front of it. Nothing good would come of that, Lev was sure. Was this the night God's house would burn?

"Don't look," said Maxim. He took his son's hand. They hurried down a narrow alley and up an incline to a small, modest house. As they climbed the steps, the door opened. Livsha, the rabbi's wife, ushered them inside. She was an astonishingly small, thin woman with a lined but kind face.

"Hurry," she said. "Come inside. How are you, Maxim? You look tired. But everyone has his own burden, no?"

Maxim removed his hat, touched the mezuzah on the doorpost, and brought his fingers to his lips. "Thank you for blessing our family," he said. "You know Lev."

"Everyone knows your boychick. He's taller than me already, although everyone is taller than me. Such a handsome man already. He's popular with the girls, no?" She pinched Lev's cheek.

Maxim rested a hand on his son's head. "The rabbi is expecting us."

"I suppose," she said. "Do you think he tells me anything? He has more secrets than I can keep track of these days. And to tell you the truth, I don't want to know what he's up to. I would worry myself sick if God weren't doing it already."

"He's a good man," said Maxim.

"You two wait here. I'll see if I can pry him from his secrets."

When Livsha disappeared down a hallway, Maxim removed a

folded blue envelope from his pocket and pressed it into Lev's hands.

"A few rubles," he said. "I wish I could give you more. This will get you by. Make it last."

Lev took the envelope and held his breath to keep from crying. He considered protesting, as he'd done with his mother, but thought better of it.

"I don't know when we will see each other again," said Maxim. "It may be a long time."

Lev wanted to remember his father's smell, his earthy, sweet leather scent. "I'm afraid," he whispered.

"Afraid is fine, but be smart," said Maxim. "And don't let anyone take advantage of you. Be as honest as you can. And find someone to love."

2

abbi Tversky appeared and gave Maxim a welcoming embrace. "You're almost late, but who's keeping time?" he said. "I thought maybe you changed your mind."

"No," said Maxim. "Lev is ready."

Rabbi Tversky wore small, thick spectacles that needed cleaning. He had the belly of a bear, but it was concealed behind a magnificent, unruly beard. To Lev, it appeared the rabbi's beard grew out of his nose to cover his mouth.

The rabbi placed a meaty hand on Lev's shoulder. "You are brave like your father. You know that, don't you, Lev?"

"I don't feel brave."

"Ah," said the rabbi, "an honest one. Again, just like your father. And before him, your grandfather, Avner, may he rest in peace. Listen, Lev, everything will be fine. We have made arrangements. Some people have gone through a lot of trouble for you, including your father. You are lucky."

"I don't feel lucky."

Rabbi Tversky laughed heartily. "I don't blame you. But all will be fine. You'll see."

Maxim took another blue envelope from his coat pocket and offered it to the rabbi. "It's all here. And some extra for your trouble."

Rabbi Tversky removed his glasses. "Thank you, Maxim. You're a cherished friend—a mensch through and through. But you know that already. We could stand here all day and have the grandest time and drink too much, which wouldn't be a bad thing. If you had come earlier, we could kibitz; maybe share a glass of wine. But it's late. You need to be getting home, too, before God forbid anything should happen tonight. Give my love to Vera. Say goodbye."

"We did," said Maxim, but he pulled Lev to his chest and kissed the top of his head. "My little man."

Maxim released his son, turned away, and hurried out of the house. To Lev, the banging of the door behind him sounded like a cannon.

• • •

Rabbi Tversky led Lev to a room in the back of the house, where he was greeted warmly by two girls his age huddled in a corner—the Shenker twins, Sofia and Sarra, whose father ran the tavern near the market. Lev had long had unholy thoughts about them. He wondered what it would be like to kiss them at the same time.

"Sit here for a while, Lev," said the rabbi. "And you," he said to the sisters, "be nice to him. He's had a distressing day. Well, like all of us."

Rabbi Tversky left the room. Lev sat next to Sofia.

"You don't look so good," she said.

"I guess you're happy about being sent away?" he said.

"Father says this is for our safety and only for a few days," said Sarra. "We'll be home before we know it."

"Do you believe that?" asked Lev.

Sofia squeezed Lev's hand. "We have to."

"It might be exciting," said Sarra.

Lev grunted. "This is forever. This is happening now. We'll never see our homes again."

"You don't have to always be so serious," said Sofia.

"If you say so."

Sarra cupped her hand around her sister's ear and whispered something. Lev pretended not to listen, but he was sure he heard, "I don't know."

"Maybe we'll all go to the same place," said Sarra. "The three of us. It could be fun. Of course, it depends on what the rabbi has arranged. He's already taken a few others. Efim Gulko was here with his little sister. We only saw them for a few minutes before the rabbi took them away."

"I'd like to think we're going to a rich family in Varapaeva," said Sofia. "They live in a mansion with dozens of rooms, a garden you can get lost in, and a bed of thick, just-plucked feathers."

"It's cold there," said Lev.

"Not when I imagine it," said Sofia.

●　●　●

Livsha entered the room, carrying a small plate. It held an apple kuchen, and atop it a single lit candle.

"For the birthday boy," said Livsha. "This will make you feel better, no?"

Rabbi Tversky followed her into the room. He clapped his hands and sang, "*Mazel tov tsu dayn geburtstog—*"

As the girls joined in singing, Lev stared at the candle and felt lonelier than he could ever remember feeling. Maybe it was more sadness than loneliness. Sadness for everything he'd never had a chance to do, for things he'd taken for granted, for the life ahead of him that was now in doubt, of being matched to a pretty girl, of his wedding night and its anxieties and promises. All of that seemed unattainable now.

"Did you make a wish?" asked Livsha, bringing the kuchen close to Lev's mouth. "Blow out the candle."

Lev closed his eyes and tried to think of something he wanted, but he could only see a gray cloud. Maybe he was being too negative. What if the girls were right, and this was only temporary?

When he opened his eyes and blew gently at the flame, a loud noise came from beyond the walls of the house. A terrible explosion. Distant screams.

"All of you, stay here," said Rabbi Tversky before rushing from the room. They heard his heavy footsteps and the front door slam.

This is it, Lev thought. The reason they were being sent away. An expansion of the intimidation. More people would be hurt tonight.

Lev sprang to his feet, startling the girls and Livsha, who dropped the kuchen. He bolted from the room, running after Rabbi Tversky, and joined him in front of the house where they were met with a wall of fire in the distance. The sky was alive with angry orange streaks and billowing smoke.

"Go back inside," said Rabbi Tversky. "You're safe here."

"No," said Lev, running away from the rabbi into the splintering night.

3

Lev imagined that he was invisible as he moved quickly through the village and away from the safety of Rabbi Tversky's house. *I'll be fine, as long as I keep going.*

The synagogue was ablaze. Fire and black smoke belched from open sores where stained glass windows used to be. Bands of burly, torch-bearing men with raised voices were defiant with drunken brazenness. Loose, frightened horses galloped through the chaos. Families with whimpering children and infirm matriarchs in tow pushed wagons and carts overflowing with hastily chosen possessions. The darkness was engulfed by the roar of the tumult. Lev felt small, insignificant.

He could have traveled less-public roads, but he was uncertain about them, so he kept to the familiar. He had come this way earlier with his father, but that already seemed like a long time ago. Where there were clumps of forest, he hid behind trees and pretended to be a squirrel until he arrived home.

The structures that had been his house and barn were gone. In their place were thick columns of flames that licked the sky and drew curling white ribbons across the heavens.

Lev ran as close as he could to the inferno until he was stopped by its heat. "Mother!" he called. "Father!"

There was no answer.

Lev sat on the ground and cried until he was limp. Then he watched the fire until only embers remained, and sunrise broke.

• • •

As Lev walked back up the hill in the early morning, Rabbi Tversky and Livsha opened the door and ventured outside

"I'll fix him something," said Livsha. She disappeared into the house.

"We were worried about you," the rabbi called. He sat on the porch and waited as Lev shuffled slowly toward him.

Lev yawned and stood limply before him. "I'm back," he said, eyes downcast.

"I see," said the rabbi. "We weren't sure we would see you again. But you're strong like your father."

Lev sat next to the rabbi. "My house," he said. "It's gone."

"And your parents?"

Lev shook his head and wiped his eyes.

"I knew you would be back," said the rabbi. "You left your bag."

The two sat there for a long time without talking. A hooded crow landed before them and pecked at the ground.

"I don't blame you," said the rabbi. "I might have done the same if I were younger. Still, everything was arranged for you last night. I was forced to take Sofia and Sarra instead. There was only room for one, your spot. But we managed. It will be harder on them, but God will make it work."

"I'm sorry," said Lev. "Where did they go?"

"It's better if we don't talk about it. But now you'll be taking their place. There's no choice in the matter."

Lev tried to speak, but words wouldn't come out. He swallowed, then coughed. "I feel sick."

"Probably the smoke. Your face is black with soot."

"I couldn't do anything," said Lev. "I shouldn't have left them."

"And how would things be different?"

"I don't know," said Lev. "Everything feels upside down." He coughed again, feeling as if a house was on his chest. A heavy curtain of weariness fell upon him.

"The sun shines brighter after a shower," said Rabbi Tversky. "But let's get you cleaned up. We have a big day ahead of us. Livsha's making something delicious. Can you smell it?"

• • •

Lev sat beside Rabbi Tversky in his small horse-drawn cart as they passed through Komenska. The destruction from the pogrom was not as extensive as the evening's fires suggested. Most neighborhoods appeared peaceful and untouched. But then they would come across a random business or home where nothing remained except smoldering wood and a stone chimney.

"They don't want to destroy everything," said the rabbi. "They only want us to leave."

"How do they choose where to burn?" asked Lev.

"Wherever their cowardice takes them."

They left Komenska behind and headed west through the open Russian flatlands in the direction of Glod, a village a half-day's ride away.

"I've never been to Glod," said Lev.

"We're not going there," said the rabbi, "although at this rate we'll be lucky to get anywhere. Solnishka is a good mare, but I can't push her. I could encourage her with a whip, but it wouldn't do any good."

Lev tried to think of other things to say because it was disrespectful to not keep up his side of the conversation. He knew he was supposed to comment about the horse or the countryside or to be inquisitive about where they were headed. But he could not shake the vision of his house and his parents inside melting into the floor. He didn't want to talk. He would have rather climbed into the back of the cart to sleep for a thousand years.

"Are you a righteous man?" asked Rabbi Tversky.

"You wouldn't be sending me away if I were a man."

"The Torah doesn't technically say who is or is not a man," said the rabbi. "What's most important is whether you are righteous, whether you believe in God."

Lev shrugged but said nothing.

"I only ask because he is with you. Or at least he wants to be with you. But he can't if you turn away from him. He is closest to those who need him, to the brokenhearted. He's an expert at saving people with crushed spirits. It's true, Lev. I've seen it over and over. He's sitting right next to you."

"There's no room," said Lev. "The cart is too small."

"There's always room," said the rabbi. "God isn't that big. He can fit in a thimble."

A short time later, Rabbi Tversky stopped the cart and turned to Lev.

"Understanding and dealing with loss is a big part of what a rabbi does," he said. "So, will you accept that maybe our thoughts are not so foreign from each other?"

Lev nodded. "Yes."

"Sometimes the best medicine is having someone on your side. But on with it now. I need to return to Komenska soon to deal with others who are grieving. You won't hold that against me, will you?"

"I trust you."

The rabbi pulled hard on his beard. "Not far away, we'll be meeting up with some people who will care for you. They have promised to provide shelter and protection, and they will be well compensated. They are different than you, Lev, but that doesn't make you better than them. Still, be alert."

"I will."

The rabbi put his arm around Lev. "You're a good boy," he said. "You don't deserve this, but this is how God tests us. He gives us what we don't know we need." Then the rabbi touched Lev's head and removed his worn brown yarmulke. "You won't be needing this. It will cause you more trouble than it is worth. God will know it wasn't your choice, so you shouldn't worry. I'll keep it safe for when you return." The rabbi folded the yarmulke and put it in his pocket.

"Will I?" Lev asked. "Return, I mean."

"If that is what you want. God listens."

Lev pondered what the rabbi said as they continued their journey. *This is an important day for me. I want to remember everything about it.*

4

olnishka pulled the cart up and over a modest incline that revealed a small clearing with a dozen brightly colored, tall, wooden medicine wagons, each with its own team of horses. Emblazoned in large yellow-and-black lettering on the side of the closest wagon was ALUŞTA TRAVELING CIRCUS & SIDESHOW OF AMAZING FREAKS.

Rabbi Tversky said, "The Roma. Or gypsies, as some call them." He handed the reins to Lev. "Wait here. If anything happens to me, Solnishka knows the way home." He climbed down and began to walk toward the wagons.

Lev called after him, "What do you mean, 'if something happens to you'?"

The rabbi waved at Lev and kept walking. As he got closer to the wagons, a tall, barrel-chested man came out to meet him. He wore a flamboyant, bright-green fedora and had a thick, long mustache with ends that curled up to circle his eyes like twin monocles. A leather sheath hung from his belt.

Lev couldn't hear them well, but it wasn't long before the mustachioed man began to raise his voice, stomp his feet, and wave his fists in the air. The rabbi handed him a blue envelope, but the man slapped it to the ground and kicked dirt on it. Lev looked at the reins in his hands and considered how best to encourage Solnishka that it was time either to rescue Rabbi Tversky or make an escape.

The rabbi continued to talk. He gestured in Lev's direction and said something that appeared to calm the man in the green hat, then picked up the envelope and held it out. The man folded his arms and shook his head but snatched the envelope from Rabbi Tversky. The rabbi offered his hand, but the man didn't take it.

As they continued to talk, Lev saw a fly land on Solnishka's back. The horse twitched, but the fly wasn't scared away. It crawled toward the horse's head and disappeared into its ear. Solnishka shook her head, but Lev wasn't sure the fly left.

Rabbi Tversky came back to the cart while the man with the violent mustache stood unmoving. The rabbi smiled and walked to the back of the cart and lifted Lev's bag. "It's been arranged."

"He looks angry," said Lev.

"Expectations," said the Rabbi. "His name is Smagin. Your parents and I had arranged for you to go elsewhere. He thought he was getting the girls. But we worked through it. He's waiting for you."

Lev's feet were heavy. "I can't get down."

"Our God who split the sea can handle this small thing," said Rabbi Tversky. "Don't fret over Smagin. He's got pins in his head. He's noisy, true, but he will abide."

Seeing no honorable alternative, Lev gathered his courage, climbed down, and took his bag from the rabbi.

"Good health to you, Lev. God willing, we'll see each other soon."

"No," said Lev. "I don't think so."

Lev moved away from Rabbi Tversky, Solnishka, and anything resembling brightness.

Lev walked over to Smagin and stood next to him. They watched in silence as Rabbi Tversky turned the cart and drove away.

"I was promised two young girls," said Smagin in a gruff, phlegmy northern accent. He pulled the brim of his hat down so Lev could barely see his eyes. "But you don't look like them. What are we going to do about that?"

Lev shrugged. "I'm sorry."

"Ah, sorry. I guess that makes everything fine. People apologize and expect the past to be washed away. But me? I don't think so. An apology is only words. It changes nothing. Whatever was present before, the apology is still there afterwards. Do you agree?"

"I—I don't know." Lev hoped his response didn't anger Smagin.

"What don't you know?" said Smagin. "Is it that you don't have an opinion, or that you disagree? Are you trying to provoke me? Is this how we will start things between us?"

"I don't know what you want me to say."

"What I *want* you to say? You can't think for yourself? Your rabbi tells me that you've had some trouble, but I have troubles too. I was counting on those young girls to help sell more tickets at the gate, make announcements in nearby towns. Who can refuse a pretty girl? And, yes, your rabbi would have paid me more. So what do I have now? Half as many workers and half as much money."

"It's my fault," said Lev. "If only I hadn't left last night, but—"

"I don't want to hear your buts," said Smagin. "Give me that." He snatched Lev's bag.

"That's mine!" said Lev, lurching for the bag, but it was too late. Smagin held it over his head, well out of Lev's reach.

"I'm thinking whatever's in here is mine," said Smagin. "Compensation."

"That's my property," said Lev. "My mother packed that bag. Give it back."

"It's my bag now," said Smagin. "It's part of the deal. Everything you have is mine, and I will keep you safe. This is our new agreement."

Lev, excited and frantic, shook his head. "Give it back and I'll leave. Please."

"You're not going anywhere. And the bag is mine."

"I don't think so." Lev kicked Smagin square on the knee as hard as he could.

Smagin grunted, dropped the bag, and reached for his leg. Lev grabbed the bag and ran.

Smagin growled, "Ungrateful!"

Lev sprinted back up the hill, down the road, and into a thick stand of trees. He settled where the trees were most dense, keeping a diligent lookout to ensure he hadn't been followed.

Then, when he felt safe, he allowed emotion and weariness to claim him. He fell asleep wondering if his parents felt pain during their last moments, or if the smoke had already put them down.

• • •

Lev woke to a series of hard nudges to his ribs. Smagin stood over him, tapping his boot against Lev's side.

Startled, Lev attempted to scramble to his feet, but Smagin pressed his heel hard into Lev's throat, pinning him to the ground.

"If I wanted to hurt you, you would already be swallowing your own blood," he said.

Lev started to speak, but Smagin pressed down harder. Lev could barely breathe.

"I'll put my foot through your neck if you struggle," said Smagin. "Then you'll be dead, and you won't have to listen to me anymore. On the other hand, if you agree not to kick me again or run away, and if you promise to listen to me, then I'll release you and we can be friends."

Smagin waved a *shashka* above Lev—a short, single-edged saber that appeared well used but sharp.

"Do we understand each other?"

Lev relaxed his body and tried to nod.

"Good," said Smagin. He lifted his boot and dropped the blue envelope on Lev's chest. "Here's your money. I won't force you to accept my protection. And I won't face every day wondering if you'll be violent or disappear. You are an impulsive young man. I can see you are stubborn and proud. Normally, I would admire that. But I was never desperate for this. I only agreed to take the girls because I understood their situation. It's the same with me. The Bolsheviks in Petrograd are blaming more than just the Jews. Most ethnicities and minorities are targeted too—Romani, kulaks, cripples, pederasts—though we're not as hated and hunted. They won't think to look for you among us. Still, they don't like entertainers like us because we're different. We're liars and cheats, they say. We'll steal their children and wives. We've been traveling west for weeks, stopping here and there to make money. But as long as we keep moving, they mostly leave us alone. Do you understand what I'm saying?"

"Yes," said Lev, rubbing his neck.

Smagin slid the shashka into its sheath. "We're communicating, you see. It's not so difficult. I am sorry that we did not get along so well, but you must understand that I accepted notable risk when I agreed to take the girls, and now you, instead. I don't like surprises, so that's why I suppose I acted a bit aggressive. I'm not normally that way. Well, I guess I am sometimes. Still, we might have had a mutually beneficial relationship. I could have used another capable hand. I don't see many whiskers on you, but I'm thinking you have a strong back and would have been a hard worker. I would have showed you great adventure and made sure you came to no harm. You would have been educated in life and love and gambling and women—all the things that make our existence worth living. But that's in the past now, and so you won't accuse me of being a thief, all your money is there, every ruble. Count it if you want. You are unharmed, and we can go our separate ways with no bad feelings. Goodbye, young man. We'll be moving on now. We have a show tomorrow near Torfyanovka. Perhaps our paths will cross again."

• • •

Unmoving, Lev watched Smagin part the brush and leave. He gazed at the sky and a lone osprey flying overhead. Then he sat up and looked inside the envelope, which was stuffed with rubles. He had never seen so much money before. He wondered how his father had managed it.

He figured he could make the money last a long time if he was frugal. There was probably enough to buy an old mule. He could travel the Russian countryside and take odd jobs, sleeping in abandoned barns. Eventually, he would change his name to Leo and pretend to be a gentile. He would apprentice himself to a blacksmith, or learn another trade that would make him respectable and earn him a comfortable living.

But hiding for the rest of his life and pretending to be someone else already felt exhausting, as if living a lie were suffocating. It would be easier to make his way back to Komenska, but now there was nothing there for him but pain and nostalgia.

Lev began to focus on Smagin's teased projections—love, life, gambling—which seemed more alluring and real than anything his life was promising. It was Smagin's last offer of women that made Lev feel as if he were underwater.

He stood, brushed off his pants, slipped the blue envelope into his bag, and walked back to Smagin's wagons.

● ● ●

All but two of the wagons were gone when Lev returned. Smagin was leaning casually against one, poking at the ground with the toe of his boot.

"These ants, they are devils," said Smagin. "We could have made camp anywhere, so of course we ended up on top of an anthill. But they were here first, so what right do I have to complain?"

Lev wanted to explain how his world had fallen in on him. Smagin should know about his parents—the delicate way his mother crossed her knees while embroidering a window curtain, how his father had taught him how to plant his feet when swinging an axe. But all Lev said was, "I'm sorry I kicked you."

"I was only going to wait a few more minutes," said Smagin. "The others are gone, but they're not too far. My wife, Natalya, said we should have ridden with them, but I said no. Why am I still here? I'll tell you why. Because I knew you would return. I'm very good when it comes to reading people."

Without saying anything, Lev pulled the fat blue envelope from his bag and presented it to Smagin, who looked at it, nodded, and scratched his chin.

"I'm not sure I want your money anymore," he said. He licked his fingers and smoothed his mustache. "I'm thinking the trouble you've already caused me and the trouble you're likely to be in the future may not be worth it. At the very least, your price should go up, don't you think?"

"This is all I have," said Lev.

Smagin's smile revealed two gold molars. He took the envelope and slid it slowly in the back pocket of his trousers. "I'm thinking that's not true," he said. "If you want to make lying one of your crimes, that's your choice. But I would be surprised if your parents didn't stuff your cheeks with a few rubles."

Lev considered running again but thought better of it. This time, he reached for the truth. "Yes, I have more money," he said. "But my father gave it to me, and you can't have it."

"Ah, but I could take it," said Smagin. He stepped away from the wagon. "I'm ready for you this time, boy. Smagin is a fast learner. Anyway, this is a simple thing. Give me the rest of the money now, voluntarily, and the moon will smile on us. If you prefer, I'll take your precious rubles while you sleep. But where is the chivalry in that?"

"I'm not afraid of you," said Lev. He dropped the bag and raised his fists.

Smagin clapped his hands and doubled over with laughter. His green fedora fell off, and an ocean of shoulder-length hair tumbled out. Then he picked up the hat and readjusted it atop his head. "You are full of surprises, boy. And now I see you are ignorantly brave. But—no matter. If it is your desire to die, then so be it. The ants will dine well tonight." He pulled the shashka from its sheath and swung it over his head.

5

Smagin was interrupted by a striking woman with long, straight red hair who came from behind the wagon, swishing her way between them. She wore a cheerful purple dress that stopped well above beaded leather sandals. Her yellow flowered blouse had wide sleeves, and a dozen gem-encrusted bangles sparkled on her wrists.

She slapped Smagin's butt as she passed. "That's enough," she said.

"I wasn't going to hurt him," growled Smagin.

"Of course not," she said, stepping very close to Lev. She placed her open palm gently on his cheek. "You've frightened the handsome boy. He's trembling."

With an exaggerated bow, Smagin said, "Allow me to introduce you to Natalya, my wife, a despicable creature who specializes in ruining my fun."

Her hand lingered on Lev's face. He felt frozen, frightened. "My, you are a pretty one," she said. "You'll be useful to lure women to our shows—young girls with dreams of kissing you, and bored wives who will fantasize about seducing such a young thing."

"He's feisty," said Smagin. "Be careful. More trouble than he's worth."

Natalya said to Lev, "Smagin thinks that because he's married to me, he can tell me what to do. He pretends to forget this is my business. Alușta is my name—not his. It was my father's circus, and my grandfather's before him. As for Smagin, well, he's a convenience. He's warm in bed, and he thinks that gives him privileges. If he were smarter, perhaps it would be enough."

"You shouldn't talk about me this way in front of others," said Smagin.

"I'll try to remember that." She ran her fingers through Lev's hair. "What's your name?"

Lev was hypnotized by her blue eyes and crimson lips, the way she smelled like frankincense. She was more alluring than any woman in Komenska. She also seemed more dangerous. "Lev," he muttered.

"It fits you," she said. "I see a lion in you, an old soul finely tuned for survival. Wary. Worried. But confident he can overcome. Your aura is very bright. But that name won't do, not if we're responsible for you. You need a secular name. We wouldn't want your rabbi to throw an Old Testament hex on us, would we?"

"He *would* do that," said Smagin. "I met that old-bearded wizard. He's a crafty one."

Natalya whirled about and quickly had her hands around Smagin's neck, her long black fingernails digging into his throat. "Do you see me speaking with the boy?" she snapped. "Did I ask you to keep interrupting? If you speak again, we'll have to take corrective measures tonight."

Natalya tightened her grip until Smagin began to cough and fight for air. She released him and held a finger to her lips.

Lev said, "Leo."

Natalya returned her attention to Lev. "Quick on your feet, I see," she said. "That's nice. From now on you will be our Leo, our ward, our son." Before he could protest, she slid a hand down the front of his pants. He inhaled sharply as she explored him with an expert touch that filled him with suffocating confusion. "Yes, you'll more than do," she said.

• • •

When Natalya picked up Lev's bag, he followed her to a wagon emblazoned with an illustration of orange explosions and billowing smoke that surrounded tall letters proclaiming THE AMAZING EXPLODING MAN. She knocked once on the wagon's door and called, "Mishal, coming in." When she pulled open the door, an odor of decay emanated from within.

"You'll start here, helping Mishal," said Natalya. "He's one of our greatest attractions. Famous throughout the world. Do what he wants, but be wary—he's tricky. There will be trouble for you if he doesn't perform."

Lev took a tentative step forward and peered into the wagon. "I can't see anything."

"He's in there," said Natalya, sounding impatient. She threw Lev's bag inside. "Hurry and climb in, or we'll be too far behind to catch the lead group before dark."

Lev stepped up and into the darkness. It smelled like something had died. The door slammed behind him, and the wagon lurched as the horses headed out. Lev stumbled over his bag and fell facedown. The floor of the wagon felt gritty.

An ancient, high-pitched voice came from somewhere in the impenetrable gloom. "I told them I didn't want an assistant."

Lev said, "It's dark. Where are you? It doesn't smell good in here."

"It's the sulfur. You'll get used to it if you stay."

The wagon was moving at a steady pace, so Lev felt comfortable enough to stand. He began to discern vague shapes as his eyes became accustomed to the dark.

"Can you light a candle?"

"Not a good idea," said Mishal. "Besides, darkness is a state of mind. Most people spend their lives rushing toward the light, trying to make money and destroying those who stand in their way. But to truly know life, and to experience enlightenment, you must embrace the absence of light. Only then can you see what's true."

Aided by a thin sliver of light that struggled through a seam, Lev was finally able to see Mishal, a miserably thin old man perched on a blue cushion at the far end of the wagon. He sat cross-legged and naked, except for the folds of loose-fitting muslin braies gathered at his waist.

"Come closer, my boy. Let me take a look at what they've thrown me."

Lev moved slowly toward Mishal, careful not to not lose his step as the wagon swayed. The sides of the wagon were piled high with wooden crates.

"You're wise to step lightly," said Mishal. "Highly stubborn chemicals in those boxes, you know. It's a wonder this wagon hasn't blown sky high with how careless the horses are, always rolling over rocks. Don't be afraid of me. Old Mishal doesn't bite. Sit. I have something very important to tell you."

A terrible odor emanated from Mishal, but Lev squatted in front of him and tried not to breathe through his nose.

"What do they call you?" asked Mishal.

"Lev, but now Leo, I guess."

"An Israelite, eh? Figures they would pair you with me. Actually, we're brothers, you know. We were one tribe in antiquity, although most people are either ignorant of that or don't want to believe it. I'm from Aqaba, a proud Arabian port. Have you been there?"

"No," said Lev. "I've lived in Komenska all my life. Never been anywhere."

"Staying in one place has advantages," said Mishal. "I am sure that you know all the secrets of Komenska, its hideaways and legends. You know the people, the butcher, the mayor, the beggar."

"I always give the beggar a kopek," said Lev. "My father said that generosity doesn't make a man poorer."

"That's what I mean. Your life is rich with family and village dwellers. Is there a girl?"

"No."

"Well, there's time for that. My life is quiet and insulated, compared to yours. True, I have seen the sands of Zanzibar and have walked the shores of Singapore. I have scaled the highest mountains of Tibet and entertained three sultans of Somaria. I have been with seven women at one time. But I'll never enjoy what you have—freedom."

The wagon swayed, and Lev was afraid crates would fall. "I used to be free," he said, "but not now. Actually, I don't know what I am. Now I'm told I have to change my name. Everything is upside down. I feel like—like—"

"Hush now, boy. Settle down. No need to get upset."

Lev rubbed his eyes. "I'm not upset. But it's good to talk about it."

Lev and Mishal sat quietly for a while. Lev felt the man's penetrating stare. He tried to decipher the writing on the crates. He wondered if Sofia and Sarra were having as much difficulty wherever they were.

"Do you feel better now?" asked Mishal. "We don't have to talk any longer if it's going to make you sad again."

"I'm fine."

"It comes down to this," said Mishal. "You're either free or not free. There's no in-between."

"Yesterday I left the only home I've known," said Lev. "Everything is gone, and I'm all mixed up."

"Then we shall be mixed up together," said Mishal. "Providence has matched us well. Two souls in pain seeking lost freedom. We can help each other. May I trust you are discreet?"

"You mean can I keep a secret?"

"I knew it," said Mishal. "The minute I saw you enter the wagon, I could tell you were someone I could confide in."

"I would never purposely betray anyone, unless—"

"That's exactly what I'm saying," Mishal interrupted. "You're a person of true character. I know that without having to pay that criminal Professor Orakam. Bah, he's nothing but a carny hack. He can't predict anything, but don't go telling him that. He's a fraud, is what he is. He'll turn the screw. But it doesn't matter, anyway. I'm through with all of this. From this moment on, I'm done with performing. I swear. Tired of all the theatrics and getting burned every performance. I'm done, I tell you. Finished. You have helped me decide."

Remembering Natalya's warning, Lev said, "You can't! Smagin and Natalya, they'll be mad. I don't know what they'll do."

"Oh, they'll be angry, all right," said Mishal. He laughed and pulled on an ear.

"Besides, you're a main attraction, right?" said Lev. "The villagers at the next stop are probably already lined up to see you."

"That's probably true," said Mishal. "I *am* famous throughout the civilized world. People fight for the best tickets. But it's too late. I can't go on any longer. I'm weary and old. Mistakes are creeping into my routine. Besides, I'm not appreciated, and the owners of this ridiculous excuse for entertainment are oppressive tyrants. I've tried to escape many times. You are certainly my last hope."

"I'll help you," said Lev, "but only if you help me. Stay a while longer. Teach me what you know. Then we'll escape together."

Mishal nodded but did not reply, other than a low grumbling noise that Lev interpreted as a noncommittal maybe. Then he reached behind him and brought out a copper hookah that he quickly lit with a mechanical flint.

"Don't look so worried," said Mishal. "It's only a small spark. Much safer than a candle or another fire stick. Even if the crates catch fire, the explosion will be so immense, we will be instantaneously blown to a million pieces on the way to Heaven. We won't feel a thing."

Mishal inhaled deeply though the thin leather hose and held it in his lungs for a long time before blowing five concentric rings. They floated away like smoke from a train's stack.

6

Sunlight from the open wagon door woke Lev, his body stiff from the floor and restless dreams. Alarmed that Mishal was gone, he hurried outside and saw the wagons had been arranged in a circle to display their promotional placards. In addition to the Exploding Man, other wagons promised The Woman Who Eats Dirt, The Astonishing Three-Headed Baby, The Snake Girl Comes Alive, Professor Orakam Knows the Future, and other equally amazing marvels. An extraordinarily large, blue-and-white-striped single-pole carousel tent was being hoisted in the center of the wagons by huge, bare-chested men wearing black wool hats.

Lev peeked inside one of the half-raised tent's peripheral arches and was immediately collared by a sledger. He had a deep crimson scar that ran across his nose from one ear to the other.

"You're the new one," he said. He grabbed Lev's arms and squeezed. "Not much meat. We'll work on that."

"I don't mind helping, but I need to find Mishal," said Lev.

"That old corpse? There'll be plenty of time for that later. If you work in Aluşta, then you work. And if you don't want to work like everyone else here, then the head of a hammer might accidentally fly off and take your scalp with it. If that's what you want, I mean."

"I'd prefer not."

"Then get to work." The sledger thrust a heavy post maul into Lev's arms and dragged him to the edge of the tent where others were sinking stakes into the ground. "The holes are marked. Pound 'em in."

Lev watched the other sledgers as they hammered the stakes. He tried to imitate their form, but the maul was unwieldy. The man closest to him forced a stake flush with just a few blows, but Lev could not discern any progress with the one he was working on. While his body concentrated on the heaviness of the maul, his mind drifted to the last conversation he'd had with his mother. He regretted the argument and wished it had gone better. *I was disrespectful,* he thought. *She died thinking I was unhappy with her.* Lev wished he could go back in time to reverse his impudence. On the other hand, he knew if he had won the quarrel and convinced his parents to let him stay, he too would be charred bone and ash. His next thought was that he was glad he was alive, and then he was ashamed.

After only a few minutes, he was unbearably hot and soaked with perspiration. He pulled off his shirt and immediately felt a breeze. He attacked the stake with renewed vigor, swinging the maul as high as he could manage and hoping gravity would do the rest.

Laughter echoed around the interior of the canvas tent. On the other side, three young girls appeared to be giggling and pointing at Lev. He wondered if they were making fun of him for his lack of hammering prowess, or maybe they were amused his physique did not measure up to that of the muscled sledgers. Embarrassed, he considered pulling on his shirt, but he didn't want them to know he was self-conscious.

Lev tried to ignore them as he worked, concentrating on hitting the stake squarely as it began to inch slowly into the ground. His shoulders already ached. When he glanced at the girls again, they were halfway across the tent, gingerly stepping over pipes and piles of thick ropes as they flirted with the sledgers. As they came closer, he saw they were grown women who appeared to be identical sisters. They were dressed the same, too, with white tops, teal dresses, and bright-burgundy scarves. Lev lowered the maul and tried to strike a confident stance.

"The hammer is bigger than you," said one as they passed Lev. The others laughed. "But you're cute. You should come to our show tonight."

They left the tent, leaving Lev intoxicated with the scent of sweet lilac swirling around him.

. . .

Lev hadn't finished hammering the stake, but the sledgers kicked him out because he was too slow. Although his pride was wounded, he was glad to be able to search for Mishal. But as soon as he stepped away from the tent, a large, clammy hand grabbed the back of his neck. *Smagin.*

"I've been looking for you, boy." He threw Lev against a wagon and leaned hard against his chest.

"They made me help in the tent," grunted Lev.

"You embarrassed me yesterday, boy," said Smagin. "Do I appreciate being treated like a dog? No, I do not. I am a man like any other, true? I am not an animal you can kick. You can call us Gypsies or Roma or whatever you want. We deserve respect, even from each other. Do you think I felt humiliated to be treated that way by my woman? And do you think she continued to treat me that way in bed last night? Yes, but that's none of your business. So, do you think I will take my anger out on you? Do you, boy?"

"I—I didn't do anything wrong."

"You being here is something wrong," said Smagin. His face was inches from Lev. He could smell garlic on the man's breath. "Everything about you is wrong. The way you act. The way you pretend to be someone other than who you really are. The way you think you can get what you want by your boyish charm and fake innocence. There is nothing I like about you. Nothing."

"I'm sorry," said Lev. "You're hurting me."

"Am I? Oh, poor boy. Such a delicate flower."

Lev looked in Smagin's eyes and saw hatred, but beyond the anger he perceived a man anchored in fear, control, and bravado that masked insecurity and pain. Lev maneuvered a foot behind Smagin's leg, then took a deep breath, closed his eyes, and shoved him with all his strength. Smagin, caught off guard, stumbled back but didn't fall.

"Leave me alone," said Lev. "I'm no threat to you. But if you touch me again, I'll make sure Natalya knows."

Smagin laughed. "Do you think I am frightened of her, boy? You have disrupted everything."

"Being here isn't my choice."

"Nor is it mine." Smagin stepped forward and punched Lev hard in the stomach.

Lev dropped to his knees and fought to catch his breath. Smagin patted him on the head.

"Give it a moment. You'll be fine, just breathe. That's it—good. I'm sorry, but that needed to be done. You must admit you had it coming. So, for now, let's call it even and we'll leave it at that. Or you can keep pushing me, and we'll take it to another level. You can dig your own grave. I can be more help to you than harm. You should worry about Mishal."

"I don't know where he is," said Lev, still on his knees.

"I don't care if you find him, and you probably won't," said Smagin. "You can waste time later looking for him. And if you're nice to me, then maybe I'll help you find the elusive bastard. But for now, you and I have a more important errand."

• • •

Lev walked two steps behind Smagin and one of the featured

jugglers as they headed out of the encampment and toward the small village down the road.

"This is Pavel Borovsky," said Smagin. "He's one of our best. It's always smart to take a taste of the carnival into town. If the people get a little excitement for free, they'll pay in droves."

"Nice to meet you," said Lev.

"So, here we are, a happy trio, no?" said Smagin. "But next time, you two will be on your own. Natalya doesn't like when I go anymore. She says I'm too tempted. There have been times that her suspicions were correct, true, but that's just between you and me. But who can blame me? Women are drawn to my mystery and magnetic personality. They are stuck at home with overweight husbands who don't know how to please a real woman. But in me, they see respite—salvation. They hope for excitement, heat, and passion, even though they know it's only momentary. Can you blame them or me? I'm only human."

Lev dug his hands deep in his pockets and didn't say anything. He didn't trust Smagin, but for now, it felt good to be out on the road with the world around him. He was free, though he knew it wouldn't last. Eventually, he would be concerned that Mishal had fled. He wondered if Natalya would truly punish him for that. As they walked, he thought about tomorrow, and the next day, and all the days after that. He considered a time when everything would be routine and his time in Komenska would be a distant memory, a prologue to all the pages in his life yet to be written.

"You're quiet," said Smagin. "You're mad at me, aren't you?"

Lev shrugged. "My mother said that people who talk the loudest have nothing to say."

"I see," said Smagin. "I would have liked to have met her. Your father as well."

"Don't—don't speak of them," Lev sputtered. "You're not worthy to even know their names. No matter how hard you try or pretend, you will never approach their kindness or wisdom."

"Is that why they abandoned you?"

"It was their greatest sacrifice," said Lev. He felt a tremendous surge of sadness.

"You're not afraid of me, are you?"

"I don't know yet."

"Well, that's something," said Smagin. "But don't be so fast to judge me. I was raised in three orphanages and then, when I was too old, pushed to the streets. I have had a harder life than you can possibly imagine. Now, stop pouting. The town is just around the bend. We have work to do."

* * *

The road widened as Lev, Smagin, and Pavel Borovsky entered Torfyanovka, a small village near Russia's western neighbor, Finland.

"We've been here before," said Smagin. "A tiny village. Small, but nice. The *traktirs* serve only wine and vodka, but that's enough. Pioneers and fishermen live here. The place wouldn't exist if weren't next to the border. Strangers come and go every day. Vagrants and wanderers are stuck here because they're denied border crossing."

As they drew closer, Lev saw the spire of a church and its yellow onion dome that stood out from the anemic skyline.

"The less you speak, the better," Smagin said to Lev as they made their way down the busy street and toward the village center. "Watch and learn. But remember this—when I call on you, say that you are afraid. Nothing more, nothing less."

"But what if I'm not afraid?"

"I don't care if you're invincible or constipated or the king of Siam. Today, you're an actor. It's pretend. Our job is to sell, so you'll sell. Understood?"

"How will I know when?"

"You'll know," said Smagin. "Blend in and be ready."

Smagin signaled the juggler, who trotted ahead to the wide wooden sidewalk in front of the dry goods store. The juggler withdrew a long knife from a deep trouser pocket and threw it impossibly high, until it nearly disappeared. Suspended in flight, the knife turned three times at its highest point and plunged violently down, where the juggler caught it cleanly by its handle before it hit the ground.

Instantly, the crowd parted and formed a circle around him. He threw the knife again.

At the knife's crest, the juggler pulled another from his pocket and sent that one flying too. Then a third. The juggler caught each knife and passed it to his free hand just in time to grab the next one. The knives were a whirl of metal and constant danger.

Smagin talked theatrically as he threaded his way through the crowd. "Behold, ladies and gentlemen," he said, "an authentic Borovsky juggler, live, here! A treat for you, famed throughout our country and beyond, and just a taste of what you'll experience at the Aluşta Traveling Circus & Sideshow of Amazing Freaks, only a short walk down the road. Did I say Aluşta? The most amazing entertainment outside of Vladivostok? I did! And now ask yourself, ladies and gentlemen, are you watching this juggler because of his skill, or because you hope he slips and a knife plunges into his skull?"

At that precise moment, the juggler stumbled. Gasps erupted from the crowd. The juggler contorted his body, eluding the falling knives as each sliced safely into the ground around him. Smagin stepped close to him. "The fantastic Borovsky!" he crowed as the crowd clapped wildly. "Some of you may have seen Aluşta a few years ago when we played your esteemed village. If you liked it then, I trust you will tell your neighbors that we are not to be missed. The highlight of the year! But now, I must tell you with a heavy heart that you may never see us again. We are embarking on a world tour and will give command performances to powerful kings. Western Europe and the Americas beckon our small company. I am afraid we may never be back. So, gather your spare rubles, just a trifle, and see us tonight at sunset.

"For those who saw us last time, you know the amazing sights that await you. For the rest, let it be said that you must not miss all the Borovsky jugglers, the exploding man who dies every night, our three-headed baby, and a beast who eats through his neck. I admit, this is not for the squeamish, but certainly no gentleman will want to be left out. Bring your women to show you are not afraid, and shield their eyes from the grotesque. As for children, we welcome them, of course, but be warned—their eyes may never be the same! Is there reason for alarm? I ask you—over there, the young man in the back! Tell me you're not afraid."

Smagin pointed at Lev. The entire crowd turned in his direction. To Lev, it seemed that they looked to him for reassurance, that he was their guide, their permission. Lev felt Smagin's eyes burning into him.

Lev exhaled. "It sounds . . . intense?"

There was silence for a moment, and then a chorus of laughter echoed through the gathering.

Smagin chuckled too. "Ha! *Intense? Frightening?* Well, maybe so. Who can blame the young traveler? He's only a pup! But you, my friends, will not be cowed, lest you be ridiculed tomorrow for missing the show. And now," said Smagin, bowing exaggeratedly, "I must bid you farewell. There is much work to do before tonight's spectacle!"

• • •

Smagin told Lev not to stray far from the village center. "Borovsky and I have an important errand," he said. "We'll be back soon."

Lev watched them head up the road. For the first time since his house turned to smoke, he felt truly alone, as if no one else in the world existed or ever would. *Anything is possible*, he thought, but he did not allow himself to act. He wasn't sure anything would be better than his present situation. He looked up at the church spire and wondered if those inside might provide sanctuary. There were commonalities among God's clerics, weren't there? Would a Russian priest be as sheltering as his rabbi? Perhaps, but the priest could be just as willing to deliver him into servitude as Rabbi Tversky had done.

Resigned, Lev wandered aimlessly through town before realizing that someone was shadowing him.

Lev had noticed him earlier when the juggler was entertaining the crowd. He stood out because of his height and slender countenance—a pale, rail-thin man dressed in a dark linen suit who stood on the edge of the gathering, a head taller than everyone else. He was aloof, the only one who did not look up when the juggler threw his knives into the sky. Lev had also marked him because he appeared not to have eyebrows, giving him an amphibian-like appearance.

Lev felt the man's eyes follow him and tried not to look in his direction as he moved deliberately down the street, but the man kept pace and didn't seem to mind if he was noticed. Lev wove his way past villagers and peddlers, in and out of shops, and down a narrow path until the man was far behind.

When Lev stopped to rest in an alleyway behind the stores, he felt a burst of chilly air. The man suddenly appeared next to him without a sound, leaning casually against a post next to him.

"You're avoiding me," he said in a menacingly nasal voice. "I wonder why. It makes me suspicious of you."

Lev turned to run, but the man grabbed his arm with a hand that felt like an iron claw.

"And now you try to flee. You can understand why I am curious about you, am I correct? You act guilty about something. Innocent people don't behave this way."

"Let go," said Lev.

"What's your name?" asked the man. "I haven't seen you before. I know everyone here—where they work, how many times they go to church, and how often they try to cross the border."

"I don't need to tell you anything," said Lev. He struggled to free his arm, but it was intractable.

"Oh, but you do," the man said nonchalantly. "It's my job to know everything that happens in Torfyanovka. Besides, I know you are connected to Smagin. Don't deny it; I'm familiar with his games. He didn't randomly call on you during his tease. You're a shill. But you're more than that, I think. What is your name? That's the second time I've asked, and I won't do so again."

Lev paused before saying, "Leo."

"Leo, eh? Why do you say it as a question, rather than a statement? I feel you are being untrue."

"That's my name," said Lev. "And I don't care what you think."

"You should. You should care very much. One of my jobs is to prevent Jews from leaving unless they pay the appropriate fees and taxes and are in possession of all necessary documentation. And you, Leo, or whatever your real name is, are as Jewish as the sky is blue. The way you talk, the way you walk. The deferential way you hold yourself. No need to deny it. I'm an expert in these things."

Lev was drawn into the man's magnetic eyes and could not look away. He felt as if the tall stranger were sucking out his soul through his forehead, and that when it was gone, nothing would be left other than a pile of clothes.

"You're with Aluşta, aren't you?" demanded the man.

Lev thought of how he should answer, but he felt compelled to utter the truth, even though it wasn't what he wanted. "Yes."

The man released his arm. "The truth brings light into the world," he said. "I'll be at your show tonight. Perhaps there are others of your lesser race working there as well."

The man turned and disappeared down the alley.

7

As Lev hurried back to the village center, he grew increasingly uncertain if the disturbing encounter had occurred. Only moments had passed since he was transfixed by the man, but it already seemed like an ancient dream, or as though it had happened to someone else.

Until the pogroms had started in Komenska, he had not been overtly aware of anti-Semitic hatred. He understood division among people; his family and everyone he knew lived on one side of the hill rise, while the Christians, politicians, and rural police lived on the other. But peace had prevailed throughout Komenska. Now, though, he felt his religion had marked him and that, inexplicably, it was something to be ashamed of, to worry about.

This is why the rabbi took my yarmulke, he thought, but the man without eyebrows had not been fooled. Lev wondered how his belief in one God was so obvious, and if there was anything he could do about it.

The street brought him back to the center of town, where all was normal. People were walking, determined, carrying bags and pushing carts and by all appearances going about their lives, the same as any other day. But Lev felt they were somehow different, as if they were sneaking glimpses at him and muttering slurs under their breath. He was certain this was only imagined, but he was worried and self-conscious.

Lev walked through the village center and observed how others behaved. He tried to observe commonalities about how they held themselves, how they moved through the streets and greeted people they knew with only a smile or wave. They *did* appear to walk faster than people in Komenska. He didn't see them stop to kibbitz on corners to share the latest news or ask how a sick person was getting along. *I must remember to walk faster,* Lev noted.

Wary of other dangerous encounters, Lev tried to remain inconspicuous. He positioned himself a good distance away from the busy village congestion, standing by the side of a building on a quiet corner but with an unobstructed view of the road.

· · ·

It was midday when Smagin and Borovsky returned. They stumbled up the street, flanked by two young men in police or military uniforms. All four carried bottles of vodka, obviously drunk. They were loud and disorderly, singing "Shiny Shine," a bawdy, well-known Russian sailors' shanty.

The sea, it brings me to your door
Your father says to come no more
You meet me down upon the shore
You share your shiny shine!
You share your shiny shine!
You share your shiny shine!
You meet me down upon the shore
You share your shiny shine!

The tide comes in and drags me down
You follow me without your gown
But just before we both will drown
You share your shiny shine!
You share your shiny shine!
You share your shiny shine!
But just before we both will drown
You share your shiny shine!

Lev stayed off the street until they came closer, then he ran out to join them. He felt an urgency to tell Smagin about what happened, but the man was clearly in no condition for a serious conversation.

"There you are, my fine boy," said Smagin, nearly shouting, his eyes glassy and half shut. His moustache, which once so proudly circled his eyes, was now plastered against his chin. "How kind of you to greet us. But should we have expected less from someone as bright and ready as you? I have entertained our new friends with stories about you, and they are equally impressed. Ah, you should have joined us. It would have been a splendid time or, well—what was I saying?"

Borovsky, who seemed slightly more sober than the others, said, "Smagin has had his share of vodka, as you can see."

Smagin shouted, "Vodka not imbibed is a sacrilege. Don't you agree, my fine friends?"

The four raised their bottles and howled at the midday sun.

Borovsky said, "I will escort the guards to their barracks. Will you take charge of Smagin and get him back to the wagons?"

"I do not need marshaling," said Smagin. "I am in full control of my senses." He bowed his head and vomited on his shoes.

Lev stepped back. "I'll get him home."

"I'm not as drunk as you think," said Smagin, leaning heavily on Lev as they headed back to the circus. "I can talk, can't I? You're Lev, and I'm pretty sure I know who I am, and there's going to be a show tonight. How could I remember those things if I were too drunk?"

Lev struggled to keep Smagin upright, half holding and dragging him along the road. He tried not to focus on the putrid odor of Smagin's vomit.

"Besides," said Smagin, "we were on a very important mission . . . I think I'm going to be sick again."

Lev kept him at arm's length and held his breath as Smagin gasped and heaved.

"I can hold my liquor," said Smagin. "And if you tell anyone I was sick, I'll slice your belly and pull out your insides." Smagin sank to his knees and appeared to lick the ground. "I'm fine."

Lev sat near him. "We've got to get you back."

"Give me a few minutes."

"I know you won't remember this, but a man in town knows who I am," said Lev. He felt relieved to tell someone, even a prostrate drunkard. "He made threats. I don't think it's a good thing—I'm pretty sure he's going to cause trouble for us."

Smagin groaned. "No one worries me, boy, but let's talk about this later."

"I don't know if there'll be a later. He seemed very serious."

"You don't have to raise your voice."

"He knew your name."

Smagin belched. "Everyone knows my name."

Lev was startled by a sound from behind.

He thought about hiding but couldn't bring himself to abandon Smagin, so he stood, put his hands on his hips, and presented what he thought was an intimidating scowl.

He was relieved when the juggler, Borovsky, came up the path.

"He makes a lot of noise, but he's a pussycat," said Borovsky. "Let's get him up."

• • •

Natalya stood, arms crossed, as Lev and Borovsky gently placed Smagin on his bed. The juggler bowed and said nervously, "Good day, Madam Aluşta. I must prepare our troupe," and then hurried from the wagon, leaving Lev to face her alone.

Natalya kneeled and rested the back of her hand on her husband's forehead. "It takes a lot to put him down," she said. Then she stood, smoothed her dress, and ran an index finger along the length of her bottom lip. "You've had an adventure today."

"Yes, ma'am," said Lev.

"He doesn't listen to me. He knows there will be consequences for his actions, but he still does these things, perhaps in spite of his punishments, often recklessly and always without thought. He knows you should be looking after Mishal, but he took you anyway, probably to show off. I think he's fond of you. Of course, he would never admit such a thing. It would display weakness."

They were disturbed by four sharp knocks on the wagon door.

"See who that is," said Natalya. "I'm sure it's the cook. Tell him I'm working on the eggs."

Lev pushed open the wagon door to reveal the tall man who had approached him in town.

When Lev stepped back, the man came inside without being invited.

"Perfect timing, I see," he said. He looked at Smagin, prone and still, then back to Natalya. "I hope I am not interrupting anything. You are precisely the three people I wanted to see, although I observe that Smagin is indisposed. Is it a coincidence you are all together? I think not."

"What is your business, sir?" said Natalya.

"My apologies. I am Grisha Krinsky, special agent with the Joint State Political Directorate. I am here under the express authority of the Council of People's Commissars."

"Naturally. And what is your business?"

"It concerns this boy, Leo, or whatever his name is, and your intentions of crossing from Russia. I have been charged with enforcing the Council's precepts."

Natalya turned to Lev. "I believe you have duties to perform. Please attend to Mishal."

Lev blurted out, "He—he confronted me in town and made threats against you."

"This is a matter between the gentleman and me," said Natalya. "You need not concern yourself. Please attend to your own business. It won't be long before Mishal will be called upon to perform." Then she added with definitive authority, "NOW!"

"Yes, ma'am." Lev tried to stay out of Krinsky's reach as he passed him, afraid he would be grabbed again.

He left the wagon, but instead of resuming his search for Mishal, as he knew would have been prudent, he hurriedly slipped beneath the wagon and pressed his ear against the floorboards. He could hear everything.

"Harboring lesser humans will not endear you to the Council," said Krinsky.

"I personally vouch for all my employees," said Natalia. "Show your proof or be on your way."

"I am never wrong about these things," said Krinsky, sounding smug.

"It must be comforting to enjoy so much certainty."

"I'm very good at my job," said Krinsky.

Natalia's voice became louder. "You're a parasite, just like the rest of your gang of thugs."

"The law is the law," said Krinsky. "That boy lives the Old Testament and, as such, must abide by the corresponding statutes. Those obligated to leave our prosperous nation must have state authorization, be in possession of the proper documents, and pay the prescribed fees. I encourage him to stop by my office tomorrow to begin processing his request. These things take time."

"As I said, he's not of that honorable faith. But even if he were, he would be caught in your government's web of contradiction. You are forcing them from their jobs and expelling them from the country, and so they can't earn money to pay your extorted sums."

"And you and your fellow Gypsies, your wretched Roma, are subject to the same edicts," said Krinsky.

"Your government—the latest government—has created travel requirements without logic," said Natalia. "They are despicable, but we are prepared to pay your price of fear. We have the required papers and your bounty of twenty-five thousand rubles."

"How unfortunate for you that the price is now, shall we say, fifty thousand rubles. And that doesn't include the boy and others like him in your company. You should come see me tomorrow, too, so we can discuss this. I know you want to ensure that your border crossing will go smoothly and with minimal interruptions. And if you don't have the financial means, I am sure we can find . . . other ways to ensure safe passage."

"You're disgusting," said Natalya.

"Only a realist."

"I'm not afraid of you," said Natalya. Lev pictured her pointing at Krinsky.

"I hope Smagin isn't dead. He doesn't look well."

"It would be lucky for you. You may go," said Natalya.

"I am looking forward to your show. I appreciate fine entertainment. Good day."

Lev heard heavy footsteps above him, then the wagon door opened and Krinsky stepped down.

Lev was careful to remain hidden, but Krinsky turned, crouched, and looked in his direction. "I know you're there," he said. "We have unfinished business." He dismissed Lev with a wave, then stood and disappeared behind the tent.

Lev tried to reconcile his first impression of Natalya—intimidating and controlling—with the one who'd defended him and did not wilt, even though the situation seemed bad for her. How could someone he didn't know him risk such great difficulty? Smagin, too, seemed slightly less the monster he was yesterday.

For now, though, Mishal was on Lev's mind. He needed to get this right. He walked around the compound and was impressed at its transformation. Large canvas banners and flags had been raised on the side of the tent closest to the road. Torches circled the wagons. As the sun faded, there was already a small crowd of villagers gathering awaiting admission.

On a whim, Lev checked Mishal's wagon, where he caught the old man taking items out of the bag his mother packed. Angry, Lev grabbed his bag from Mishal, who gave it up without a struggle.

"I was putting everything back," said Mishal in his sing-song voice. "I didn't think you'd mind. It's a harmless way to learn about people. Someone packed it with care."

"My mother."

"I wasn't sure I could trust you, but now I see you come from a good home with parents who cared for you a great deal. I didn't find anything that would make me worry. But there is a modest amount of money in there."

"I know."

"You can count it if you like. I didn't take anything."

"You had no right."

"I am truly sorry. I can see you are upset. I couldn't bear losing your trust so early in our relationship."

"I didn't rummage through *your* things, even though I had the opportunity."

"It says a lot about you that you didn't. I think most people would have because of curiosity that originates from a dark place. I wouldn't have minded. I have no valuables, nor anything to hide. Are you aware there is a letter to you in the bag? It's still sealed, don't worry."

"A letter?" Lev dug into the bag and found it at the bottom—a small, folded envelope with his name written in his mother's compact, shaky script. He brought the envelope to his nose and thought he could smell her familiar scent of soap and fresh-baked bread. He opened it carefully and heard her voice again.

Lev. If it is true that a drop of love can bring a sea of tears, then I am certain we all will drown. I do not know what the future will bring, but God willing, let only good things come our way. We deserve something good if there is balance in this world, as they say. I know you are upset, and I don't blame you. But I hope your anger will fade. I could not live thinking that you will stay mad at us forever. Our hearts are equally broken. Please do not doubt that you are the most loved person in our world. We will miss you every day, every meal, every time your voice would normally be pestering us with questions. But knowing you will be safe helps calm our panic. We are counting the days until you return. Rabbi Tversky has told us the name of the town to which you will likely be taken. If things settle down here, perhaps we will try to visit you there, although it may not be possible. In the meantime, please make smart decisions. We cannot wait to hold you in our arms again and hear all about your adventures. I'm sure we won't recognize our boy and that you will be an independent man when our eyes next rest upon you, with the grace of God. Goodbye, my sweet love.

Your loving mother.

Lev breathed through the pounding in his ears. He wiped his face and read the letter again. He doubted the pain would ever subside.

"Tears are sacred," said Mishal.

Lev slid the letter back in the envelope. "Thank you for finding it," he said quietly. "I didn't know it was there. I'm sorry for being cross with you."

"Words of support from loved ones, no?"

"Yes," said Lev, "and sad."

"One and the same," said Mishal. He poured two glasses of dark liquid from a slender decanter. "Drinking is frowned upon by my homeland, but it was also the cradle of wineries through antiquity. I reconcile the two by only drinking occasionally. Now is a suitable time.

It's medovukha. Honey and water never tasted so good." He held out a glass of the deep maroon spirit to Lev.

"I shouldn't." He reached for it anyway. "My father used to let me drink a little on the Sabbath. Sometimes more than a little."

"Let us drink to our parents. To yours and mine." Mishal dipped his tongue in the medovukha. "I can't tell you how good it feels to be done with this terrible job. For the first time since I can remember, I feel free. A great weight has been lifted, and I have you to thank. Do you know what I'll do now, Lev? I am going to watch the show from the audience. I have always wanted to see it from a different point of view."

"There are people lining up out there expecting to see you. You can't disappoint them."

"I'm through with it," said Mishal. "Done. Over. Kaput."

Lev set the glass on the floor and considered the withering person before him. He thought of his parents' sacrifice, and how Natalya had defended him against Krinsky's threats. He recalled his early Talmudic studies about responsibility. Starting with Adam and Eve, it was clear there was no hiding from God, who expected people to follow through on their promises.

He stepped closer and lowered his voice to make sure Mishal knew he was serious. "I have had enough of people ordering me around. That goes for you too. You're important to the sideshow, and you know it. Don't take advantage of me. You would have retired a long time ago if you could, but you waited until I got here. Stop trying to manipulate me."

Mishal frowned. "I haven't told *you* what you must do. I am only saying where my destiny awaits. I choose for me."

"You'll perform if I have to drag you there," said Lev. "Do you think you're the only one with responsibilities? They gave me one job."

"This has nothing to do with you."

"It has everything to do with me. You will perform, and I swear that on whatever god you worship. What do you think Natalya will do with a clumsy failure that causes them problems?"

Mishal shrugged. "That's of no concern to me."

"I'm serious."

"I can see that."

"Don't patronize me."

Mishal was silent. He sipped some medovukha, scratched his neck, and, Lev thought, looked defeated. "For you, I'll do it. But only this one time. After this, I'm through. But this is bondage, and you'll have to live with knowing that you are my master today. I'm giving up my freedom for you, young man. You are no different than all the others who have enslaved me. I thought you were better than that."

"I'm not," said Lev.

"If only you understood my sadness," said Mishal.

8

Mishal rose, drained his glass and, with a pathetic flip, tossed it to the floor, where it tumbled and rolled away without shattering.

"Ah, so be it," said Mishal. "That is emblematic of my life. If I'm to perform a final show, then I shall make it my best. Help me into my costume, boy. Once again into the fire!" He pushed the fabric off his shoulders. The braies dropped to his ankles, revealing a naked man with pronounced ribs and limbs like twigs. Immediately sad for him, Lev regretted speaking so harshly. "In the corner. The metal chest. Help me dress. You can do that for me, no?"

Lev opened the top of the weathered box. There, atop a bed of red fabric, was a folded garment. He lifted it up to reveal a faded golden jumpsuit with blue sequins sewn into the seams. He held it open as Mishal stepped into it, then buttoned the back to create a gaudy picture of baggy excess.

"Now the cape," said Mishal.

Lev pulled the red fabric from the chest. It was surprisingly bulky.

When he raised it high, it unfurled with a metallic clanking sound. The outside of the cape was smooth, crimson velvet, charred and patched in numerous places with small black holes throughout. Sewn into the other side of the cape was a hidden wire frame of hinges and metal plates that carried four heavy steel tubes.

"Hold it there a moment," said Mishal. He opened one of the wooden boxes and withdrew several pieces of thin explosives. He inserted one into each of the cape's pipes and connected them with lengthy pieces of fuse. Then he screwed thick black metal caps into the ends of the pipes. "The trick is to simulate a delightfully horrific explosion while staying safe. The pipes contain the combustion, rendering them harmless to me. It's a noisy and impeccable illusion, I'm pleased to say."

"It looks dangerous," said Lev.

"Not to worry, my friend. The black suppression caps are carbon steel. I had them and the pipes specially fused with iron and nickel by a very skilled Khabarovsk blacksmith. I'm perfectly safe, although sometimes, yes, the heat can cause minor burns. But the secret to delivering thrills is to make the illusion simple and repeatable. Things go wrong when elements are overly complex, or when one must count on precise timing or a particular skill. That's the beauty of my show, and I've done it more times than I can count. You'll see. I climb the central pole. At its zenith, I ignite the apparatus. The people below see smoke, a blinding flash, and a very loud bang that causes them to recoil and blink. They can't help it. At that precise moment, I escape through the top flap."

· · ·

Lev watched from the staging entrance as the audience filed into the tent, chattering with anticipation as they took their seats. It wasn't long before it appeared to be filled to near capacity. As Lev scanned the crowd, looking for Krinsky, a large hand slapped him on the shoulder.

Smagin looked weary but infinitely better than the last time Lev saw him. His moustache was again standing at attention, ringing his half-open eyes.

"Watch me carefully, boy," said Smagin. "I've performed in worse shape, but if I pass out, prop me up and throw a little water on my face."

"You don't look so good," said Lev.

"I'm a professional," said Smagin. Then he strode past Lev and into the center of the tent, extended his arms as if holding Atlas's immense globe, and shouted, "Ladies and gentlemen, lend me your ears!"

The audience stopped talking immediately. There was supreme silence in the arena.

"Those words, first spoken by Mark Antony in William Shakespeare's *Julius Caesar*, were uttered before a wondrous funeral. And here, within this great tent tonight, we will conduct our own funeral. Here, we shall bury the mundane, the ordinary, the ubiquitous sloth of daily routines. Together, we will dig down six feet and throw dirt upon everything trite and predictable. So be it! For our small company knows why you have come, and we intend to fulfill your deepest desires, your darkest hopes, your simmering wishes of observing brutish beasts. Here, you will witness the world's most incredible mysteries. Do not doubt me, whether you are young or old. I am here to speak the truth. And now, a small warning for the weaker sex, or even, perhaps, boys and men with delicate constitutions—know that what you are about to behold may shock and sicken you, so do not hesitate to shield your eyes if necessary and ask a companion to narrate what you're missing. But enough talk, my friends. You are duly warned and fully prepared for an evening of scandalous and unprecedented spectacle. Behold, the Indian Snake Charmer!"

Smagin bowed deeply, backed out of the tent, and slumped to the ground next to Lev. Breathing shallowly, he appeared physically spent. Lev kneeled and saw that Smagin's eyes were closed.

"Do you want me to help you back to your wagon?" asked Lev.

"I'll get through it," whispered Smagin. "Get me up when the box is opened."

"What box?"

Hurrying past them was a Hindu man wearing a tall, ochre-colored turban. He held a thick wooden pungi flute and rolled a long, multicolored crate into the center of the arena. He sat next to the crate, crossed his legs, and lifted the pungi to his lips. He blew into the instrument, which emitted a reedy, mournful sound, a hypnotic melody that weaved in and out and repeated without end. The audience leaned forward in their seats in excited anticipation. Like everyone else, Lev could see that the man was directing the wordless song toward the box, as if trying to wake whatever was inside. After a few minutes, the turbaned figure slowly began to rise and pointed the pungi to the sky as he continued to play. Then he walked around the crate and played faster, evoking a sense of urgency.

The top of the crate snapped open, and its sides collapsed to reveal an abomination—a naked woman with no arms or legs. She was facedown and squirming to the music, swaying to the song's rhythm. The man with the turban crouched next to the woman and played directly to her. Fleshy stumps bobbed where her legs should have been. Her shoulders were swaying, absent of appendages. She held her head up and looked straight ahead.

A great noise rose from the crowd as they talked, called out, and pointed.

Lev said to Smagin, "The box."

Smagin's eyes snapped open, and he stood.

"Is she real?" asked Lev.

"There's never been a more real person, my boy."

Smagin walked into the tent and stepped close to the performers. "Ladies and gentlemen, behold! The astonishing snake girl! If your eyes are shielded, then you are missing what is truly one of the wonders of the world. And for our young guests, we graciously offer this as an invaluable education. And now, for my promise! If you don't agree that this show has already been worth your rubles, then please see me for an immediate refund."

Smagin helped the man fold up and attach the sides and lid of the crate. Then the man pushed the crate out of the tent.

"That is only an appetizer!" said Smagin. "Next, as we shared with you in the village today, you are truly fortunate to see the most accomplished athletes you will ever encounter. The Borovskys and their knives of death!"

Pavel Borovsky ran into the tent, trailed by five other men and a goat on a short leash. They were dressed identically in skin-tight, flesh-colored mesh leotards that presented their impressive muscles. They surrounded the goat, standing shoulder to shoulder, and began tossing knives to each other in frightful arcs that threatened to impale the defenseless animal.

Smagin shuffled out of the tent and approached Lev. "Where's Mishal?"

"He was here a moment ago. He's ready."

"If he were ready, he would be here. Do you know how much money I've been forced to refund because of him? He's missed several performances over the past few months. Tonight won't be one of them. I suggest you find him. He's on soon."

Lev turned but was stopped by three women standing in front of the exit, those who had made fun of him earlier in the day while helping the sledgers drive stakes. He remembered how they'd smelled of lilac, but now it seemed more like lavender, nearly overpowering, as if they had bathed in it and brought the steam with them. They stepped closer and began to circle him. One touched his ear.

"You're in a hurry," said one of the women, but he didn't know which one. They were indistinguishably dressed in identical black robes. Their faces looked painted on, especially the ruby red of their lips and ivory teeth that he believed could devour him.

"You're going to miss our show if you leave," said one. "Why would you want to do that? Don't you want to see us?"

"I—I d-do," Lev stammered. "But I need to f-find . . . I mean I have to go. I need t-to—"

"Shhh," said another. She put a long finger against his lips. It felt warm. He wanted to know if it tasted of sugar or salt. "We're famous, you know, though no one ever sees us."

"True," said another. "We're stuck under the floor as it's wheeled out. We operate the three-headed baby. Our cries are so realistic, you'd swear the puppet is real."

"You're fresher than those tired workers we know so well," said the woman closest to him. "You should come see us after the show tonight."

Lev felt a hand brush against and then linger on the back of his pants.

"I have to find Mishal," he said. "I'm serious."

The sisters came closer to Lev. They pressed their bodies against his and locked him within their triangle. "He smells like a newborn baby. But you're not one, are you?"

"I'm not a baby," said Lev. The lavender fragrance was making him dizzy, as if the women had cast a spell upon him. He felt his stomach filling up with a delirious emptiness. "If I don't find him—Mishal, I mean—it'll be bad for me."

"Oh, fah," one said. "That old man has been causing trouble forever."

"We'll let you go, but only if you come see us tonight. We'll be at the fire. Find us there."

"Yes," said Lev.

"Do you promise?"

"I promise," he said. The sisters took a step back, allowed him to pass, and he hurried from the tent. When a voice came from the sky, he thought it was Eros calling to warn or entice him. But it was only Mishal, who was standing atop the tent near a rope ladder.

"I was looking for you, young man," said Mishal. "Inspecting things up here to make sure the exit works well. It should have been your job, but I couldn't find you. I'm too old to be climbing ladders every day. Help me down."

• • •

Smagin, now more tired than drunk, addressed the crowd for a final time. "My friends, as if you have not been astonished enough, we present to you our finale," he said, his head back and arms outstretched, as if he were about to ascend to heaven. "We have traveled far over the years, from the Sea of Okhotsk to Ekaterinburg in the Ural Mountains. We have played to crowds large and small, great cities and villages, fabulous pageants, and the tiniest of private celebrations. Our wandering troop of talented nomads has changed over the years, but one thing has remained constant with Aluşta—a show so remarkable that it ceases to exist with every show, somehow reborn time and again to trouble the eyes of those who behold its perfection. You come to conquer your fears and to see things you believe are only rumor. But let us be truthful with each other, shall we? You come to tempt fate, to see ugliness and monsters—and if you're lucky, to grasp death. Shall I disappoint you? Of course not. Why? Because you've come to see the Amazing Exploding Man, have you not?"

Transfixed, Lev watched as Smagin turned in circles, his arms extended as the audience whistled and clapped. Into the din strode Mishal, who appeared much taller and confident than Lev had seen him. In his golden jumpsuit and heavy crimson cape, Mishal stepped with exaggerated grandeur as he and Smagin traded places. Mishal, his sequins sparkling and each boot landing with purpose, walked close to the cheering audience, raised his arms, and clasped his hands in triumph. Lev thought he looked like he was taking a victory lap in advance of his accomplishment.

Mishal recognized the adoration by bowing and nodding, then moved to the ladder that ran up the center pole. There, he hung his head as if in prayer, and the audience became very quiet. There was silence for an interminably long time, until, finally, Mishal raised a hand and rested it on a rung. Then another hand. And suddenly, he began a slow ascent up the ladder, stopping occasionally to wave to the crowd. Lev watched carefully, admiring Mishal's showmanship, thinking that maybe he could learn to entertain people the same way.

When Mishal reached the top, he waved a final time and pulled the cape tightly against his body.

Then, there was a loud pop, an arresting flash of white light, and a deafening explosion that brought screams from the audience.

The top of the tent was awash in billows of smoke and fire, and bits of debris streamed down. After the initial scare, the crowd settled down, and, like Lev, watched as the cloud dissipated to reveal a large, jagged black hole in the tent where Mishal had been. A roar of approval erupted from the audience.

● ● ●

The audience, exhausted and satisfied, stood, stretched, and slowly began to leave.

Lev went outside and waited by the rope ladder, where he'd earlier helped Mishal down. When he did not appear, Lev decided he had missed him and that he was already sucking on the hookah tube.

But the only thing he found in Mishal's wagon was an earthy smell and a strange emptiness. Lev felt uneasy.

He glanced around the cluttered space. Horrified, he saw the four black steel containment caps that he'd helped secure. They were on Mishal's faded blue cushion, arranged in a tight row like posed matryoshka dolls.

Lev jumped from the wagon, hurried to the tent, and scurried up the ladder to see that the canvas roof was splattered with a fine mist of blood and small, scattered clumps of tissue.

Lev observed the horrible carnage and swallowed. His eyes watered. Acid rose and stung his throat, but he fought it back.

He sat on the edge of the tent next to the ladder, legs dangling. *I'm not getting off this roof*, he thought. *Let the moon take me far away and back to my small room and the brown furniture, the chores and candles, the Torah and arranged marriages, the mandel bread and people who didn't need to verbalize love to express it.*

Lev remained there for a very long time, sorting the past from his future, until a sledger slapped his foot. "The tent must come down now, boy."

Without protesting, Lev climbed down. He walked around the tent and into Smagin's wagon, where he found him and Natalya sitting at a small table, drinking Ararat brandy from thimble-sized glasses. Smagin was struggling to remove a boot.

"Help me with this confounded thing," he said, his voice tired and raspy.

Lev straddled Smagin's boot and pulled up on the heel until it slid off.

"Something is wrong," said Natalya. "It is written on your face. Why so glum? You did well, coaxing the old man to please the crowd. It was a good show tonight. You pulled your weight."

"He's gone," said Lev.

"I know," said Natalya. "He won't be bothering us again."

"He wasn't a bother," said Lev, surprised at her harshness. "He was a good man. I should have listened to his ramblings about freedom. I didn't know he was serious."

"You're not making sense," said Smagin. "He was aiming for *you*. For all of us. He was a threat and had to go. No one will miss Krinsky. We'll be long gone before he's found. Other slimy government spies from Moscow will wonder why he disappeared. They'll eventually come looking for him, but they'll be too late."

"Krinsky?" said Lev, confused.

"Some things you handle with persuasion, others with a knife," said Natalya. She motioned to a shashka hanging from a crooked nail. It was smeared with something that looked like red chocolate. "This is how we survive."

"Krinsky?" Lev said again, but then he understood.

Natalya rose and came close to Lev. She touched his face. "You're upset," she said. "Don't be. We have to take care of men like Krinsky who stand in our way. They won't find him, and he probably won't be missed for several days. You don't have to worry."

"I meant Mishal," said Lev. "He didn't use his containment caps. On purpose."

"What?" said Natalya, her face suddenly ashen. "Are you sure?"

Lev hung his head. "I think it was something I said to him. I forced him to perform. I didn't see how serious he was about quitting. It's my fault."

Smagin slammed his fist on the table. The glasses bounced toward the edge. "That goat of a shepherd's bitch!"

• • •

When the tent came down and was packed away, a large fire was struck in its place. The flames lapped at the sky and warmed the faces of the performers and crew, who gathered around it to toast another successful show and boast about what they would do with their share of the gate.

Lev stood apart from the others, transfixed by the fire's rising bands of red, orange, and blue. He inhaled the smoky fragrance, which reminded him of the paraffin candles his mother lit at dusk on Fridays. She would stand before the twin candles, her eyes nearly closed, drawing her hands over the flames while asking God to illuminate her family's eyes and pray for a gentle and well-deserved day of rest. But the fire before Lev only seemed to separate him further from an omniscient deity that would permit so much desolation. He felt disconnected from everything. He was even numb to the three women who slipped away from the fire to join him.

One of them placed her hand on his shoulder. "No use being upset, sweet thing. It doesn't help."

He was aware of them and their sickly sweet lavender, but he did not move away as they came close to him.

"We decided you weren't going to come," said another.

Lev wanted to say so much. That he'd had a very bad day. Several very bad days. That he was tired and sad and felt as if he would explode. That he felt lonely and captive and anxious. That he hadn't forgotten the three women and was hoping he would see them at the fire. That their smell blinded his thoughts and burned his blood.

He had been taught by Rabbi Tversky and the Talmud that a man was to marry at eighteen. It was a *mitzvah* to do so. His parents were aware of this, and he himself was anxious about it. Lately, he had begun to look differently at girls his age. Would one of them be his bride? Whom would he be alone with at the mysterious *cheder yichud*, in private, in the quiet moments after being wed? He was nervous about the carnal union between man and woman, but he had been taught it was reserved for the marriage bed.

"You're shaking," said one of the sisters. "Are you cold?"

"No," said Lev.

The women touched him. One kissed him lightly on the neck. Another wiped moisture from his face. Without objection or resistance, Lev let himself be herded to a wagon with an interior draped in bright Khokhloma textile fabrics displaying berries, leaves, and outrageously colorful flora. The air was filled with the thick smell of fresh rose petals.

The women whispered their names in his ear. "*Irina Khorkov. Raisa Khorkov. Gorana Khorkov.*" They led him to a padded straw mat, where they removed his clothes and caused his body to fill with a sweltering melancholy and unbearable expectancy. He was drowning in flowers.

Then, with tender hands and synchronized expertise, the Khorkov sisters ushered him across a forbidden bridge of pleasure that lasted until daylight.

• • •

The Aluşta caravan, heady and bloated from the night before, rumbled down the hill, its wagons rolling noisily into Torfyanovka toward Finland.

Weary and contemplative, Lev sat atop one of the last wagons, Mishal's, as the procession of horses, wood, and wheels moved slowly through the village. He watched people come out of shops to investigate the noise. Some held up their hands. Lev waved back, but he was scared they would see how frightened he was to be leaving so much behind. He imagined the residents of the town were looking on jealously at what they assumed was an exciting circus lifestyle, at the freedom to pull up stakes and travel the world, at the luxury to cross the border without probing questions and extortion. Perhaps under ordinary circumstances, Lev would be celebrating and wryly bragging to others, but he felt no joy, only a disconnection from everything. With Krinsky gone, he'd assumed that leaving Russia would be a simple matter, but he wondered if they would encounter another intimidating government official to take his place. He could not help wishing that they would not be allowed to leave the country. Watching the Russian landscape fall away behind him, he felt overwhelmed by a loss he could not name.

Lev looked back as the wagons reached the far end of the town. The villagers were still standing there, watching the wagons exit their lives forever. The people appeared as if in a painting, silent and motionless. Lev knew they would resume their routines as soon as the dust had settled. All that remained would be stories about a goat that had escaped falling knives and a man with a trick that made him appear as if he truly exploded.

The wagons continued down a narrowing lane that wound through sparse vegetation and a few scattered homes until it reached a small border crossing, attended by two armed men. Lev was some distance from them, but he could see them well enough to tell they took their jobs seriously.

They leveled their rifles at the lead wagon and called loudly, "*Ostanovis!*"

When Smagin approached the two men, their demeanor changed. They lowered their weapons and exchanged what Lev judged to be warm greetings. Then they began to talk and laugh. The three kept at this for some time, but their voices did not carry far, and Lev could not hear them.

Smagin gave each of them a small package, after which they shook hands and slapped each other on the back. A bottle appeared—vodka, Lev was sure—and they took turns passing it around.

It wasn't long before the three embraced and Smagin returned to his wagon. The two guards waved goodbye, and the horses leaned forward to pull the line of wagons down the road and into Finland.

When Lev's wagon approached the crossing, he recognized the two guards as the men Smagin had been drinking with in town the previous day.

And then, quite suddenly, they were across the border. Lev looked behind him as his country grew smaller. He saw the sky collapse upon the Russian landscape and everything he'd known and been.

PART TWO

KRISTIANA, NORWAY

9

By the time the Aluşta circus arrived in Kristiana, only Natalya, Smagin, Lev, and one wagon remained. The rest had been shed during the four-month journey from Russia. The Borovskys jugglers were the first to leave when they and two wagons joined a struggling street fair in Karhumäki, Finland. The rights to the human oddities, including the Snake Girl, the Human Skeleton, and their wagons, were purchased by a horse show in Stockholm that desperately needed to draw larger crowds. The remaining assets—notably the Khorkov sisters and their Three-Headed Baby act—had been sold to an underground beer hall in Lillehammer that entertained locals during the long winters.

The Aluştas had not planned to dismantle their troupe but had little choice once the Borovskys left. The trio hadn't wanted to be far from Russia, in case the political winds changed again. When the brothers brought a shockingly high offer for their act, the other performers began to see different futures as well. It hadn't helped that Mishal's death had made what was once a modestly enjoyable profession seem tawdry and depressing. At the same time, Natalya and Smagin grew weary, and sought a comfortable retirement if they could realize enough money.

Standing on the dock near Akershus Fortress at the head of the great Kristiania Fjord inlet, Lev and his two keepers gazed at the SS *Hellig Olav*, an impressive, five-hundred-foot black steamship with a single, red-striped funnel and two masts. Smagin placed his hands on Lev's shoulders.

"You've been a good man and true to your word," he said. He sounded old and nearly beaten, a tired carny who already seemed to regret giving up the only thing he knew. "I never told you this, but your rabbi promised you wouldn't be any trouble. You haven't been."

Smagin pulled him close and hugged Lev so tightly that all the air in his lungs fled.

"You're a sentimentalist," said Natalya.

"I can't help it," said Smagin. He released Lev and rubbed his eyes.

"I guess I am too," said Natalya. She kissed Lev on each cheek. "Now, remember what I told you. You're to find my aunt Elizaveta when you get there. She still carries my name."

"I won't forget," said Lev.

"Your English?" said Natalya. "How good is it?"

"I studied with my parents," said Lev. "They dreamed of moving to America one day. I won't have a problem."

"You were meant for America, then," she said.

"Tell me again why you can't come?" asked Lev.

"Our lives are in Russia," she said.

"So is mine," said Lev.

"Your destiny is in the New World," said Natalya. "You'll be hunted as long as you're here and with us. This is true with your kind. But America? It will be different. We are fulfilling our promise to your family."

"Never mind that," said Smagin. "He'll do fine in America. He's a survivor. Lev, did I or did I not give you everything I promised?"

"You did," said Lev.

"Including women, heh?" Smagin laughed heartily and slapped Lev on the back.

Lev didn't need to be reminded about the Khorkov sisters. He'd ached for them. The women were interchangeable, but their names were not. *Irina. Raisa. Gorana.* The most beautiful names in the world. He had seen them many times over the past months. He would lie awake in Mishal's wagon at night, thinking of them, his body restless, crazed, and possessed by turgid spirits. He was powerless to resist sneaking to their wagon, where it would always be dark and welcoming. He never knew who was touching him, whether it was one or all of them. He liked it this way. These were evenings fraught with blindness and no restraint. He would have walked to the end of the earth to find them and their lavender, their soft caresses, their urgent reckoning, their incessant kisses, their creative and skillful passion that resembled love, their penchant for calming him by saying, "Beautiful boy." Then he would slink back to his wagon, drained of madness and finally able to sleep.

"Don't mind him," said Natalya. "The ship will be leaving. If there is trouble and Elizaveta can't help, then send a message to us at the Russian consulate. We'll check now and then if we can."

Smagin stepped close to Lev and presented him with a slender object wrapped in purple velvet. "It's a kinzhal," said Smagin. "Nothing fancy. But it's served me well for many years. I have more daggers, but this one has proven its worth more than others."

Lev removed the velvet to reveal a short, curved weapon in a jewel-encrusted scabbard. It was very old, and its handle was made of smooth, well-worn ivory. He slid the dagger from its sheath to reveal its double edge. It appeared rusty but lethal.

"Thank you," said Lev. "I hope I don't need it."

"And I hope you do!" said Smagin. "You're not living life unless you acquire a few enemies."

"Don't mind him," said Natalya. "He means well."

Lev nodded, wrapped the kinzhal, and slid it into his bag. He knew he would never see the Aluştas again. They were already ghosts to him. Good ghosts, but ghosts all the same.

"To America, then."

. . .

Lev stood in line at the edge of the dock, waiting to sign the ship manifest. He had never been this close to something this big before. It loomed above him, dark and mysterious, as tall as a mountain and so long he could not see both ends at the same time. How did something so large remain upright and stay afloat? Beyond the ship, the water looked cold and dangerous. It smelled of fish and seaweed.

The past months had hardened him. The routine of traveling, caring for horses, and raising and lowering the tent had delivered a semblance of stability to his new life, though the work was demanding and difficult. Still, he had grown to enjoy working with the sledgers each day, which made his upper body lean and sinewy. But the greatest change in him was that he was no longer afraid. He had been inoculated from death and did not fear it. He had learned the trick of blending in with people by mimicking them and using their phrases. He did not know what he would find in America, but he felt equipped. He imagined great opportunity, but despite not yet being on the ship, he already missed the relative safety of the traveling circus.

When it was his turn, he stepped forward and presented his papers to the chief purser standing behind a podium. He was wearing a dark-blue uniform and impossibly thick glasses, which made his eyes appear unusually large.

"How many of there are you?" he asked in a throaty Danish accent, beautiful and precise.

"Just me."

The purser began to transfer information from Lev's identity papers to lines and columns on a page in a large book. "Leo. Okay. How do you say your last name?"

"Aluşta," said Lev.

"That Cyrillic alphabet is nothing but trouble. I'll spell it like it sounds. You can sort it out in New York, but it will always cause you difficulty if you don't simplify it. A-L-U-S-H-T-A. That'll do. Says here you're eighteen."

"Yes," said Lev, though it was untrue. It was one of many lies in the forged papers that Smagin had purloined for him.

"Is your profession still construction?"

Lev was ready for this question, but he wouldn't answer as Smagin had urged. "Tell the bastards that you can swing a hammer and raise a tent with the best of them," Smagin had told him. "If that's not construction, I don't know what is."

Lev felt the purser look at him with doubt. *You're not a carpenter,* Lev imagined him thinking. *You're a runaway, a mongrel, a liar.*

"Yes."

"Not sure that will pass muster when you get to New York. They're looking for skilled workers these days. People who will contribute to society. But they're building things, I guess. And I see you have a relative there, this Elizaveta, so maybe that'll be enough. Anyway, that's your problem." The purser leaned close to the manifest and signed his initials. He put Lev's papers on a stack of other identity documents.

"I need that," said Lev. He regretted saying it almost immediately, certain that he'd called unnecessary attention to it.

"You'll get it back after we've looked it over," the purser said. "Is that a problem?"

"No," said Lev.

"Third class. Cabin 418."

10

At the top of the gang plank, a crowd had gathered around a uniformed crewman who was welcoming passengers. "The SS *Hellig Olav* is big and all steel," he said. "We have more than two hundred crew to make you comfortable. She was built in 1902 in Glasgow, and she's the pride of the Scandinavian America Line. She's ten thousand gross tons, and you'll find her fitted with the latest technology, from radio telegraphy to electric lights. Speed is what this ship is good at. It'll make fifteen knots in the twelve days it takes to get to New York."

Lev walked past first-class rooms, a library, a smoking room, and other salons. Then he went down a level to the second-class accommodations, which were adjacent to private aft promenade areas. Third class, where Lev was headed, was four floors down, far less glamorous, and segregated from areas frequented by those in first and second class. Still, it was a meaningful improvement from the recent past. Lev had heard stories about how those who paid the least were once crammed into steerage, in great, open compartments with little privacy, rampant diseases, and extended periods of darkness.

Lev stood on a promenade deck as the ship left the dock. He tried to spot Smagin and Natalya, but the crowd was too large. He waved anyway. He watched the dock grow smaller, then took the stairs two steps at a time down through the decks, passing families carrying babies and heavy trunks. It was exhilarating. Here, no one knew anything about him. He could go anywhere. Be anything.

At the lowest passenger level, he roamed the narrow hallways, looking for his room, which he found down a long passage, nearly to the stern. Inside, he found an empty, small but clean four-person room with two stacked iron bunks on either side of a porcelain washstand. The mattresses were very thin, but they were supported by springs. Lev hoped they would be more comfortable than wagon mats. Everything in the room was starched white, except the blue blankets and pillows on each bed.

Lev sat in a bottom bunk to test its softness. *This will do fine*, he thought. It almost seemed as nice as his bed in Komenska. He peered out the small porthole as the ship slipped south down the Kristiania Fjord.

Suddenly, two men bounded into the room. They were older than Lev, but not by much, and they both wore gray-checked flat caps. One was a bit taller than the other, and he had the beginnings of an anchor beard and mustache. The other had a large wine-colored birthmark on his cheek. They seemed surprised to see Lev, and they stood silently for a moment and looked at each other, nodding. Then they moved to the opposite side of the room and sat on the bottom bunk.

"Is this your room?" said the one with the short beard.

"Yes," said Lev. "I'm Leo. Pleased to meet you."

"I'm Karl, but you don't need to know my name because you're a Jew, aren't you?"

Lev knew he was supposed to deny it, but he remained silent.

"No answer? I knew it." Karl elbowed the one sitting next to him. "See, Walter, what did I tell you? This is exactly what I was saying. This whole boat is filled with the hook-nose bastards. As soon as we stepped in here, I could smell him. First they lost us the war, and now they're fleeing Europe like rats. We're being forced to sleep with them. Do you think that's right?"

"Nope," said Walter. "It's not right at all."

Karl pointed at Lev. "Do you think it's right, Leo? Where's the fairness in that? We paid good money for our tickets. Probably more than you. I'm thinking you should find somewhere else to sleep. Walter and I need a private place in this beschissen boat to get away from all of you."

Lev wondered how easy it would be to retrieve Smagin's kinzhal from his bag, but he figured they would be upon him if he made a move for it. He knew his father would have turned the other cheek and walked away. Lev imagined him saying, *"If they don't want to be around me, then I don't want to be around them, either."* Lev was sure his father would have found a way to avoid a physical confrontation by apologizing, leaving the room, and asking to be accommodated elsewhere.

Lev stood. "Whether I am Jewish or not is none of your business."

Walter and Karl got to their feet. "That's an angry tone. Wouldn't you agree, Walter?"

"I would," said Walter.

"In fact, I think it's threatening," said Karl. "Am I right?"

"Definitely threatening," said Walter.

Lev said, "I'm not threatening anyone. But this is my room and I'm staying here. If you think there's been a mistake, then you can take it up with a steward."

Karl took a step toward Lev. Walter joined him. "Like I said, I'm feeling very threatened," said Karl. "I would be within my rights to defend myself. You're a witness, Walter."

"No one could blame you," said Walter.

With the situation unraveling, Lev considered backing down. It was senseless to fight bigoted, unintelligent people. They were incapable of learning, so all actions would be wasted. But Lev felt he would lose self-respect and a sense of himself if he were to shrink from them. Besides, he already hated them.

"Nothing good will come of this," said Lev. "Let's sit down and talk it through. There's been a misunderstanding. We might have more in common than you think. But no matter what, Jewish or not, I'm sleeping here."

Lev saw anger take hold of Karl's face. It looked as if he would explode. Walter slid a hand in a pocket and withdrew something metal. They rushed at Lev and wrestled him to the ground.

Lev resisted fiercely, kicking them and yanking Karl's hair. He flailed at them and caught one squarely on the nose. But the two held Lev down and began pummeling him in the stomach and face. Lev tasted blood and knew he could not fight them off.

Karl hissed, "Kike," and began to slam his fists into Lev's face. Walter spit on him and kneed him in the groin. Lev, now nauseous and limp, his eyes puffy and closing, could no longer defend himself, but the two did not stop. Karl stood and kicked Lev in the head, and then there was darkness.

• • •

Lev's mother came to him in a dream. He was nine years old. She was lightly dabbing a wet cloth on his face, cleaning a wound.

"We won't tell your father," she said. "It would upset him very much."

"He would have wanted me to stand up for myself."

"Your father believes that anger is fear in disguise, and that it is best confronted with faith."

"What would the rabbi say?"

"You're going to have a large bruise here. I don't think we can prevent your father from seeing it."

"I don't care if he knows. A man has to be a man. I know he'd be proud of me."

"You're my little Lev." She kissed his forehead. "We'll always be proud of you, no matter what."

"Even when I do bad things?"

"This wasn't a bad thing. But boys like you shouldn't be fighting over such silly things."

"What things are worth fighting for, then?"

"I would fight for you, and your father. That's all. Everything else can be replaced."

11

Lev woke from an extended sleep to someone gently lifting his eyelids. "Your eyes are fine, which is something you should be happy about. You're very lucky. You could have easily lost them both."

At first, Lev could see only a blur of light. Then he blinked and discerned a vague blob of color, which came into focus as a bulbous nose.

"That's the good news," said the man in a deep Scandinavian accent. "Please don't try to move your jaw. Relax. There's nothing to be overly concerned about. You should make a full recovery. You have some nasty bruising to your ribs. But here's the worst of it. Your jaw has a troublesome fracture that needs time to mend, otherwise you could lose some teeth. I've wired it shut."

Lev, still only half aware of his surroundings, felt sore all over. His tongue probed a web of thin wire that wrapped around his upper and lower teeth.

Lev tried to say, "Where am I?" but it came out, *"Air uhm uh?"*

The man came closer again. He was wearing a white jacket. "I'm the ship physician. I'm sorry," he said. "I asked the captain to turn around, but we were already too far and in a narrow lane. I've tried to make you comfortable."

Lev, now fully awake, tested his jaw and confirmed that it was tightly secured together. He could breathe through the sides of his mouth, but he was forced to mostly use his nose. He tried to sit up, but a sharp pain in his side forced him flat.

"Give it time," said the doctor. "Chief Purser Vestergaard has been here several times already. He's very concerned about your condition and wants to know who's responsible."

"I am," Lev struggled to say.

• • •

Lev rested on the small infirmary bed for longer than he should have, even though the doctor encouraged him to stand and test his balance. But Lev didn't mind staying under the blanket, sinking into the pillow, closing his eyes, and cursing himself for not avoiding the fight.

He understood why it happened. Karl and Wilber embraced Jew-hatred propaganda and were hunting for someone to exorcize their fury. But Lev knew he could have avoided it. *Why didn't I?* he wondered. Why hadn't he fled the room at the first hint of trouble? Why had he invited their anger by standing against them? What had he been trying to prove? Lev pondered these questions but found only unsatisfying answers relating to pride and the necessity to stop evil. But the wires in his mouth and the rigidity of his jaw told another story. *I was stupid.*

After a while, Lev curbed his self-pity and rose to his feet. Only then did he notice he was naked and wearing a loose medical gown that was open in the back. His clothes were folded neatly on a metal stand beside the bed, and his bag was hanging from a hook on the wall. Beside his bag, a porthole revealed the water rushing by the ship. Lev drew closer to the small circular window and marveled at the world where the infinite ocean reigned and made him feel lost in time.

Lev contemplated the ocean, then walked across the room to a full-length mirror that framed a tall, eye-level beam scale. He had bright-purple bruises around his eyes and the left side of his face. His jaw was alarmingly swollen. Lev thought he appeared as if he'd gone a few rounds with a professional boxer. He lifted his hospital gown to see bruises on both sides of his torso, where he had been kicked. He knew his mother would have been horrified, but he thought he appeared manly and rugged.

A young woman came into the room carrying a tray. Lev quickly lowered the hospital gown and gathered it behind him.

"You're up," she said in a delicate Swedish accent. "Wonderful. We were worried about you, Leo."

Embarrassed, Lev backed up and sat on the bed. He worked to enunciate, "I'm okay. Thanks."

"That's better than I could talk if I had my jaw wired shut," she said. "I brought you dinner."

"I can't eat."

"You're on a strict liquid diet," she said.

She came close to the bed and lowered the tray, which held a tall metal tumbler with a straw. Lev peered inside the glass to see thick brown sludge, then raised his eyes to admire the presence of the girl before him. She had the features of a perfect porcelain doll, with iridescent blue eyes and short-bobbed, blond hair. Lev decided she was the most beautiful girl he had ever seen. She did not appear to be as earthy or worldly as the Khorkov sisters, but she had an alluring innocence and femininity that was instantly intoxicating, and he felt the same uncontrollable suffocation of desire that had driven him to the Khorkovs' wagon.

"Meals through a straw from now on," she said. "Tonight, it's whipped liver and carrots. I know, doesn't sound very good. I'm sorry."

"It's fine," said Lev. "Are you a nurse?"

She laughed. "I work in food service. Mostly in dining. Sometimes cabin delivery or catering amenity areas."

"Will you always bring my food—I mean, my drinks?"

She laughed again. "Maybe." She turned to leave. Lev was taken by the graceful way she moved and how precisely she grasped the door handle. He imagined her taking his hand the same way and was certain it would be charged, like the moment a spark caught a candle's wick.

When she was gone, Lev realized he hadn't asked her name. He hoped it wasn't a fatal mistake. He knew it was preposterous, but he already wanted a life with her, to wake up every day next to her, to survive only on her kisses.

Lev took his bag off the wall and looked through his things to make sure Karl and Walter hadn't stolen anything. His clothes and money seemed undisturbed. He slid his hand toward the bottom and found his mother's envelope.

Lev opened the letter carefully, as if it were a delicate antique. He knew it would make him sad, which was what he wanted. He had trouble picturing his parents, other than how they might have faced their last moments. Lev decided they were on the floor, breathing smoke and holding hands before the fire engulfed them. He imagined their souls rising to the heavenly court, while their physical bodies ascended through the flames as curls of ash before floating down to the small village where they were born.

I will save this letter forever.

Overcome with a new wave of grief, he leaned against the porthole to watch the night and the invisible ocean that was revealed by occasional silver sparkles. He wondered how he would manage to be worthy of his parents' sacrifice.

Suddenly, Chief Purser Vestergaard burst into the room in a bluster. He was the man who'd confiscated Lev's identity papers on the dock—the same documents he was now waving above his head as he confronted Lev.

"*A-answers!*" he stammered, his thick glasses vibrating down his nose. "I don't care how out of sorts you're feeling, I demand answers this moment, or I'll drop you into the water without a life vest, you bugger."

Lev knew the purser wasn't serious about throwing him overboard, and so was not cowed by the threat. "It's hard for me to talk."

"Don't give me that excuse, you insolent liar." He tapped the papers. "Your identity papers are fake. Forged. Phony, I say. There's nothing about them that can be substantiated. Your age. Your name. Everything."

"They're real," said Lev calmly. "My father acquired them on my behalf from a reputable agency."

"Another lie. I've radioed both sides of the Atlantic. You don't exist."

"I'm as real as you," said Lev. "I'm pretty sure I exist."

Vestergaard shook with rage, his face turning radish red. "Gentle Moses! Are you trying to provoke me? I won't have it. You must have eaten nails!"

"I'll gladly answer all your questions," said Lev. "I haven't given you cause to be angry."

The purser paused, exhaled a mighty gale, and rubbed his eyes. "I've gone down with the flag this trip, I have. More trouble than usual. I was hoping for an easy ride this crossing. But I suppose you're right. What's done is done. We'll let the authorities in New York handle you. They're very adept at dealing with stowaways."

"I'm not a stowaway."

"If you're not who you are pretending to be, then you're an enemy of King Christian the Tenth. And you'll be treated as such aboard his ship."

Lev reconsidered his strategy of denying the purser's accusations. Sooner or later, he would be found out. "I don't want to go to jail." He sat on the bed and feigned resignation.

Vestergaard nodded and smacked his lips, evidently proud that he'd wrangled contrition from Lev. "You're not the sharpest knife in the drawer. There's no jail on the *Hellig Olav*. Any empty storage room will do for something like that if needed. Anyway, you're not going anywhere. The Atlantic is a stellar guard. Now, fess up and be done with it, or I'll go cucumber on you again."

"My parents are dead. I'm going to live with an aunt. She's my only relative."

"Is your name really Leo?"

"Yes."

The purser looked at Lev hoping to gauge his honesty. "Well, you do have a stowaway look about you. Maybe it's the truth, maybe not. The captain will decide. But on to other matters." He folded Lev's identity papers and put them in his coat pocket. "Who did this to you?"

"I can't remember."

"Those two Germans sharing your cabin. Say it was them, and we'll put them in the closet. Or worse."

"If I knew for certain, I would tell you," said Lev. "Don't you think I would want protection? I'm not going to say it was them if I'm not sure."

Vestergaard considered Lev's rationale. "I can't think of a reason you wouldn't tell me, unless you started the confrontation."

"I didn't start anything."

"Anyway, I spoke with them and they denied it," said the purser. "One of them took a blow but blamed it on a stumble. I don't believe them. Nor you. I'm going to be keeping a close eye on them. They've been asking about you."

Lev didn't hear what the purser was saying because he was too busy trying to figure out why he hadn't fingered Kurt and Walter. He wished only terrible things would happen to them. He wanted to crush the life out of them. But Lev questioned his own culpability and so remained silent. It was also true that he was thinking about something else.

"Sir," said Lev. "I am sorry for all the trouble I have caused you. You have every right to be upset. During the rest of the voyage, I would like to do what I can to make amends and be helpful. I couldn't sleep otherwise. If it would be of service to you, may I suggest that I work while aboard? Perhaps in the kitchen? I am a very hard worker. I can wash dishes, wait on tables, and deliver food. Whatever needs to be done."

12

Lev was roused from a deep, dreamless sleep by a hand on his shoulder.

"The captain wants to see you."

Lev slowly let go of the night web that held him fast. "Captain?" He opened his eyes to a plain-faced young man in uniform.

"It's not a good idea to keep him waiting."

"What time is it?" asked Lev.

"Time to get out of bed," the petty officer said, which sounded the way he meant it—sarcastic. Then he relented. "Three in the morning. Let's go. Captain Peronard is an impatient commander."

"Three?"

"I won't say it again. I'll be blamed if you don't get up right now. I'll dress you myself if I must."

Lev pulled on warm clothes and followed the petty officer out of the infirmary, down a corridor, up a flight of stairs, and outside. The wide promenade deck was void of passengers and crew, and the star-filled sky and frigid air made Lev feel as if he were on another planet. Lev exhaled an icy cloud when he spoke. "Why does the captain want me?"

"The captain doesn't need a reason."

The petty officer walked fast. Lev hurried to stay with him up another flight of stairs to the upper promenade deck and the cramped maze of pitch-black passages and rooms behind the wheelhouse. It was so dark that Lev grabbed the petty officer's sleeve so he would not stumble or get lost. Lev was pulled left, then right, and into a space that, like everything, was entirely dark.

"Stand here," said the petty officer, who pushed Lev's hand away. "Don't move until you get your night vision. I'll be back." Lev heard him walk away, leaving him feeling insecure and exposed. He strained to see, but there was only frightening black everywhere. There could be people within reach, and he wouldn't know. Lev shivered.

It took a long time for his eyes to grow accustomed to no light. After several minutes, he began to see formless shapes around him. He was in a large room with great glass windows opening to the bow and beyond. There were several tall, vertical objects in the room that remained vaguely outlined but which the suffocating darkness made almost indistinguishable.

Minutes passed. When his eyes finally adjusted adequately, Lev could discern people hovering close to several instruments. In the center along the windows was the ship's large main wheel in front of a binnacle with steering compass. On either side were other tall telegraph instruments—engine order, relay, and docking, and another used only for emergencies. Behind Lev was an array of radios and other installations. Attending to the navigation instruments were officers of the bridge. All were quiet. The scene, cast only in shades of dark gray, was ghostly.

The petty officer returned when Lev's eyes were fully acclimated. "This way," he said. He opened a door on the side of the wheelhouse and motioned for Lev to exit. "Captain Peronard is outside. He's expecting you."

Lev stepped through the door into the cold and onto the navigation bridge, a wood-planked area that extended the full width of the ship, port to starboard, and was open to the elements, except for an awning that provided shelter from rain. The navigation bridge had an identical set of ship's wheel and telegraphs. The night was quiet but for the sound of water rushing by the ship.

Lev was surprised at how well he could see. Forward, the Atlantic loomed menacingly, owning everything, as if land never existed. A lookout officer stood on either side of the navigation bridge, both engrossed in searching for ocean hazards. In the center of the bridge, standing alone before the wheel, was a tall, distinguished-looking man with a neatly trimmed gray beard. He was dressed in a knee-length formal uniform coat and military cap pulled down to the bridge of his nose. Without turning toward Lev, he said, "Come closer, son."

Lev joined the captain at the wheel. "I'm sorry for the trouble I've caused, sir."

"Quiet," said Captain Peronard. "Now's the time for listening. What do you hear?"

"Hear, sir?"

"Out there," said the captain, pointing into the night. "The brine bitch. You can hear her talk if you understand her language."

"I don't know what I'm listening for."

Captain Peronard looked hard at Lev. "Not another word."

Lev nodded and tried to concentrate on the sounds of the ocean. He wondered if there was something in particular he should be listening for other than the quiet, incessant hush of the ocean. He struggled to separate the wind from the water. He wondered if birds migrated across the North Atlantic, and if they made an audible sound. If there was something else out there to be heard, what could it be? Lev shrugged but was afraid to verbalize his inability to hear anything specific.

The captain exhaled through his nose. "Then what do you see? You have your night vision, correct?"

"I guess," said Lev.

"Any nearby light will ruin it," said the captain. "And without anything bright in the area, the eye is tricked into changing. It's chemical. Now tell me what you see out there."

Lev gazed at the ocean. It appeared calm, almost welcoming. "What am I looking for?"

"Ships in distress. Whales. Icebergs. Dead bodies. Someone on a raft. Anything that endangers the ship."

Lev returned his attention to the water. He desperately wanted to spot something so the captain would approve, but there was too much water to see anything else.

"Oh my Lord, they're out there," said the captain. "I've seen them every trip. Bergs so big that you can't breathe when you spot them, so large that you discover just how afraid you are. Have you ever been afraid, boy?"

"Yes," said Lev. "Quite a lot lately."

Captain Peronard clasped his hands behind his back and leaned forward in a way that suggested he might fly forward over the ship and into the water. "Fear is a useful thing. It's what keeps us alive. Without it—fear, I mean—we'd go soft and miss something important. Nearly eight years ago, this ship wasn't too far from here. Came across three monstrous icebergs, some smaller ones, and a field of ice that would freeze your veins. Sailing by those, no matter how slow you're going, is like being on the moon, a landscape so terrifying, so menacing, that the only thing you can hear is the beating of your heart high in the throat. That's what fear will do to you. It'll turn you white as bones, and as bloody as a walrus battle. It was near high noon when we saw those blue monsters, floating there so close, as if they were friends. Nothing unusual about them. They weren't hiding. Right there in the alley, just waiting to snag themselves a tasty morsel. I have spent half my life worrying about those Satan fuckers. I do more than dream of them, boy—I bleed them.

"And eight years ago, when we spotted that ice from hell, we called it in right from this bridge to let other ships know. I remember the number—41° 43' latitude, 49° 51' longitude. Those numbers nag at me like a sea witch. And as I said, we called it in. A day later, those sirens grabbed the *Titanic* and pulled her down fast. You can't say they weren't warned. I can show you the call log if you don't believe me."

"I believe you, sir," said Lev.

"Do you know what happens when a ship like that goes down? I'll tell you—*violence.* The sound is outrageous. The groaning of metal. Water rushing to fill every pocket of air. Lots of fire, though you wouldn't figure it. Screams of trapped passengers and crew who die in seconds with their eyes open. It's bloody and terrible, and there's nothing serene about it. And when it does go down, when the last painted piece bubbles under, everything stops. No sound. Complete silence, except for random survivors calling someone's name.

"This is the fear every captain lives with. We don't sleep well. And truth be told, when we make land, we huddle together with cigars and curse the invention of ocean travel. It's a silly idea. Dangerous. Fraught with obstacles. Honestly, it's a miracle any ship makes it across. If the bergs don't get you, then you'll catch pneumonia standing outside like this looking for them, and you'll die in bed coughing up green sputum. I give credit to God for keeping us afloat sometimes. Do you believe in God, Leo?"

Lev was surprised—and concerned—that the captain knew his name. "Very much so."

Captain Peronard nodded. "That's good. I wish I could be as certain as you, but I can't think of another reason why most ships make the crossing safely. We're dancing on devil's knives out here. And I don't need you distracting me from this gruesome business."

Lev stood quietly, worried about where this was headed and wondering if the captain was always this reflective. The captain seemed to have finished speaking and was now staring off into the distance. The long pause was difficult to endure, so Lev said, "I'm sorry, sir. I never considered the dangers."

Captain Peronard looked at him warmly. "Ah, don't mind me, boy. I'm an old pirate at heart and jaded by the ocean's majesty. Now, what is it you want?"

"You called for me, sir."

"I did. Vestergaard has been bending my ear about you. And I see why. I'm sorry about your injury. I'm told you won't rat on those responsible."

"I'd rather not, sir," said Lev. "I mean, I don't remember."

"I see. Well, just between us now, I wouldn't either. A man must fight his fights. And though there may be harm, being a snitch is the lowest of human qualities. I admire your gumption, boy. But that doesn't erase the mystery of who you are, and if you're aboard legally. The hardnoses at Ellis Island will make those decisions. For now, as Vestergaard says you suggested, you can work while aboard. It'll do you good. Something about joining our food service?"

• • •

It took two days of washing dishes in the ship's main kitchen for Lev to figure out there was an art to it. The secret to a well-washed bowl was to first submerge and soak it in the large industrial sink, then scrub it well before rinsing it again. Skipping the first step resulted in more work. Submerge. Scrub. Rinse.

Lev enjoyed the mechanical nature of the process. Dirty dishes on the left, clean ones on the right. It was honest, mindless work that Lev felt was cleaning his soul. For each dish he scrubbed, he methodically chipped away at the lies contained in his travel papers and his inability to avoid fighting with Karl and Walter. He regretted distracting Captain Peronard from his important duties.

He had already washed too many dishes and silverware to count—large cast iron skillets, copper saucepans, cutting boards, butcher knives, measuring cups, mixing bowls, oversized Dutch ovens, baking sheets, casserole dishes, stock pots, even a Russian samovar that reminded him of home. But throughout his time in the kitchen, he had not yet seen the angel who had delivered his liver and carrot shake. He watched for her, always aware of who was nearby. Women of all ages flew in and out of the kitchen, but not her. He supposed he could have missed her if he was looking down while concentrating on a particularly stubborn pan. He began to worry that her duties would not bring her near him. Maybe there was another kitchen.

The doctor allowed him to continue sleeping in the infirmary, so he worried less about inadvertently encountering Karl and Walter. Nor did he give much thought to the pain in his jaw, or the hunger pangs that gnawed at him because eating through a straw was not filling. He did not worry about what would happen to him when they arrived in New York. If the immigration authorities allowed him in, he was unconcerned whether he would be able to find Natalya's aunt, Elizaveta. Nothing worried him except finding the girl who had laughed at him and said, "Maybe."

Lev knew it was silly to obsess over a person he'd only fleetingly met. He didn't know her name or anything about her. But the thought of her filled him with yellow butterflies, and he had to lean against the sink while washing dishes to hide his passion.

At the end of his afternoon shift, he was relieved by Bartel, a lanky twenty-year-old with long red hair, with whom Lev had struck up a friendship. Bartel told Lev that he had left his home in Leiden because his father never came back from a hunting trip and his mother had invited a cruel constable to her bed. "I will never go back," he told Lev. "It's an infected place." Bartel said he was hoping to meet a rich heiress on the ship. "I will please her and she will take me away from this poverty."

Lev confided in him that he was looking for a girl, too, but he doubted she was wealthy. When he described her, Bartel shrugged, said couldn't place her, and chided Lev for not being brave or quick enough to have asked her name.

Bartel asked Lev if he had seen her. "Not today," said Lev, "and not since the only time she delivered my drink. Maybe she doesn't exist."

"You can't be passive when it comes to women," said Bartel. "They want strength. They want aggressive men to erase their fears and fulfill

their deepest desires that even they may not be aware of." He elbowed
Lev and said, "Women are most content and happy when you give
them a good shove every night. They'll give you everything. I'm serious.
But you have to be bold and go after what you want. You might wait
your whole life if you're waiting for this girl to magically appear."

13

Lev strolled the decks after his shift in the kitchen, keeping close the railing and the sea. He wondered if icebergs were nearby and what Captain Peronard would do if one was spotted. He heard music coming from an open door and explored its source. Lev entered and found himself at a recital in a music salon. He stood at the back of the room and was surprised to finally spot the girl who had brought him the liver and carrot shake. She appeared to stand at polite, unobtrusive attention to the side of the upright piano, her hands clasped loosely behind her back. Lev watched her scan the guests who were listening to a man at the piano play a rapturous melody.

A woman in front him whispered, "That Willem Andriessen is heavenly, wouldn't you say?"

Lev's attention was entirely on the girl as she fetched a glass of wine or helped an elderly passenger up from the velvet, tufted banquette sofa. He saw her watching for empty plates in need of another helping of caviar and thin wafers. But mostly, Lev saw that her attention was focused on the pianist, Willem, on his hair, which rested in thick boyish waves atop his head, and his lithe fingers that danced across the keys. Lev guessed she was waiting for Willem to glance at her and smile. *They're lovers,* Lev decided. She had curled up to Willem in his cabin the previous night, resting her head on his chest while listening to his adventures at a conservatory. She wanted Willem to love her again, to make her feel as if they were the only two people on the Atlantic.

If only she would look my way, thought Lev.

She was more alluring than Lev remembered. He tried to catch her eye, but she didn't look in his direction. *Soon enough,* he thought. *When the music ends, I'll cross the room and take her hand. I'll tell her that I have not stopped thinking about her since we met. That I took a job in the kitchen hoping I would see her. That I searched for her until Providence led me to the music room, where her face was full of light and her presence stirred my soul. I must ask her name immediately.* Lev thought these things and more as he waited for her to notice him.

Willem played the last note and held it with the piano's sustaining pedal as the guests in the room clapped in appreciation. He looked up at the girl, reached for her hand, and kissed her fingers. "I chose that melody for you," he said.

A weakness fell upon Lev. The blood rushed from his body, as if the bottom had fallen out of a great tank of water. An emptiness took hold of his stomach, and he felt like he was going to be sick. He leaned against the wall and grew angry. At her. At the usurper and his piano. At himself.

When the clapping faded, she returned her attention to the passengers, scanning the room for anything that required her to provide service. She smiled with recognition when she finally saw Lev. She waved at him, and Lev was immediately thrust back into the fire.

I must get her away from him, he thought.

• • •

Lev hurried from the music room and to the railing of the starboard promenade. There, looking out at the ocean where it bled to the horizon, he tried to figure out a way to hate the girl who still did not have a name.

Lev knew that Smagin would have laughed at him and told him to grow some courage. *"Wanting and getting a woman are two of the same things!"* he'd growl. *"If she's the bauble you desire, then what are you waiting for? A man's not a man if he doesn't take what's rightfully his."* But then Smagin would look over his shoulder to ensure Natalya hadn't heard him. *"Of course, it would be best to temper your actions with a dose of servitude."*

Mishal would bury his advice in cryptic puzzles. *"The things you desire can be traps,"* he would instruct. *"This is often true, but you will be unable to see it. You think you have an understanding of what's right and what will bring you happiness. But happiness is unknowable. It can never be achieved. This is always true. And it is the reason we are so rarely content. We always want something more. If it is a woman you want, then first consider whether you intend to make her a possession. And if so, why? Are your desires noble, or infected?"*

Lev did not have to wonder what his mother would have said. *"A relationship sewn from love has nowhere to go. You're too young to make a wise choice in a wife. Choosing someone yourself is wrong. It isn't done. What is the benefit to our family if you choose your own wife?"*

Perhaps more than anything, Lev was embarrassed for thinking she would be interested in him. He replayed the moment in the infirmary. He could have invited her to stay longer, thanked her for bringing the shake, or asked her to help him get dressed. He wished he had touched her hand and stolen a kiss. He wondered if her lips tasted like cherries.

But he realized now that she hadn't seen him. He was a passenger like any other. *I hate her,* he thought, but was unconvinced. She remembered him. He'd seen it in her face in the music room when she'd waved at him.

Lev wished he had a stone so he could heave it into the ocean. He knew it wasn't rational to dislike the man at the piano, but he did. *He's not good enough for her.*

He rushed back to the music room but didn't enter. He stood beside the door and waited until she came out. He thought of all the things he could say. *I enjoyed the performance. I didn't think you'd recognize me. What was your name again? I've been looking for you. I've fallen madly in love with you, you know. I shouldn't say it, but I was insanely jealous when you kissed the man playing the piano. He's no good for you. I'll challenge him to a fight.*

But the first person to come through the door was Willem. Lev recognized him right away. He quickly caught up to him.

"That was good playing," said Lev.

Willem stopped and turned to Lev. "Your accent has the music of Russia, no?"

"I was born there."

"I envy you. Stravinsky, Shostakovich, Prokofiev—especially Prokofiev. Sergei is a friend of mine. You come from a land unrivaled in this century for bringing true and authentic melodies to our ears. Are you a musician?"

"No."

"That's a shame. It's in your blood. Your birthright. Well, in any case, you're very nice. I'm Willem." He extended his hand. Lev looked at it as if it were a poisonous snake but shook it anyway. He was surprised at its softness.

"Leo," said Lev. "You probably didn't see me in there."

"Sadly, that is true. I am mostly oblivious when I am playing. May I ask what happened to you? The way you talk, I mean."

"Some people don't like Russians."

"Some people don't like themselves. They hate what they see in the mirror and vent their frustrations in order to compensate. I feel sorry for them."

Lev hadn't expected such compassion, and he felt his hate for Willem falling away like shekels through a beggar's hands. *I don't want to like him.* "I'm a Jew."

Willem shrugged. "I'm Evangelical Lutheran, but I don't go around announcing it. The Church of Denmark would find that immodest."

"I mean that's why my jaw is like this. I was in a fight."

"I gathered that," said Willem. "But I am envious of you. I must avoid such confrontations. My hands are everything to me." He looked down at his hands and made them into fists. "My father was a composer. My brother too. We were not allowed to play with other children. I don't know why I am telling you this. I have had a few drinks."

"I liked your playing. I wanted you to know."

"You're a fine fellow. Would you care to join me for a cigar? Your female friend is welcome too."

"I'm traveling alone."

"A handsome young man like you? I don't believe it."

"There is someone I'm interested in, but she doesn't feel the same toward me."

"Nonsense," said Willem. "Have her join us. I'll talk you up. She'll be yours in no time. Cigars on the observation deck. Say a half hour?"

14

ev found Willem on one of the long rows of chaise lounges lining the observation deck. He was wearing a wide-brimmed straw boater and smoking a cigar. The girl, *his* girl, was sitting next to him. They looked comfortable together and appeared to share the secret nonverbal language of lovers—a quiet laugh, a raised eyebrow, a touch.

"Ah, my fine man," said Willem. "I wasn't sure you were coming. I hope you don't mind that I've started without you. Dory, this is the young gentleman I told you about."

She had a name. *Dory.* It was simple and delightful. It fit her so well. *I will dream of that name,* he thought.

She smiled broadly at Lev as he approached. "I saw you at the recital, Leo. How are you feeling?"

"Hungry," said Lev, struggling to open his mouth wide enough to make conversation. "Dory, that's such a pretty name," he said. "Suits you."

Lev was close enough to see that he had not been wrong about Dory's beauty, but she might as well have been an ocean away. She was so obviously with Willem. He tried not to show his disappointment.

"Poor thing," Dory said. "But you're looking so much better. The bruising is almost gone."

"Sit," said Willem. He held up a long cigar with a red and yellow oval band. "It's an Optimates. Quite smooth."

Lev sat next to Willem. "I don't smoke."

"You mean not yet," said Willem. He lit a phosphorus match and dipped the end of the cigar in the orange flame. "A good cigar can soothe the soul, Leo. Kipling wrote that 'a woman is only a woman, but a good cigar is a smoke.' There's truth in that. I've written some of my best pieces after relaxing with a cigar." He turned to Dory and said, "But of course, I've also written sensuous piano concertos after being with a fine woman."

"I think they're nasty," said Dory. "But your lips are always sweet." She leaned into him and they kissed with open mouths. Lev looked on with hot jealousy.

Lev took the cigar and slumped back on the chaise lounge. He observed Willem as he puffed on his cigar, then took a deep drag on his own. Willem said, "Don't inhale," but it was too late.

The smoke filled Lev's lungs. He coughed and could not get any air, as if someone had slid an arm down his throat and was pulling the life out of him. His mouth throbbed and strained at the wires keeping his jaw shut.

"That's how you learn," laughed Willem. He moved to help Lev, pushing him forward and lightly patting his back. "Breathe through your nose."

"Poor thing," said Dory. "He's turning white."

Lev could barely hear them because he was stuck in a fit of coughing and nausea. His eyes watered, and he continued to cough until his energy was gone. Then he closed his eyes and reclined on the chaise lounge.

Dory sat next to Lev and rested her palm on his forehead. "He deserves better," she whispered.

"I know what you mean," said Willem. "There is something

unusual about him. I don't often talk with people who stop me like he did when we met. When he looked at me, I couldn't tell if it was in admiration or disdain, as if I'd always known him or was supposed to know him. It's strange. I can't explain it."

Lev, now very weak and exhausted from coughing, breathed easier but only barely heard their voices. He was, however, acutely aware of the warm hand on his forehead. He knew it belonged to Dory, and he felt her energy flowing into him, healing the burning in his chest and giving him renewed hope that she cared for him. *That's what love is,* he thought. He rested quietly and wished for her touch to last forever.

Lev was intoxicated by Dory's touch and queasy from the cigar. Bleary-eyed, he saw how warmly Willem regarded her and wondered if they had been intimate, or if they'd engaged in the lewd ring-toss game the Khorkov sisters had taught him.

Willem appeared happy and contented. *I want that,* thought Lev.

"Dory, can you help me get to the infirmary?" Lev asked. "I don't feel so good. You don't mind, do you, Willem?"

Willem shook his head. "I need to practice for tomorrow, anyway," he said. "The captain asked me to entertain the passengers in third class. You should come. I could use a steady hand to turn pages."

"I have to get back to work too," said Dory. "The infirmary is on the way."

Willem offered his hand to help Lev up. "I'm sorry you're not feeling well, my friend," he said. "Please let me know if there's anything I can do for you. I hope you can help at my recital tomorrow."

"I'll be there," said Lev as they left Willem, thinking, *You're not making it easy to despise you, but at least I will be alone with her.*

• • •

"I'm glad you like Willem," said Dory as they headed up the stairs. "I haven't seen him take to someone so quickly. Well, other than me, I guess."

But Lev was barely listening to her. He was trying to figure how to reach for her hand in a nonchalant way that she wouldn't mind. He wondered how Willem captured her heart, and he could not stop thinking about them being alone together. *Does she want an aggressive lover? Should I stop her on the stairs and try to kiss her?*

He had learned about intimacy between a man and woman by observing his parents. They were not overtly romantic with each other because it was frowned upon in Komenska. Lev had rarely seen them hold hands. Even within the confines of their home, Lev could not recall seeing them kiss like Dory and Willem—at most, maybe a peck on the forehead on an anniversary. But they were considerate in unspoken ways, helping each other with small tasks like cleaning up after dinner as the day's light gave way to stars. Lev often saw them standing in the kitchen next to each other, passing a wet dish into a dry towel. They seemed genuinely interested in each other's answers to questions, and he rarely heard them quarrel. When he was older, Lev would listen for the creaking bed at night. He did not doubt they were in love; they seemed entirely comfortable with each other. That's what love was, he concluded, being so comfortable with another person that you could be yourself and not try so hard at everything.

When they reached the infirmary, Lev said, "Thanks for coming with me, Dory."

"Dorete," she said. "Willem calls me Dory, though I don't like it. It sounds like a little girl's name."

"Dorete, then," said Lev, regretting that he'd lured her to the infirmary. *Only Willem gets to call her that.* By not allowing him to call her Dory, she had made the boundary between them clear. Willem, with his talent and confidence, had won the right to call her Dory, to kiss her anytime he wanted, and to lace his fingers between hers. "They've been very nice about me staying in the infirmary. I think they feel responsible for my jaw. They want to keep me away from the ones that did it to me."

"They should," said Dorete.

Lev leaned his back against the wall. "I'm sorry I brought you here. I didn't know what else to do."

"Leo?"

"I mean you and Willem. I don't blame you. He's a wonderful guy. I think everybody must feel the same."

"Oh," said Dorete after thinking for a moment. "I see. Leo—I didn't know you saw me that way. You're wonderful too. But—"

"I'm stupid. I'm sorry."

Dorete took his hand. "Please don't be upset."

"I'm not. Well, I am a little. I can't help it. I'm an idiot."

"You're a sweet boy," said Dorete. "There's something sad about you that makes me want to help. But Willem and I are together."

"I know," said Lev. "It's obvious. Don't mind me."

"He's fond of you."

"I wasn't looking for that."

Dorete released his hand. "I'm fond of you too."

Lev wanted to run away and hide in a dark corner of the ship. "My mouth hurts from talking. I should go to bed."

Dorete smiled at him, but Lev couldn't interpret it. "You'll feel better tomorrow. I'm sure of it."

When she was gone, Lev undressed, slid under the blanket, and cursed everything he could think of—his youth, his presumptuousness, and the rabbi's horse, Solnishka.

15

Lev was roused in the morning by Willem, who sat on the edge of Lev's bed and playfully punched his shoulder. "I'm not leaving until you're up and ready to attack the day," he said.

Lev pulled the blanket over his head, embarrassed to face him. He was sure that Dorete had told him what happened. "Please go away," he said. "I don't feel well."

"Maybe if you stole my girl, you'd feel better, eh?"

Lev slid the blanket down until his eyes were uncovered. "Are you going to hit me?"

Willem laughed. "I might poison your food. But violence? Never. Besides, she's stronger than me, and she's free to be with whom she pleases. For now, she's with me, and I like it that way. I'm a lucky man. Don't take it personally, Leo, but you're a bit green for her anyway."

"I'm not too young, if that's what you mean. But I get it. She's your girl."

"That's very European of you," said Willem. "Old-fashioned. But I don't own her. I think she'd give me a jaw like yours if she heard me suggest otherwise."

"You're not cross with me?"

"Cross? No. Irritated by your deviousness? I suppose so."

"I didn't mean anything by it. I just thought a girl like her and me, you know—"

Willem stood. "Can I ask you a question, Leo?"

"I suppose."

"And get a truly honest answer? I won't get angry."

"You look mad already."

"I'm not, only I want to understand something. Promise me you'll be truthful."

"I will," said Lev.

"You stopped me yesterday after my recital so you could get close to Dory—true or false."

"I don't know," said Lev. "But I saw her kiss you. I didn't know what else to do."

"I come from Zeist. Do you know of it?"

"No," said Lev. He sat up and swung his legs to the floor.

"It's a fine town, but very provincial. Unsophisticated. A bit narrow-minded, I admit. But they're good people. Solid as a stump, and they take things seriously. They have only two ways of looking at things. Yes or no. Right or wrong. Good or evil. When it comes to stealing a woman, they settle things with fisticuffs. And if both men are still standing, then they face off with cricket bats. The first one with a bashed-in face loses."

"You are going to hit me, then, aren't you? I suppose I deserve it." Lev stood, raised his chin, and closed his eyes. "Go ahead."

Willem clenched his fist. "I might. You could use a good lesson. But, really, you seem a bit too wounded already. Besides, I like you. And anyway, if I put you on the ground, I would lose someone to turn the pages at my recital this morning."

• • •

Lev was filled with a terrible sense of dread as he and Willem descended to the lowest passenger deck and the memories of his encounter with Karl and Walter.

"I don't like it down here," said Lev.

"That's why I agreed to do this," said Willem. "Dory told me what happened to you here. I have found that music heals. It brings people together."

"Some people have too much hate for music to penetrate."

"When you heard me play yesterday, what did you think?"

"That you were better than me," said Lev. "That Dorete was right to have preferred you over me. That I could never measure up to you. That you were talented and rich and more worldly than I could ever be."

"And all that while listening to me play. That's my point. Music—and all art, really—is a force for personal change. When I'm at the keyboard, I'm barely there. I'm almost always taken someplace else, to a pristine beach or a mountaintop with views more beautiful than you can imagine."

"Hate is stronger than music," said Lev. "I've experienced it firsthand."

"You may be right," said Willem, "but we would be no better than they if we weren't to try."

When they arrived on the lower deck, Lev and Willem turned into the main passageway, where placard announcements of Willem's recital were affixed to the bulkheads:

A FREE CONCERT TO

CELEBRATE

OUR IMMINENT ARRIVAL IN

THE UNITED STATES OF AMERICA!

WEDNESDAY 10 A.M.
MAIN DINING SALOON
THIRD CLASS

WORLD RENOWNED DUTCH
PIANIST AND COMPOSER

WILLEM
ANDRIESSEN

PLAYING POPULAR MELODIES FROM THE USA!

NOCTURNE, OP. 45
JOHN KNOWLES PAINE

ALEXANDER'S RAGTIME BAND
ARTHUR COLLINS & BYRON HARLAN

OVER THERE
GEORGE M. COHAN

LET ME CALL YOU SWEETHEART
LEO FRIEDMAN & BETH SLATER WHITSON

YOU MADE ME LOVE YOU
JOSEPH MCCARTHY & JAMES MONACO

AMERICA THE BEAUTIFUL
KATHARINE LEE BATES & SAMUEL A. WARD

THE STAR SPANGLED BANNER
FRANCIS SCOTT KEY & JOHN STAFFORD SMITH

The largest of the third-class deck's dining saloons had been cleared, except for the long white tables bolted to the floor. The space was now crowded with passengers, almost all immigrants, who had been promised a recital of American music. At the far end of the room was a brown upright piano.

Captain Peronard greeted Willem warmly when he and Lev entered the room. "You do us a great honor this morning," he said to Willem, vigorously shaking his hand. "As you can see by this large gathering, there is great anticipation for you."

"Shouldn't you be guiding the ship?" asked Willem.

"It's a clear morning," said Captain Peronard. "My officers are more than capable. It'll get a bit dicey this evening, to be sure, and there's warning of a tricky ice flow. I'll be attending then, I promise you. For now, I thank you for this."

"The honor is mine," said Willem.

The captain spoke to Willem but faced Lev. "I see you've met our wounded friend."

"Hello, sir," said Lev. "I'm turning the pages for him."

"Then I suggest you get turning."

The crowd parted for Captain Peronard as he strode through the gathering. When they reached the piano, the captain faced the passengers and raised his hand as if testing for rain. "If you were outside right now, you would see a gathering storm," he said. "But in here, we are safe, warm, and among friends. Even better, the *Hellig Olav* has arranged for a grand treat for you. When we learned the esteemed Dutch composer Willem Andriessen would be traveling with us, we imposed upon him for a few select performances to make the long voyage a bit more pleasant. With the United States of America just a few days away, Maestro Andriessen will be treating us to melodies by composers native to the continent. Please welcome him."

The passengers erupted in sustained applause as Willem bowed and sat on the piano bench. "Stand here directly next to the piano," he said to Lev. "Your job is to watch me, not the crowd. Pay attention. If you miss my signal, the composition will be interrupted. I will look at you and nod my head when I'm ready for you to turn the page." Then he addressed the music, his hands hovering over the keys. The crowd grew silent.

After what seemed an interminable wait, Willem's fingers gently dipped into the keys and the delicate, halting notes of Paine's *Nocturne Op. 45*. The gorgeous music, with a returning melody that Willem teased, was unlike anything Lev experienced in Komenska, where music originated in the synagogue with the cantor's mournful voice that sought the attention of God. Outside the house of worship, klezmer and clarinet dance music made weddings and other celebrations joyous. But the sounds emanating from Willem's hands were altogether different, angelic.

Alert to Willem's warning, Lev kept his attention squarely on the musician, who seemed as if he and his instrument existed in another world and were oblivious to everything around them. Lev gazed at the man who had taken Dorete from him, but he no longer resented him. *If I were a woman, I would want to be with him too,* he thought. Willem was too suave, too friendly, too welcoming, too genuine to dislike. The music, quickening and now soaring, underscored everything wonderful about him.

Lev, mesmerized by Willem's intensity and immersion in the music, was caught off guard when Willem lifted his head just enough to meet his eyes. Willem appeared to be intoxicated, though he wasn't. Lev thought he looked desperate, his eyes wet and pleading. He was somewhere else, so involved in the composition that he had been absorbed into its beauty and was nothing more than a host to Paine's creation. Lev was so surprised by Willem's sadness that he almost missed his cue.

A moment passed before Lev remembered his task. He reached over and turned the page.

There was a noise, a rustling, steps, people jostled and protesting with quiet grunts. Lev looked up to see Karl and Walter only a few yards away, leaping toward him, launching over other passengers in a frenzied attempt to attack.

Before Willem was aware of the commotion and Lev could take a defensive stance, the men were upon them, eyes flashing and teeth bared. Karl jumped onto the piano's keys and lunged at Lev. Walter barreled through passengers and hooked Willem around the neck as the piano toppled over in a loud chord of chaos.

16

With low, menacing clouds pressing overhead, a persistent mist of light rain and sea spray fell upon the small group of officers and passengers gathered on the exposed port promenade deck for the funeral service. Black umbrellas were held high as they faced the railing, along with the tightly wrapped body of Willem Andriessen, which rested on a raised bier beneath the Dutch flag's white cross on a field of blood red.

Captain Peronard stood next to the body, head bowed and hands clasped behind his back. Behind him, his officers stood silent in two tight rows, all wearing their blue dress uniforms, none shielded from the elements. Off to the side, within the loose group of passengers, Lev and Dorete looked out to sea, but not at each other.

"This is every captain's least favorite duty," said Captain Peronard slowly, deliberately, lifting his head as if addressing an audience in the Atlantic. "But it is one we are prepared to do, because it is sadly too common. We usually lose passengers due to illness. In the days of unsanitary cramped steerage, which still exist on many ships, there would be several such ceremonies a day. But rarely like this, where hatred and ignorance are the diseases." Captain Peronard paused a long time, mumbled something inaudible, and nodded. "This is a very sad day. A great loss to a cultured civilization. I did not know Mr. Andriessen well, but I experienced his warm heart and willingness to share his talent for the benefit of others. He died in service to his country, to our commercial enterprise, and to me. I will forever feel remorse, regret, and guilt about this great loss and personal tragedy."

Lev tried to swallow but could not. He tried to abate his tears but could not. He tried to find the courage to grasp Dorete's hand but could not. He was lost in grief and the unrelenting vision of Willem falling beneath the piano, the terrible sound it made when landing on his head.

Captain Peronard removed a small, worn black book from his inner jacket pocket and thumbed through it. He cleared his throat and began to read. "Eternal Lord, who created the heavens and the raging sea, vouchsafe to take into thy almighty and most gracious protection our ship, all who serve therein, and our precious cargo of human souls. Preserve them from the dangers of the sea, and from the violence of the enemy, that they may be a safeguard unto all nations, and a security for those who pass lawfully on the seas. We pray that all who are aboard this vessel, and all acquaintances and loved ones on land, may in peace and quietness serve God. Let us be ushered through calamities, known and hidden, and be protected from the dangers of the deep, monsters lurking in cold darkness, and sirens, whose songs lure ships to dash upon rocky reefs. Amen."

The captain closed the book and looked to the gathering. "Would anyone like to say a few words about Mr. Andriessen?"

"I didn't know him, but I enjoyed his music," said an elderly woman leaning on a cane. "I heard him play in the salon the other day. He was very talented."

Lev wanted to speak but thought it would be inappropriate. He felt responsible for Willem's death. *They were after me, not Willem. If I hadn't befriended him, this wouldn't have happened. If I hadn't been jealous, I wouldn't have spoken to him.* He was preoccupied with self-pity, unaware that people were looking at him.

Dorete patted his arm. "Shh," she said, trying to quiet him. "Leo, it's okay. It's over now."

But Lev could not stop his sobbing. He hung his head and tried to will the ship to sink so he could be with Willem and the others who had died in his wake. In his heart, he knew he was not the cause of Willem's death. Karl and Walter were, of course. But he also knew that he was at the fulcrum of this disaster, and he could not live with it.

Lev felt a presence, and he raised his head to see Captain Peronard standing inches from him. "Buck up, son," he said. "Man proposes, but God disposes. Be strong now. We're with you. Those thugs won't be seeing daylight until we get to New York. The authorities there will deal with them, I promise. Murder is murder."

Lev sniffed and held his breath. He had an urge to vomit, but he swallowed it back and looked at the captain. "Yes sir."

The captain turned, stepped back to the still figure beneath the flag, and opened the book again. "We therefore commit Willem Andriessen's body to the deep as we look for the expected resurrection in this, his last day among us. We gaze at the present and the life of the world to come through our Lord, at whose second coming in glorious majesty judges us all. At that time, the sea shall give up her dead, and the corruptible bodies of those who sleep beneath the waves shall be changed to reflect his likeness. The Lord, glorified in his mighty work, subdues all things unto himself. Amen." The captain motioned to his officers, who stepped in unison to the bier and lifted it to the railing.

Captain Peronard said, "Godspeed," and the body, still bearing the Dutch flag, was gently lowered over the side and into the water, where it floated for a few seconds as if being held high by an invisible hand. The flag's white cross billowed around the corpse until, waterlogged, it slipped below the surface and faded into the depths.

• • •

The rain thickened, driving the passengers and crew to quickly disperse once the funeral was over. Only Lev and Dorete remained. They stood at the railing and continued to stare into the water.

Captain Peronard addressed them as he walked away. "Leo, come see me later," he said. "I have a job for you."

"What kind of job?"

The captain didn't answer, saying only, "I'll be expecting you before dark." Then he left Lev and Dorete to themselves.

"I'm sorry," said Lev.

"Don't say it again," said Dorete. "I can't bear to hear you say it."

"I'm a horrible person. I know it. And there's other reasons you can legitimately hate me forever."

"I don't hate you."

"I was up all night thinking about how, with Willem gone, I could be with you. That's how awful I am. I can't even mourn him properly. I'm thinking of you and me being together. I'm disgusting. Go ahead and say it."

"We can't be together," said Dorete quietly. "I loved him. I miss him. You're a nice boy, Leo, really. But I don't see you that way. I can't, especially now."

Lev rested his arms on the railing and his chin on his arms. "Don't you think I know all that? That's where my brain goes. I don't like the person I've become."

Dorete looked to the horizon, then again to where Willem had disappeared. "I can't help but think of him down there. It's cold and wet and dark. He's lonely and scared."

So am I, thought Lev.

• • •

Lev retreated to the kitchen, where he took refuge in the comforting routine of washing dishes. But each submerged utensil reminded him of Willem's watery grave, and he grew increasingly despondent as the dishes piled up. Bartel tried to engage Lev in conversation but could not reach him.

In the late afternoon, a petty officer came for Lev, the same one who had taken him to see the captain a few days earlier.

"It's not among my listed duties to keep after you," he said. "I'm not a nanny. The captain's waiting for you."

"I know," said Lev.

Without protest or question, Lev walked with the petty officer as they made their way to the bridge.

"I've made eight crossings with Captain Peronard," said the petty officer. "I've rarely seen him have a passenger to the bridge, let alone twice. And now this. Humiliating, if you ask me. It took me years to get here. Now you show up, and it's as if he's adopted you. I'm not threatening you or anything, and if you tell the captain I said anything, it'll be a problem between us."

"I don't want to cause trouble," said Lev.

"Then we understand each other."

When Lev arrived on the bridge, he was fitted with a long blue crew overcoat that fastened with thick brass buttons. A wool hat was pulled over his ears, and he was taken outside to the navigation bridge. It was still light out, but the sun was threatening to set behind a bank of dark gray clouds.

The petty officer pointed to a spot by the starboard rail. "Stand here and look to the ocean," he said. "Hold the rail if necessary, but keep your place. The captain will be along shortly."

Unsure but uncaring about his task, he turned to the water and faced its enormity. Although it was overcast and approaching dusk, he could see to the horizon. The ocean appeared calm, even welcoming. But closer to the ship, where the ocean had been divided by the prow, the water was riled and foamy.

Lev was startled by a heavy hand on his shoulder. He grabbed the rail. It was Captain Peronard, who addressed him warmly.

"You're looking north, Leo, though I don't blame you. It seems logical to stand against the rail and watch for dangers, but they won't come from that direction, because we're not heading there. Turn this way." Captain Peronard forced Lev to square his shoulders and move his left foot back. "Stay northwest. That's where icebergs pose the biggest problem because they're not as obvious. I've got others who will watch due west, where most dangers lurk. But those a bit to the north are sly. The current can draw them into unpredictable runs. They try to sneak up on you, the bastards."

Lev saw determination in the captain's eyes. *I'd best not say anything,* he thought, but could not remain silent. "I don't know why I'm here."

"You're on the Lord's watch with the rest of us," said Captain Peronard. "Once we get through the night, we'll be clear to the Statue of Liberty."

"That's not what I meant."

"I know what you meant," said the captain. "You're here because I said so. You're here because it's my pleasure. You're here because it'll be a reckless night, and I could use an extra pair of fresh eyes."

"Not because you want to keep an eye on me?"

The captain grunted. "Well, that too. Now look alive, sailor. The sun is leaving us, and we have important work to do."

• • •

The sun threw blinding, golden arrows where it touched the ocean and began to dip from sight. Lev imagined the ocean would part and the ship would tumble down to the dry seabed. He had no reason to question lessons about the flight from Pharaoh, but here, in the middle of unimaginable vastness, Lev doubted that any deity could divide such waters. He wanted to believe, but the small classroom tables of Talmud study seemed so long ago, as if someone else named Lev had pored over the ancient texts.

He knew that God's compassion and wrath, as violently manifested in the parting of the Red Sea, was central to Judaism. The celebration's

"Song of the Sea" was repeated every morning in synagogue. Lev knew it by heart.

In the greatness of your majesty you threw down those who opposed you. You unleashed your burning anger; it consumed them like stubble. By the blast of your nostrils the waters piled up. The surging waters stood up like a wall; the deep waters congealed in the heart of the sea.

Now, as night fell upon the ocean, Lev silently repeated the prayer to himself and its concluding phrase, *The Lord reigns for ever and ever.* In doing so, he felt closer to his religion than he had since leaving Komenska. But, standing at the edge of the world, high above where Willem slept, Lev wondered if the water vexed him, and if he would be punished. Hadn't Jonah, amidst a similar ocean, challenged God and been punished by a mighty storm that laid bare his disobedience? He had accepted his demise and went willingly into the maelstrom, only to be swallowed whole by *dag gadol,* a fish so massive that Jonah could breathe and survive in the monster's cavernous belly.

Lev was certain it wasn't a coincidence that here, at his darkest hour, the ocean had become his universe. He knew the ship was moving swiftly through the water, but it might as well have been motionless because the ocean disguised any progress toward a destination.

He held tight to the rail and stared ahead until, gradually, night vision came to him. The ocean was a slowly rippling velvet blanket that appeared geometrically uniform. The sky hung low, filled with heavy clouds. It was a silent, gray scene, which reminded Lev of glimpses through a traveling kinetoscope that had once stopped in Komenska on its way to Minsk with very brief, otherworldly halting images of horses running, people sneezing, and blacksmiths working an anvil. The scene beyond the ship's railing provided a similar timeless view that seemed immediate and unreal.

Lev stayed true to northwest and looked for anything that appeared to be out of place. He glanced at the other scouts on the navigation bridge and saw they were silent and still as statues. Guilty, Lev snapped back to his own lonely post and tried to see what was different from the moment before.

Something had changed.

Near the horizon, Lev saw a bright speck. But more than a speck. It was wider than what would have been expected in a white-capped wave, and it was persistent, except for the undulation of the ship, which made it appear to bob. Lev blinked to see if it would go away, but it was still there—and maybe larger. Perhaps it was a whale, Jonah's great fish making straight for the ship so it could gobble up Lev when he was thrown overboard.

But the object did not behave like a fish, nor did it dip or roll like a large piece of driftwood. Whatever it was, it appeared comfortable in the ocean, at home. And the longer Lev watched it, the closer it came, and the more he became certain that it was dangerous.

Lev knew he should call out, but he did not want to be wrong, so he continued watching the distant object until, finally, he could clearly see that it was an enemy to all ships.

Lev pointed at it, cleared his throat, and said loudly, "Iceberg!"

Before Lev could take another breath, Captain Peronard was next to him. He casually draped an arm over Lev's shoulder and lowered his head to Lev's height. The captain did not appear flustered.

"Show me what you have, son," he said calmly.

"Out there," said Lev, pointing. "It's getting closer."

The captain raised a spyglass to his eye. "The question is, Leo, is it getting closer to us, or are we getting closer to it? They're tricky, to be sure, and they don't like to be spotted. They'd rather hide beneath the surface and snag themselves some metal. They're ornery that way." The captain stopped speaking and held his position. Lev didn't hear him breathe. Then the captain whispered, "Ah, there she is. A fine catch, Leo. She's stealthy, that one. Crafty. I know her kind. Aiming for our lane." The captain lowered the spyglass and moved swiftly to the tall brass engine order telegraph. He slid the handle up and down three times to demand flank speed and rapid acceleration, triggering a series of bells. Then he disappeared into the wheelhouse.

The crew on the navigation bridge had not moved. Each remained steadfastly looking out to the ocean. Lev did the same, returning his attention to the iceberg, which was measurably closer.

There was a very loud screeching sound, and Lev felt the ship lurch forward and perceptively increase speed.

The captain returned and again peered through the spyglass. "Hard to tell what's beneath her, but that's the way with most things. She could be a pussycat or mad like piss. We can't turn toward her because we won't gain the radius. Turning away will only make us a bigger target. But the Olav can outrun her, believe me, Leo. She's built for fifteen knots, but we can get a hell of a lot more out of her when necessary."

Captain Peronard's calculations were spot-on. The iceberg continued its movement undeterred, but the ship was cruising fast, and it became obvious that neither would meet.

When the ship was well ahead and out of danger, the captain stood tall. His posture suggested satisfaction.

"That's how it's done. You can see the beauty of teamwork and grit, can't you? As long as everyone does their job, our vessel is very much impervious to the elements. I'm proud of you."

"Thank you," said Lev.

Catching himself, the captain coughed and said, "I don't mean you in particular. I meant it as in everyone. Now look smart, Leo. The night is young, and your watch will take you to sunrise. Stay on your mark. You'll work here until we reach New York."

"Yes sir." Lev watched the captain turn back to the telegraph to slow the ship.

Lev looked again to the ocean and his lonely yet satisfying task. He pulled his collar tight around his neck and leaned into the long night.

PART THREE

NEW YORK

17

ev was on the navigation bridge and was dumbstruck as the sun rose, clouds parted, and passengers crowded the decks of the *Hellig Olav* as it entered Upper New York Bay and sailed up the Hudson, past the Statue of Liberty and Ellis Island. Through his clenched jaw, he uttered, "Oh my" when seeing the jagged New York skyline for the first time, with its closely packed, impossibly tall buildings. From this distance, the city appeared serene, beautiful, and full of hope. At the same time, its enormity was intimidating. *It must be easy to get lost there,* he thought. He wondered how he would ever find Elizaveta, Natalya's aunt.

To his left, Lev beheld Liberty and the infinite varieties of freedom she promised. He wondered how moved his parents would have been at this moment, had they been aboard. His mother would weep, his father standing stoic, struggling to remain composed.

Lev wanted to feel the same way, but he gazed at the monument and could not summon awe. Instead, he felt remorse at his loneliness and uncertain about everything. His entire life had been mapped out for him in Komenska where he would have continued his studies and apprenticed with his father. He would be betrothed to a beautiful stranger, but when married they would fall in love and quickly have children of their own. He would join his father in drunken vodka dances, and then bury him when he passed away. Lev would become a respected pillar of his community and be known for his kindness and wisdom in his old age. When he himself died, his family would gather around him and tell stories. Close friends would wash his body, wrap him in a peasant's shroud, and bury him in a simple wooden coffin that would quickly decay and return his remains to dust.

All this had been taken from him.

Now, traveling up the Hudson, he was unable to summon any future. Lev knew he should be relieved, even happy, because Captain Peronard said he was considered a crewman and was therefore exempt from any investigation related to falsification of travel documents. It was an immunity of sorts. He would disembark when all the passengers had left, and he would not be subject to probing immigration questions or the specter of deportation or quarantine.

Earlier, before sunrise and with New York only a suggestion of lights, the captain shook Lev's hand. "I'd be proud to have you on the return trip, Leo, though I suppose you're determined to stay."

"I am, sir," said Lev. "I have a relative here. I'm expected."

"Of course you are. That's the way it should be. Family is everything, if you haven't figured it out yet. But the ship is my home. You'll find yours." The captain dropped a few coins into Lev's hand. "It's not much, but this will get you started."

Lev passingly thought about staying aboard. He pondered sailing back to Kristiana on the ship's return voyage. He would look for Smagin and Natalia, then undertake the arduous journey back to Komenska to restart his life. This idea quickly evaporated. He knew there was nothing for him in Russia.

"Home is a good thing," said Lev. "I'm going to make one."

"I have no doubt that you will," said Captain Peronard.

The ship dropped anchor and tied up at Scandinavian America

Line's dock at the foot of Seventeenth Street in Hoboken. Almost immediately, Lev saw wealthy passengers depart with little delay, but all the third-class passengers were herded onto ferries that would shuttle them to a nearby island.

• • •

Dorete was waiting on the dock, holding a small white paper sack. Lev saw her as he walked down the gangplank, thinking that she appeared especially beautiful. She waved to him, and he tried to appear happy when he greeted her.

"I thought I might have missed you," she said.

Lev shrugged. "I thought about looking for you, but I didn't know if you'd want me to."

"Where will you go?"

"I have an address in New York," he said. "You?"

"I have to stay. The ship needs to be cleaned for the return trip."

"I thought you would stay here."

"I was always going back," said Dorete. "My life is in Europe. My family is there. It might have been different, but not now. Mind if I walk with you?"

"I was hoping," said Lev.

Dorete slid her arm in his as they walked down the boardwalk toward the streetcars. Lev hoped they would appear as a couple to passersby.

"You could stay," said Dorete. "It's easier going east."

"Are you asking me to stay with the ship?"

"You could if you wanted. I'm not saying we'd be together. But I would be there. We could spend time together. It might be nice."

"And talk about Willem?"

"I suppose," said Dorete. "And other things. I don't know."

"The captain asked me to stay with the ship, but I don't think he expected me to say yes."

"Neither do I," said Dorete. "But it's sad that you're leaving. I'm going to miss your crooked smile." She touched his cheek with the back of her hand. "You should see a doctor as soon as you can to get your jaw looked at."

"I have something important to do in New York," said Lev.

Dorete pulled closer to Lev. "I know."

They continued down the boardwalk, past dock workers pushing heavy handcarts. Other ships were lined up, some with passengers leaving, welcoming crews, and people heading to faraway destinations. Peddlers were selling boiled sausages.

"I don't suppose I'll see you again," said Lev.

Dorete stopped and flung both arms around Lev. "I'm sorry about everything," she sobbed.

Lev touched the back of her neck and could not help but think of what might have been. He felt sad too. "I think we will," he said. "Meet again, I mean."

Dorete dropped her arms and wiped her eyes. "This is for you. I've crumpled it a bit." She gave him the paper sack. "My address is in there. You can write me if you want. And a *banketstaaf*. Two, actually."

"I'll write you," he said. "I will."

Dorete looked sad and lonely. He imagined that she felt similar to him in many ways.

"I need to get back," she said.

Lev stepped close to her, and without hesitating or asking permission he closed his eyes and kissed her as if it were the last day of their lives. Her lips were soft and warm. At least for that moment, before they parted, he understood all that love offered and why it was so powerful.

Lev watched Dorete walk back up the boardwalk and disappear into the mass of people. He imagined her boarding the ship, going to her room, and changing into clothes she didn't mind getting dirty. He saw her wiping down tables, cleaning cabins, and arranging items on shelves, all while quietly humming a melody. He already missed her, the ship,

Captain Peronard, and the small infirmary bed. He tried to fix everything in his mind so it would remain vivid and accessible in the future.

He opened the sack and saw the two pastries. He wasn't hungry, but he knew he would want them later. Atop them was a small, folded paper. He removed it and smiled at Dorete's delicate handwriting and the delightful street name, which he instantly committed to memory—

Dalbygatan.

He slipped the paper into his breast pocket and withdrew a similarly folded slip. He had looked at this particular small sheet a dozen times during the journey. It was heavily creased and still somehow smelled of Natalya.

Elizaveta Aluşta, 97 Orchard Street, New York.

18

A ferry across the Hudson and a shared cab through New York, and Lev was standing on the corner of Orchard and Hester, dizzy from the stench of humanity and the rumbling of a nearby elevated train. Pushcarts crammed together in narrow streets offered everything imaginable: vegetables, shoes, hardware, jewelry, glasses, books, lamps, tablecloths, candlesticks, jackets, luggage, Judaica, furniture, yarn, and more. Proprietors talked loudly and waved their arms to attract attention amidst the throng of shoppers, and animated haggling in an overlap of languages sounded like a large flock of antagonized ravens.

Beyond the bedlam, storefronts promised high-quality goods and services that advertised butchers, theaters, candy, and clothes. Above the shops on either side of the street, red-and-brown brick buildings reached several stories into the sky, fronted by rickety fire escapes.

This is the aftermath of Babel, thought Lev.

His bag slung over his shoulder, Lev stepped into the chaos and pushed his way up Orchard as the address numbers rose, maneuvering around pushcarts and long lines while being careful to avoid elderly women and young children. When the mass of people was too dense, he doubled back and went around them, often raising the ire of people who threw elbows and insults at him. *Shmendrik! Putz! Beheyme!*

Lev was mostly oblivious to those around him as he concentrated on finding his destination. He crossed Grand Street and fell into a rhythm of looking for small openings or following people who weren't afraid to push their way through the deluge.

Why do I feel so alone when there are many people around me?

After crossing Broome Street, Lev was overcome with weariness and hunger. He moved off the street and paused on the corner to rest between a bakery and a store selling towels and shams. Among the baskets and makeshift stands that filled the walkway, he leaned against the facade and dug into his bag, removing one of Dorete's banketstaaf pastries.

"That looks good."

The voice came from a young boy to his left whom Lev hadn't noticed. Barefoot and dirty, he wore knickers, a ragged white shirt, and loose suspenders. A small yarmulke topped his bowl-cut mop. Lev thought he looked sickly.

"I have another," said Lev.

"Yes, please," said the boy.

Lev removed the remaining banketstaaf and set his bag at his feet. He offered the pastry to the boy, who grabbed it and stuffed half of it in his mouth. Sugary flakes fell from his lips.

"*Gabes eye uhmanz,*" he said through the food. He chewed, swallowed, and tried again. "Tastes like almonds."

Lev nodded and ate his, though much slower, taking small pieces into his mouth and sucking them through his wired teeth. "My girlfriend gave them to me."

"I wouldn't give them up, whether I had a girlfriend or not."

"I shouldn't have said she's my girlfriend. She's a friend, though."

"That counts," said the boy, who looked Lev over head to toe. "You're new here."

"I am," said Lev. "It's been a long trip."

"My name is Aaron, but my friends call me Air."

"I'm Lev, but lately, Leo."

"A lot of people have two names. The one they came here with and a new one that doesn't stick out so much."

"Where were you born?" asked Lev.

"Here," said Aaron.

"New York?"

"I mean right here. This building. Third floor. I had a twin, but he died when we were born."

"I'm sorry," said Lev.

"Yeah." Aaron finished the pastry and licked his fingers. "You want to see something most people don't know about?"

"Sure," said Lev.

Aaron pointed up. "See the top of the building? The very top? If you look carefully, you can see a number. That's when it was built. Do you see it? This one says 1890."

"I don't see it," said Lev. He shielded his eyes from the sun and squinted.

"It's up there," said Aaron. "Right in the middle. All the tenements have them."

Lev tried harder. He managed to see something but couldn't discern whether it was numbers or letters. *Aaron's lucky,* thought Lev. He had an address and knew when his home was built—two numbers that no one could take from him.

"Maybe my eyes aren't as good as yours," said Lev, still struggling to see the letters and numbers.

Then he looked down and saw that Aaron had run into the street and was swiftly moving up Orchard, easily weaving through the crowd. He was holding a familiar worn bag.

It only took a moment for Lev to understand that something was wrong. He looked at the ground to see that his bag was gone.

• • •

Lev launched into the teeming street but had already lost sight of Aaron, who had been swallowed whole by the mass of people and pushcarts. Without regard for civility, he forced his way through the crowd, throwing elbows and clawing his way while thinking only about the contents of his bag.

Lev headed blindly up Orchard and was about to surrender when, not far from him, he spotted Aaron's head bobbing through the crowd. Lev locked onto him and pushed faster through the madness as curses fell upon him.

When he grew closer to the boy, he reached out to grab him but was thwarted when Orchard intersected with Delancey. The boy turned left, sprinted by the last tenement on the block, and scurried into an alley.

I've got him, Lev thought, following Aaron into the alley where he found the boy surrounded by a large group of other children of various ages. The oldest, who looked to be fifteen at the most, was a head taller than the rest. He stood among them, holding Lev's bag.

Lev, very much out of breath, stopped a few yards from them and considered his options. The boy with his bag wore pants that were too short, and his shoes looked two sizes too big.

"Ashkenazi or Sephardic? Where are you from?"

"That's my bag," said Lev. "Aaron stole it."

"You talk funny," he said. "Say something in Spanish."

"He tricked me so he could steal what wasn't his."

"I'm thinking this is my bag now. What's with the clenched mouth?"

"My jaw is wired from a fight," said Lev sternly. "And that bag doesn't belong to you." He took a step toward the boys, who all responded by picking up rocks.

"Wired shut, huh?" said the one with Lev's bag. "My uncle Ira is a doctor and can help you with that. I'll take you to him if you want. But these are our streets. We don't like it when newcomers from Turkey and Spain shove their way in where they're not wanted. They say they're like us, but they're different. Are you different, mister? Where are you from? What's your name?"

"I can tell you everything that's in that bag," said Lev. "There's money. Not a lot, but it's mine. Clothes. And a knife given me by someone with more dignity than all of you combined. I'm not going to give them up without a fight."

"I don't think you're in any position to make demands, mister. Are you gonna give up your name, or not?"

Lev was infuriated but unafraid. He didn't doubt that the small boys would throw their rocks. He cared little about his possessions, but he would do anything to retrieve his mother's letter. "My name is Lev and I'm from Komenska in Byelorussia. I'm here to find my aunt who lives nearby. I'm not from Spain or Turkey, and I don't speak Spanish. I don't care if that makes me the same or different than you, but that's my bag and I'm going to take it back."

"Lev from Byelorussia," said the tall one. "I'm Harvey from the Lower East Side. Nice to meet you. And like I said, this is our neighborhood." He turned toward Aaron. "Is this his bag?"

"Maybe," said Aaron.

"Maybe means yes or no," said Harvey. "If you are from where you say, then you're one of us. But not if you cause trouble, and certainly not if you don't help us. If there's a knife in here like you say, then we'll use it to make you a blood brother. Are you good with that? Say yes or we'll stone your eyes out, because we don't give a shit about your speeches."

"I want my bag back. That's all."

"If you're afraid of a little blood, then fine," said Harvey. "But that just means you're a chicken, which is worse than speaking Spanish."

"I'm not afraid," said Lev.

Harvey opened the bag, reached inside, and withdrew the kinzhal Smagin had given Lev before boarding the *Hellig Olav*. "Damn fine knife," he said. Without hesitating, he flicked the tip of his index finger across the point of the dagger, and a glob of blood dripped down the blade.

Lev took a step back, but the boys immediately swarmed him, pulled him close to Harvey, and forced his hand up. Harvey said, "It only stings for a second." He grabbed Lev's thumb and jabbed it with the kinzhal.

Red splattered his hand. Harvey held Lev's hand and, despite Lev's struggles, he licked the blood from Lev's thumb, then he pushed his own finger between Lev's lips and smeared blood across his teeth.

"Salty, huh?" said Harvey. "The Indians used to do that during initiation ceremonies."

The boys released Lev, and he tried to spit out the blood. It dripped down his chin.

"We're brothers now," said Harvey. He dropped the dagger back into Lev's bag and tossed it to him. "You're one of us. Let's be friends and go see Uncle Ira."

• • •

America is no better than any place else. Violence and coercion. Stealing and lying, Lev thought as he tagged along with his newfound hoodlum blood brother. *I wish I were home.*

Lev longed to walk Komenska's gentle roads, watch his father stretch cowhide, and help his mother scrape wax from a candleholder. He yearned for innocence and wished he knew nothing of the outside world and could go back to waking up in his bed, hoping he could sleep a little longer before being roused for chores.

Loneliness was why Lev clung to the boys, and why, once the taste of blood was gone, he acquiesced and walked with Harvey and Aaron out of the alley and back up the street to 97 Orchard, a six-story brick tenement anchored by a hosiery store and a millinery on either side of the front steps.

"Twenty families live here," said Harvey as they walked up to the stoop. "Maybe not families, because Mrs. Katz lives alone since her husband died last year. He fell off the fire escape when he was cleaning his feet. I don't think one person qualifies as a family. She's on the fourth floor, and she's about as old as anyone you ever met. And 5A doesn't really count because it's only used by Mr. Yonkel's business that finishes coats from the loft factories, although nobody's supposed to know about it. It runs day and night—except on Saturday, of course—and even though it's crammed with workers, I wouldn't call it a family, except that there's a lot of people."

Lev removed the folded papers from his pocket. The one on top displayed Dorete's Dalbygatan address. Beneath it was the slip Natalya had given him, and he showed it to Harvey. "This is my address too," said Lev. "My aunt Elizaveta lives here."

"Elizaveta, huh?" said Harvey. "Here? I doubt it. I know everyone on this block. Have you heard that name, Air?"

Aaron shrugged. "Nope."

"My bubbe Bertha will know," said Harvey. "She's like a walking encyclopedia of everybody who's ever lived here. She's not my real grandmother, but she might as well be. She's everyone's. Uncle Ira takes care of her, and like I said, he'll fix you up."

They stepped inside the building and into a small vestibule with burlap-covered walls of faded cream. Two small, round paintings on the wall depicted pastoral landscapes. Lev leaned in close to inspect one; it appeared to be a small Russian country cottage. It was set among lush vegetation and a sky filled with puffy clouds. *I would like to be there.*

As they climbed the narrow wooden stairs, Harvey said, "This isn't a bad place. Better than most. Worse than others. But if there was room, my family would move here from across the street, because this tenement has better gas and two bathrooms on each floor. If electricity comes, it'll be berries. It's kinda like I live here already, because I'm up and down these stairs all the time."

They climbed two flights to the third floor where Harvey led the way to a door he opened without knocking. They entered directly into a cramped kitchen with a worn linoleum floor, a leaky stone washtub and sink, and cabinets stacked with plates, pots, and ancient-looking tarnished objects. The room smelled of dirty laundry and mold, and Lev felt an oppressive thickness in the air.

"There's usually something good cooking in here," said Harvey. He lifted the lid of a pot on the stove and leaned over to sniff it. He quickly covered it and held his nose. "Onions and garlic."

To the left of the kitchen, an open doorway led to a tiny bedroom, where an extremely large woman with thick ankles reclined on the bed, her arm draped over her eyes. "Who's there?" she said in a deep, gurgling voice.

"Bubbe, it's me," said Harvey.

"Is that you, Favvy? Raful? Velvel?"

"It's me, Harvey."

"Oh, my little Harvela, of course. Come give your bubbe a kiss." She moved her arm away to reveal an immense head and long, disheveled white hair.

Harvey stepped closer, leaned over, and touched his lips to hers. "You're not feeling well?"

"If I felt any worse, I'd already be dead and having rugelach in heaven with my grandparents," she said. "I can't catch my breath. And do you see how swollen my neck is? Ira says it's probably my thyroid, whatever that is, and now I have that to worry about, as if I'm not burdened with enough troubles. I need it like I need a hole in the head. On top of that, I have dinner to worry about, and Ira hasn't brought the groceries. And so, you see, I could be a lot better off. But what am I saying? I sound like a spoiled child. I'll survive. Help me up."

Bertha stood and squealed at the sight of Aaron, who hugged her about the legs and said, "I can almost get my hands around you."

"I was svelte in my youth," she said, "and considered the prettiest girl in Novogrodek. You can ask Ira. His friends would come over to look at my bosom. He was mortified, but I didn't care. I liked giving them something to look at."

"This is Lev," said Harvey. "He's new here but we gave him the going-over. He's a good egg."

"A good egg?" she said, looking at Lev as if he were a petri dish specimen. "Hard-boiled? Soft-boiled? Or fresh out of a chicken? Rotten eggs aren't allowed."

"A normal egg, I think," said Lev. "Nice to meet you."

"Of course it's nice to meet me," said Bertha. "What's not to like? My door is always open, and there's usually something to eat, as long as Ira brings the groceries. If you're a friend of Harvey's, then please, stay, sit for a while. I'm about as nice a person you're likely to find in this crowded city. Did I say anything about the way you talk? Of course not. I'm too polite to do that." She grabbed Lev and pulled him close, smothering him against her chest. She smelled of lye.

"He says he has a relative in the building," said Harvey. "Her name is Lizard or someone like that."

When Bertha released him, Lev said, "Elizaveta Aluşta."

"Oh, that's Liza Lusty," she said. "She stayed with the Malamuts on the sixth floor for a while when they had that big order for drapes. Took them forever because the lining wouldn't cooperate. She came from Russia, but she wasn't Jewish. She was nice all the same. She was a good worker, but a sickly thing. Coughing all the time. I must have heard her real name once or twice, but she changed it to Liza Lusty when she took to whoring. I haven't seen her in months, but last I heard she was working on Allen Street with the rest of her criminal sisters, if you know what I mean. I'm not telling anyone what to do with their life, but spreading your legs for money isn't God's work. I'm not judging. You won't hear me saying a bad word about those slutty girls, but it'll serve them right when they all die from those night diseases. I won't cry about it."

Harvey nudged Lev. "I know all the ladies in the creep joints—not that they would give me the time of day, me being too young and all. But I'm gonna save me a few dollars and go visit one or two of them one day. I'll take you there to find your Liza friend."

19

Lev wanted to rush to Elizaveta. He didn't want to accept that
she was an Allen Street whore. But before he could demand that
Harvey take him there, a door on the other side of the kitchen
opened, and a man exited with his arm in a sling. Following him
was a balding, squat, square-shaped man who had a salt-and-pepper
toothbrush mustache and a veiny red nose. "Change that when you get
home," he called after the man in the sling. "Soap. Lots of soap. Keep
it clean. Come see me if it starts to smell."

"That's Uncle Ira," said Harvey. "He'll fix you up faster than a
beggar can eat a cheese blintz."

Ira saw the man out of the apartment and then came back into the
room, saying, "Are you feeling better, Mother?"

"You didn't get the groceries like you promised."

"I'm sorry," he said, looking straight at Lev.

"What does sorry get me?" said Bertha. "You can't eat sorry. These
are hungry boys. You're going to send them away with empty bellies?"

"I wouldn't think of it," said Ira. "I'll send this little one out."

He dug in his pocket and withdrew some folded money. He put it in Aaron's hand. "What do you need?"

"What do I need?" said Bertha. "What do I always need? Good food that people can eat and be happy about. A chicken. A nice golden whitefish if you can find it. Pickles. Pastrami, but not too expensive. Knish—get a dozen. Chopped liver. Red onions. Two challahs from Malcom's cart, not the bakery. Belly lox. And cheese, I don't care what kind as long as it doesn't have green on it."

"You're expecting an army?" said Ira.

"You want to eat? All of a sudden you're questioning my cooking?"

"I don't want to argue."

"So don't argue," said Bertha. "Bring the food so we can survive another day. Is that so hard?"

Ira stuffed more bills into Aaron's hand and pushed him out the doorway. "Hurry up before we're scolded again."

"Scolding?" said Bertha. "What scolding?"

Ira continued his consideration of Lev, who felt he was being inspected.

"Hello, sir," said Lev.

"Your mouth is clenched," said Ira. "I can fix that."

"It's wired," said Harvey. "He said it happened after a fight. He'll be good to have on our side."

"Our side, eh?" said Ira. "Step inside my office and we'll see what we shall see."

• • •

The parlor was on the other side of the kitchen. It was a bright space, the only space in the tiny three-room apartment with windows. There was a long wooden table in the middle, which was covered by a colorful floral quilt and a thin pillow. A narrower table, which ran along the wall, held a variety of shiny metal medical instruments.

Ira patted the quilt. "Hop up," he said to Lev.

"I'm fine," said Lev. "I don't want to be a bother."

"You want to live the rest of your life talking like that?" asked Ira. "Unless there's a good reason for that wire, you'll be stuck like that and need to have your temporomandibular joint forced and maybe broken so you can eat and talk normal. A lot of people who call themselves physicians don't know the difference between a fracture and a harmless contusion. I see you're hesitant. I don't blame you, but I was a renowned physician in Krakow. I had the largest practice in the city. My clientele were among the highest positions in government. Now look at me—I'm mostly treating gout and bunions. Scraping by. I'm the finest doctor in this tenement madness. You're lucky you found your way to me. Now, please, let me help you."

"He set my arm last year when I broke it," said Harvey. "You're not scared, are you?"

Lev could not think of an argument against complying, so he sat on the table and tried to stay calm while Ira touched his face.

"This shouldn't hurt," said Ira. "A little pressure maybe, is all. If you feel sharp pain—any pain, actually—let me know." Ira ran his hands over Lev's jaw with increasing pressure. He pushed his fingers deep into Lev's flesh to test bone and teeth. "Any discomfort?"

Lev wasn't sure how to answer. He wouldn't call it pain, more a dull throbbing near his temples. "I'm not sure," he said. "I don't think so."

"On your back," said Ira. "I need to examine you while you're resting and not working to hold your head up. We must control your neck muscles."

Lev reclined, and Ira began a more aggressive examination. "Does it hurt here?" he asked, hooking a thumb under his jaw and pulling up.

"It's uncomfortable."

"Of course it is; I'm jabbing you with my bony fingers. I'm feeling for hot spots. Sometimes it's possible to feel a fracture."

Ira's face grew nearer to Lev. He could see bits of food and dirt in his mustache. The pores on his nose looked cavernous, and his eyes were bloodshot, dirty-brown pools.

Ira leaned in closer. "Can you feel this?"

Lev felt a sharp jab in his inner thigh. He moved his leg, but the pain increased. "What?"

"It's a small scalpel," said Ira. "Almost nothing. But I can slice your femoral artery with a flip of my wrist. You'll bleed out in seconds. Or, for a more interesting surprise, I can easily slice up and you'll be an instant eunuch and of no use to women."

Frightened, Lev didn't move. He felt the blade puncture his thigh. "Why?" he said, struggling not to scream.

"I think you know why," said Ira. "You greasy Jews from lower countries sneak into our neighborhoods and try to push us out. You pretend that Jews are Jews wherever they come from, but you know it's a lie. You can try to squeeze us with your smarmy smiles and pretend to be real Jews, like us. But all you want is to push us out like Blacks to Harlem. But you will lose this gamble, because we're staying put. This neighborhood is a cesspool, true, but it's our cesspool."

"You don't have to cut him," said Harvey. "He's already a blood brother. We sealed it."

"Good," said Ira. "Then a little more blood won't hurt." He slowly pushed the scalpel deeper into Lev's leg. "I know it's uncomfortable, but there's no other way to ensure you'll tell the truth. Now, tell me, before I rip this straight up to your groin. Where are you from and why are you here?"

Lev worked hard to fight the blinding pain. He held his breath and moaned.

"Pain is your signpost," said Ira. "It's your steady friend. It helps you see clearly and to separate fact from fiction, the tsar from Rasputin, lies from truth. So embrace it, my good fellow. Fall into the pain. Focus on it as I push the blade in more. Just a little deeper until the point hits the bone. You'll know when it happens. Now, do yourself a favor and admit you are a liar and that your Russian accent is fake. You embrace the other tribes. Admit it before I fuck you to hell with this."

Lev, now held fast by pain so intense that he could not think, tried to summon something that would satisfy Ira. His eyes overflowed, and he felt lightning strike his leg. It consumed his entire body, and he coughed up a thick gob of bile that rocketed toward Ira and landed on his glistening forehead.

Ira pulled the scalpel out of Lev's leg. "He is one of us," he said. "Now let's get that wire out of his mouth."

With a tenderness that belied his resolve, Ira stitched the incision in Lev's leg, pulling gently on the catgut to tie three precise knots. "I don't take any pleasure in this," he said. "I don't want you to think I'm some kind of monster. But those *farshtinkeners* have placed spies among us before. I'm doing what I must to make sure we stay pure, whatever it takes. Mama wants it that way. Now let's take a look at the wire. Don't mind my fingers."

He inserted a thin needle-nose cutting tool in Lev's mouth and started to clip the wires. "Your jaw isn't broken. Never was. No evidence of trauma, and your teeth are straight. Maybe it was swollen, but we can't have so-called doctors wiring up people left and right. You're thin as a rail because of it. But Mama will put some meat on your bones, I promise." Ira clipped the last wire and carefully pulled it from Lev's mouth. "Now, don't go jabbering away and opening your mouth wide. A little at a time. These things can't be rushed. You hear me?"

Lev rubbed his jaw and tested it. He opened his mouth a little and felt resistance. "This is as far as I can open it," he said.

"Give it time," said Ira. "Didn't I just say that? Now scoot. Mrs. Apfel will be coming along shortly. She has a rather sweet vagina vault prolapse that requires an expert hand. Gather your gang of hooligans, Harvey. I'll see you later, like usual. Lev should come too."

• • •

Harvey invited Lev to his home across the street. It was a similarly cramped tenement, only older and somehow damper. His mother, a silent, severe woman with a pinched face, served a small meal of spinach-filled borekas and fried artichokes. Harvey's father, Boris, was an expansive man who wore glasses so thick that his eyes appeared huge and grotesque.

"We live modestly," he said, "and I regret our table is not overflowing. But the good book tells us to welcome strangers to our table."

"He's not a stranger," said Harvey. "He has a name. He knows Uncle Ira. He arrived straight from Russia. He's like family."

"So you say," said Boris. "I'm not protesting. We're glad to have you, Lev. See? I know his name. But maybe don't eat so much."

"Yes sir," said Lev. "I'm not hungry anyway."

"Eating is overrated," said Boris. "But it was the same in the old country. We slave all week to put food on the table. Your mother bakes all day. And what do we do? We consume everything in a few minutes. It's backwards is what it is. And what thanks do we get?"

"Thank you," said Lev.

Boris pushed his glasses up his nose and frowned. "A thank-you I get from a total stranger, but my own son? Not a word. He runs around town at all hours as if he doesn't live here. We don't see him for days. Is this a hotel?"

"I'm sitting right here," said Harvey.

"And then you'll be off after you stuff your face, and we won't see you until morning. When was the last time you helped clean up after a meal?"

"I help sometimes," said Harvey. "But I have important things to do."

"Important things? I know what you're up to. Do you think I'm blind? That Uncle Ira of yours, who's not a blood uncle by the way, that shyster lawyer . . . I know what he's doing."

"He's a doctor," said Harvey.

"Doctor, lawyer, same thing. He's up to no good, like he's the Pied Piper."

"He's a good man," said Harvey. "A great man."

"What am I, chopped liver?"

"You're my father."

"So that means I don't know anything?"

"I didn't say that."

"I'm hungry," said Boris. "I don't need this aggravation. But if someone comes knocking on my door with news about you, I won't come running."

"We're helping protect our community."

"Protection shmection," said Boris. "A terrible waste of time. Do you know what you should be doing instead? You should be reading the Talmud."

"Again with the Talmud. Like a broken record."

"You should be spending time in shul. When was the last time you went? Don't bother answering; I know the answer. Never. Just down the street is the Eldridge Street Synagogue, a beautiful monument to everything we didn't have in Russia. Here, we are not ashamed. We worship openly and without fear. You go by the shul every day. But do you go in and bother to learn anything? You disrespect your religion. I don't know why I waste my breath. What you and your friends are doing enriches no one."

"If a Turkish family moved into our tenement, you'd think differently," said Harvey. "You would scream when they offered the landlord more money, because then our rent would go up. You'd be singing a different tune."

"Nobody's singing," said Boris.

Lev put his fork down. "It's nice of you to have me for dinner," he said. "I appreciate it very much. And I hope you don't think I'm out of place by saying this, but I don't understand why everyone is so impolite to each other. Maybe it's the way of America, but my parents never talked to me this way."

Boris took his time chewing on an artichoke. Then he wiped his mouth, cleared his throat, and stood. "You can both go fuck yourselves," he said.

2 0

ev walked with Uncle Ira, Harvey, and a three dozen other children
to Seward Park, a three-minute walk up Orchard. Lev had never
seen a playground like it, set amidst the cramped urban squalor
of dilapidated tenements and shoehorned shops. It was a large, cinder-
topped playground with open areas, swings and maypoles. Lev thought
it must be busy during the day, but now, at night, it appeared to be a
frozen graveyard, with abandoned swing sets transformed into great
looming spiders and shadow giants.

Uncle Ira, wearing a long, black, bulging overcoat and a wool
Stetson Temple fedora, stepped confidently. Harvey would have been
the oldest and tallest of the boys if Lev had not been among them.

"Stay alert," said Ira. "This is where cowards hide. They employ
vicious tactics without regard to anything resembling common decency.
Vicious! They won't think twice about flinging one of their piccolo
knives. You won't hear or see it, but suddenly one will be sticking out
of your neck and you'll be dead before you hit the ground. So, safety
in numbers, my young but capable army."

The boys moved tighter around Ira. Several put their hands to their necks as they moved deeper into the park as a tight pack.

"We know they're here," said Ira. "That's our advantage. They know we're coming. That's *their* advantage. But we're young and nimble and unafraid. We have been blessed and anointed by God because we're on the side of light and righteousness and goodness. Stay close to me, boys. That's good. You don't keep what's rightfully yours by being meek and hoping things will fall your way. Because they never do. It's sad that life doesn't work that way. It doesn't seem fair." Halfway across the park and heading toward the Pavilion, Ira raised his voice. "If anyone is listening, behold our small battalion of defenders. We will not pick our noses while you encroach upon what we built." And then even louder, "We will be strong and hold hands to protect our mothers and fathers, our bubbies and zaydies, our children and jobs and culture and religion—*our* religion, not the one you pretend to wear. Our world is beautiful, but people like you make it ugly."

They approached a large building on the east side of the park that looked like a grand ship resting on the ocean floor. It had ten immense, open-arched columns. The clear, moonless sky threw ink into the structure, giving it a haunted, dangerous appearance. When only a few yards away, the dark spaces between the columns softened into the shapes of many men. Big men. Men with beards and large stomachs. One, standing in the center at the top of the steps, lit a cigarette. The flame threw light on his face, revealing a weary, serious expression.

The man stepped from the shadows. He was large, as wide as he was tall and with a beard that reached below his belt. He wore a furry ascot cap. "The Pavilion is ours," he said in a gravelly baritone voice. "We told you we would take it, and we have done so." The other men, too many to count, came forward as well. They carried clubs, sticks, and baseball bats.

Ira stopped ten paces away and laughed. "Vitali the Vulture. Of course. Who else would have the chutzpah to take the Pavilion? Did I say chutzpah? I meant stupidity. Do you see us living and working in there? It has no use to us. You are welcome to enjoy it."

"I don't like that name," said Vitali.

"You mean the Vulture?" said Ira. "Who wouldn't want to be associated with the nasty scavenger? It's an honor."

"I don't like it," Vitali growled. "It's an insult."

"Do you hear that, boys? He doesn't like his name. If I were lucky enough to have a grand name like that, I would never tire of it. Vulture!"

"I mean it," barked Vitali. "Stop saying that."

Ira threw his hands in the air and brought them quickly to his sides. "If you say so," he said. "But let's talk seriously for a moment. If you think we're going to let you move in on a place we built, then you're delusional. We were here first. We won't be pushed out by you and your money. That's what vultures do."

Vitali lurched forward, but the boys swarmed around Ira to create a human barrier.

"That's it, my boys. Show the vulture you're not afraid. Challenge them to do harm to unarmed children. Even vultures won't cross that line."

Vitali nodded. "Hiding behind kids is cowardly. It won't stop us. We have every right to rent in your buildings. This isn't your community, Doctor. Quack doctor. You say you've built it, but it's a lie. Germans lived here long before you. And before them, thieves and whores and natives. You're only the most recent to nest here. Did they protest when you moved in? We worship the same God. Why do you resist us?"

"We don't resist," said Ira. "We simply have an aversion to the stink you bring when you walk down the street."

"It's a cold night," said Vitali. "Your boys are getting taller. Do your parents know you're out so late? Maybe you should all run home to your mothers' aprons before you get hurt."

"Stay where you are," said Ira. He unbuttoned his overcoat to reveal rows of pockets sewn into the lining from chest to tail. Heavy rocks were nestled in each pocket. "Load up, my boys," said Ira, who held his overcoat open as each boy hurried to remove a rock. "Minerals are elegant weapons. They take out eyes and teeth, then fall to the ground without incriminating evidence. And when focused, they can be extremely deadly." Ira lifted his head to address the men. "I wouldn't test them if I were you. They're itching to heave their stones. All I need to do is give the word and they'll open the sky with hard rain. Isn't that right, boys?"

The small hands of Ira's diminutive army raised their rocks to the sky. They chanted, "Our homes, not yours! Our homes, not yours!"

"We're small but mighty, and we're not going anywhere," cried Ira, who then emitted a guttural sound and appeared to swat a fly away from his ear. But the fly was a small, thin knife embedded to the hilt below his jaw. Lev, who was standing directly behind Ira, heard the whistle of the knife and caught a splatter of blood as it entered Ira's neck.

Ira grasped the knife, slowly slid it out, and collapsed. He fell against Lev, who gently lowered him to the ground and cradled the wounded man's head in his lap.

Ira looked up at Lev. "Am I bleeding?" he asked weakly.

"Yes."

"Put pressure on it," said Ira. "Maybe it will stop."

Lev pressed his palm over the red fountain. It felt hot and sticky. "You'll be okay," said Lev, unsure. "We'll get you home."

Vitali, who hadn't moved, said, "There are risks in any confrontation. But we don't want trouble. We never asked for this. All we want is to enjoy America's freedom, the same as you. We demanded it, true, but we offered to do it peacefully. Now we will leave you. Think about what we have said. Take this message back to your parents."

Vitali and his men disappeared back into the Pavilion, leaving a deathly silence behind.

The boys gathered around Lev and Ira, rocks still clasped in their hands. Their fire and bravado had evaporated. Now they stood quietly, waiting for everything, waiting for nothing, afraid to move until a sliver of moon appeared and they carried Ira home to Bertha, who washed his neck and treated it with Dr. Fenner's medicated ointment.

"It was a short knife, otherwise I'd be dead," muttered Ira. "But even then, I was lucky."

"Luck has nothing to do with it," said Bertha. "God is on our side."

• • •

Although he was bone tired and emotionally drained, Lev ventured out to resume his primary task of finding Elizaveta, despite Bertha's fervent demand that he stay. In the dead of night, he found Orchard to be strangely quiet. The crowds, pushcarts, and tumult were replaced with an eerie sereneness. The wind played with a pickle wrapper. A rat scurried across the road.

But Allen Street, one block up, was crowded with customers and practitioners of sex trades, a seething population of degenerate cripples, hunchbacks, wealthy hoteliers, nervous young virgins, repressed husbands, mobsters, cornered women, politicians, tourists, enlisted military, businessmen, entertainers, and ill-tempered brothel owners. The police, who might otherwise be busy arresting everyone, looked the other way; they received pleasure without payment. Layered atop this human activity, the elevated train made everything noisier and more intense.

The moment Lev stepped foot on the street, a woman sitting on a nearby corner stoop said, "How old are you?" She had only recently lost her beauty. Drawn-on eyebrows and too much rouge amplified the youth that had abandoned her.

"I'm not looking for that," said Lev.

The woman laughed and parted her knees. "You are, whether or not you want to admit it," she said. "Why else are you here? You're a handsome young thing."

"I'm looking for someone."

"Everyone is looking for someone. We all need a little attention. A warm body. A shoulder to cry on. Someone to tell our secrets and desires. Come sit with me. Show me what you have. I give discounts for virgins."

"I'm not."

"Fine with me," she said. "We can play that game."

"I'm not a virgin," said Lev. "I would tell you if I was."

"It doesn't matter to me, either way."

"I'm looking for Elizaveta Aluşta," he said.

"I'm not an information service."

"I'm sorry," said Lev. "I only thought that—"

"That because I'm a woman on Allen Street, and a whore at that, I happen to know everyone here?"

"That's not what I meant. I was only asking."

"I know what you were asking."

Lev raised his voice. "I'm not here for sex. I'm looking for somebody, like I said."

"I don't know anyone named Elizaveta, if that's all you care about."

Lev looked down and idly kicked a pebble against the curb. "That's not all I care about," he said. "I'm sorry. I'm not thinking anything bad about you. I have to find her."

"All you boys are the same," she said, bringing her knees together and folding her hands on her lap. "You brag to your friends but can't find the courage when it counts."

"You're a pretty lady," said Lev. "Anyone would be lucky to be with you."

"You're only saying it now because you have to," she said. "You seem to be a good boy, but you only care about finding this Elizaveta. I've already told you that I haven't heard of her."

"Liza Lusty, maybe?"

"Is that who you're looking for? Liza? Why didn't you say so? Of course I know her, but I haven't seen her in ages. Down the street a block. The tenement with the blue awning. She worked there, last I knew."

"Worked?"

"Yes, worked," she said. "It's Allen Street. We're all working. Selling what we own. Use your imagination, but no judging. Because if that's why you're here, you can go home alone and sleep with your hand. No one needs to be insulted."

"I'm not saying anything."

"Keep it that way."

"The blue awning?"

"As blue as your balls, I'm sure."

•   •   •

The awning was a rusted metal canopy that sheltered the front steps of a tenement building on the south side of the street, but the color had faded to a muddy gray, barely hinting at its original azure.

Lev stood in front of the building, which looked no different than any other, except for a crumpled dollar bill tacked to the front door. He wondered if Elizaveta was inside, and if she was entertaining a customer. He hadn't met her, but he hated to think of her that way. He took a step back and considered turning away. He had already connected with people who seemed somewhat welcoming and who had offered him shelter, so there was no urgency to find her. But his fondness for Smagin and Natalya caught him.

He proceeded up the steps. Maybe he didn't require help from Elizaveta, but perhaps *she* needed rescuing.

There was no one inside the building foyer or on the steps leading to the second floor, but he could hear vague, muffled noises from upstairs. Lev called, "Hello?" but the only answer was his own voice echoing up the central staircase.

He moved through the small foyer and had barely begun to climb the steps when he paused to listen. He was as still as possible. He focused again on the sounds coming from above. They were human noises, but he could not discern their genesis—lovers, perhaps, writhing in ecstasy, or people squabbling and throwing books? Sounds of pain or pleasure? He imagined there were many women in the tenement's apartments, each of them locked in a transaction, and he felt a wave of jealousy toward the men who might be with them. No matter their reason for seeking sex for money, it was sex all the same. Was the physical act any different, whether or not coins were exchanged? The mechanics were the same, he reasoned, even if the heart was not committed.

Standing on the steps and absorbing the noises brought the vividness of the Khorkov sisters to him. A wave of desire washed over him, and he wanted to be in their wagon again with the darkness, their invisibility, their instructive hands. He missed them with a blinding intensity, even though he understood that what they shared was not true intimacy. It was carnal and convenient, but it had nothing to do with love. But this insight did not make him think less of them.

He continued up the stairs, rounded the half landing, and was startled by a woman of striking beauty standing on the top step, blocking the way to the second floor. She was middle-aged, had fiery red hair, and though she was blessed with warm features that lent her an aura of kindness, her eyes betrayed exhaustion. She inhaled a long drag from a cigarette and blew the smoke toward the ceiling when she saw Lev.

"I don't want to know how old you are," she said dramatically. "As long as you don't say it, I can live with myself. Or maybe Bennie sent you?"

"I don't know who Bennie is," said Lev.

"You would remember him," she said. "He's quite unforgettable."

"He didn't tell me to come."

"Of course not," she said. "Why should Bennie send someone to help me when I'm perfectly capable of minding the stairs on my own? It's not like I have anything to do other than to manage every goddamn thing that happens in this building. Staffing the girls, cleaning the sheets, moving the money, doling out discipline, attracting guests when things are slow. Like I said, I stand around all day twiddling my thumbs. Why should Bennie give a flying fuck if I also have to stand here and sort through tricks?"

Lev wasn't sure if she was complaining or bragging, so he said, "That's a lot."

"Understatement," she said. "That's a good quality. It means stability of character. Trustworthiness. Your feet are planted firmly on the ground, no?"

"Yes, ma'am."

"Yes, *ma'am*? Please don't. As if I'm an old hag whose age demands artificial respect. I'm Stolia. Some call me Madam Stolia, but that makes me sound like a clairvoyant."

"I knew a real one," said Lev. "Or—*maybe* he was real. Professor Orakam. He could predict your future by turning cards and throwing sticks."

Stolia tugged on her ear and took another drag from her cigarette. Lev felt he was being studied. "Did he read yours?" she asked. "Did he see that you and I would be talking, and that you would agree to work here?"

"I'm not looking for work."

"Everyone needs a job," said Stolia. "You need money, don't you?"

"I don't know."

"You're in the most expensive city in the world. You look like you could use work."

"What kind of job?"

"That's better," she said. "See? You're already thinking like a New Yorker. You have to be opportunistic to get by. And if you want to make it to the top, you have mix it up. Are you getting my drift?"

They were interrupted by the sound of a creaking door opening somewhere above them, then slow, heavy footsteps came down the stairs. It was a very old man, who rounded the stairs and stood behind Stolia. Lev thought he looked ready for death, but he tried to push by Stolia, who stood her ground on the stairs and did not let him pass until, behind the man, a woman wearing a slight, transparent pink robe appeared. She nodded to Stolia, who then moved aside to let the codger pass. Lev looked away as the man brushed past him and continued down the stairs and out of sight. A scent of cheap perfume trailed him.

Lev felt the woman's eyes undressing him. "For me?" she asked.

"We haven't determined that yet," said Stolia.

"No," said Lev. "I'm not here for that."

"For what?" said the woman, who opened her sheer pink robe and exposed her breasts. "You don't like these? Old man Ketzle was just sucking on them, but he ran out of breath."

"I'm here for a job." Lev looked at Stolia. "Tell her."

"I don't think we've determined anything," said Stolia.

"You're a muzzle, then?" said the woman in pink.

"I'm not anything," said Lev.

"Oh, you're something," she said, pulling the flimsy gown around her. "You're cute as hell, is what. Give me a few minutes to clean up, and I'll be ready. You've got money, right?"

"No."

"Because you're better than me, is that it?"

Stolia said, "Yetta, he's too young to mean anything."

"The younger they are, the harder it stands and the quicker they finish," said Yetta. "But I know what he meant. Look at his eyes. He's judging us. Well, let me tell you, you punk baby, we do what's necessary. I'm supporting my family and putting shoes on my kids' feet. We get by, is what we do. We wring the sweat from sheets so we can save and get out of this stinking place."

Yetta turned and headed back up the stairs. "Don't mind her," said Stolia.

"I didn't mean to offend her," said Lev.

"She's not mad at you. She's mad at all men. She wants you to know who's boss. You haven't revealed your name. You know Yetta's. You know mine."

"Lev."

"Lev. And you're not here looking for pleasure. No—you're looking for someone, aren't you?"

"Yes."

"I'm thinking you are the famous Lev from Russia, and you're looking for Liza. Don't ask me how I know because I won't tell you just yet. But I know all about you and Liza. She warned me that you would show up, and look who's in front of me. Lev from Russia."

"I need to find her," said Lev.

"We all need things. I propose a trade. You agree to work here, and I'll tell you about Liza."

21

It was a marriage of convenience—information about Elizaveta in exchange for a cot in the basement and working at the tenement brothel. *A fair trade*, Lev thought.

He sat on a wooden bench atop the second-floor landing, counting his money. He'd never earned his own before, and he liked the weight of the coins in his hand. His job was simple. No one could go down the stairs unless the worker—that's what Stolia called her girls—signaled that she had been paid, and customers were not allowed up unless there was a worker to invite him to bed. Lev earned ten cents per transaction.

When the building was full, there were often a few men standing or sitting on the steps below Lev, waiting their turn—some embarrassed, others bragging about their prowess. They'd say, "I'm hoping Grunthilda is next. There's so much to hold," or, "As long as it's not my wife, I don't care."

In this manner, Lev became known by the women in the building. Sometimes they would sit with him when their bed was empty and no customer was waiting. They combed his hair with their fingers and said they would give him a discount. One said she would nurse him if he was hungry. But he was often disgusted by the men who went to their rooms, and he thought it unsanitary—and certainly not kosher. Still, the hours sitting there, surrounded by people on their way to and from physical satisfaction, left him feeling hollow, disheartened, and lonely.

Despite the circumstances, he listened carefully to every footfall from below, wondering if it was Elizaveta. Stolia had said it was possible, if unlikely, that she would return.

"She left several weeks ago," Stolia had told him when they struck the bargain. "She was a good person. Beautiful. Popular among customers. But she was sick and said she was going for help. Before she left, she said there was a good chance that you would come looking for her. *Lev from Russia,*' she said, and under her niece's care, no? She wanted to wait for you, but her cough grew worse, and I promised her I would watch for you. She may come back, or she may not. But she said she would send word, either way."

Lev thought about those words—*either way*—as he worked his job, counted his money, and waited for Elizaveta.

Past midnight, a customer from an apartment down the hall came lumbering out like a drunk elephant, dragging his suspenders and buttoning his shirt. One of the workers, Gerta, followed him and said to Lev, "He's good to go, and a quick one at that."

She was a beautiful, raven-haired woman, and her high eyebrows gave her a contented and centered appearance. As the man barreled down the stairs, she sat next to Lev and dropped a dime into his palm. "If I was any more tired, I would have to invent the bed," she said.

"Yeah."

"You're not very talkative," said Gerta. "Our last gatekeeper wouldn't shut up. He'd talk up everyone and tell customers about our special talents, as if we have any. Zelda can swallow a kielbasa, yeah, but we all have the same equipment. And he would sing. I'd be busy with a customer and I'd hear his voice from under the door, missing the high notes. But you? You're a quiet thing."

"My mother taught me that listening is better than talking," he said.

"A momma's boy, huh? They make the best lovers. So attentive. So caring. So purposeful. Come back to my room. It won't cost anything."

Lev thought she would look prettier if her hair weren't mussed, but she had an appealing dignity about her that he thought compelling. "I shouldn't," he said. "Stolia said not to leave the stairs unattended."

"There's no one waiting," said Gerta. "It's fine if you're shy."

"I'm not shy."

"Life is short," said Gerta. She touched his shoulder and ran her fingers down his arm to his hand. "My father lived his whole life waiting. He saved his money so he would have enough in his old age. He denied himself pleasures so that he would appreciate them when the time was right. He refused to socialize because he felt that friendships fade. He did not treat my mother well because he said there was time for that later. He planned and he plotted and he calculated the exact day that he would allow himself to start living. Finally, the day arrived. It was a Sunday, and I remember it well because my mother braided my hair with six violet ribbons. We went to the market without my father because he said he had a special chore to perform on the first day he was allowed to enjoy life. He said it was a surprise. We walked to the town center and bought fabric and apples and a small butterfly pendant. When we returned, we found him dead at the bottom of the stairs, where he'd fallen after hanging a banner that said, LIFE AND LOVE BEGIN TODAY. He was quiet and cold, and his left arm was broken in half.

"You don't forget things like that. I'm telling you this because you will suffer the same fate if you find excuses to postpone happiness." Gerta opened her gown to reveal a small metal butterfly that hung on a chain around her neck.

"That's a sad story," said Lev. "I'm sorry."

"I'll be waiting for you in my room," she said, and walked away. Lev listened to her footsteps and held his breath until he heard a door open and close. He pictured her smoothing the bed and waiting for him. Maybe she was dabbing perfume behind her ears. He knew he wouldn't go to her room, but he thought about her anyway, contemplating her experience and wondering what secrets she knew that the Kharkov sisters did not.

It was strangely quiet in the tenement brothel. No customers were waiting, and Lev could not hear any of the usual human murmurs that were almost always present in the building. He felt as if time had stopped, and that he was the only person aware of it. If he peered inside one of the apartments, he was sure he would catch naked lovers frozen and tangled. He could walk in without them being aware of his presence and brush the woman's hair from her eyes. If he wanted to, he could pry the customer away and take a turn without anyone knowing. When he was finished, he would return the heavy man to his place and leave.

Lev remained on the stool and listened to his heartbeat grow louder and rise in his chest until he could feel it in his throat. He was unable to swallow, could barely breathe. His eyes hurt. He stood without intention and walked without desire, but he stood at Gerta's door and entered without knocking. She was sitting on the bed, wearing only the butterfly necklace.

Gerta stood. "You took longer than I expected," and undressed him. She reclined on the bed, guided him to her, and lightly kissed his neck. She whispered, "Don't make too much noise because we'll be discovered."

"I won't," he said.

But Lev and Gerta were not quiet and were discovered by the other women. It quickly became routine that at the end of an evening, when no customers were waiting, Lev would be invited to join one of the women, who also longed for the stamina of youthful, nondesperate love. Sometimes he declined, but he would often accept because, hypnotized by the unceasing sounds that filled the tenement, he would overflow with desire.

Lev did not look forward to such random, loveless episodes—quite the opposite. Each evening after a fevered hour of flesh, he would swear never to do it again. He felt dirty. He imagined that his parents disapproved from their righteous perch in Heaven. But feelings of self-loathing faded each evening as midnight approached.

Lev admired and desired all of them, but some more than most. He was grateful they took turns offering their bed, but he came to prefer those who were aggressive and not shy about instruction. They contorted their bodies, demanded to be taken in impossible positions, and were not satisfied until his tongue was sore. He also liked those who called him "big boy" and ate him up from head to toe. Some tossed him around the room like a sack of potatoes.

He was most comfortable with Gerta, his first tenement lover. She was gentle but insistent, and always seemed thirsty for his kisses, no matter how many men she'd turned that evening. She wasn't satisfied until he couldn't catch his breath. Only then would she cover herself and softly sing, "Let Me Call You Sweetheart" with a verse that Lev thought romantic, yet unattainable.

Birds are singing far and near
Roses bloomin ev'rywhere
You, alone, my heart can cheer
You, just you

Lev, lazily gazing at stains on the ceiling, wondered what it would be like to be in that field of roses that extended to the horizon, their color caressing but their thorns haunting. Did the person who wrote the song wander through such a place? And were the skies filled with tree pipits and their aggressive *speks* that sounded like squeaky shoes? For the songwriter to be oblivious to these, he must truly be in love. It was certain that one must be an expert in love, to have enjoyed its rapture and suffered its sorrow, to faithfully portray it in verse.

Gerta reached for his hand and laced her fingers between his. "Tell me what you're thinking," she said. "You're far away."

"The song you're singing," said Lev. "It's nice."

"One of my customers was singing it when he was on top of me earlier," she said. "Now I can't get it out of my head."

"I wish you hadn't told me that."

"You asked."

"I didn't."

"You mustn't fall in love with me."

"I won't," he said, but he wasn't sure he meant it.

Gerta moved closer to him and rested her head next to his. "What are you looking at up there?"

"The water stains," said Lev. "I was wondering how they got there. There are three floors above us and somehow water came down through them. I think it makes the building unsafe, and we're underneath it."

"It could be anything," she said. "A bath that overflowed. A kitchen mishap. Who knows? What concern is that of yours?"

"Just wondering."

"You're a strange one," said Gerta. "Like an old person in a young man's body."

"Is that a good thing?"

"Maybe," she said. "But you'd be happier if you didn't make up stories about the building collapsing because of a common ceiling stain. Do you want to go again? We can if you want."

She kissed his neck and slipped her tongue inside his ear. It sounded like the ocean and that made him wonder if Captain Peronard was crossing the Atlantic at that very moment, and if his crew was watching for icebergs.

"Yes," he said.

• • •

The next evening was unusually quiet, with many of the women profoundly bored without customers. Some passed the time by congregating on the second-floor landing, where Lev kept watch on the stairs, waiting for the rush of men who did not arrive.

"They'll be here," said Stolia. "All men come here eventually. They can't help it."

Maybe the rain is keeping customers away, Lev thought. Maybe the world had grown so melancholy that even those who were the most sexually frustrated could not bring themselves to part with their money. Outside the small world of the cramped tenement, he imagined that everything was larger and somehow more important. People led meaningful lives out there, beyond the trains and bridges, beyond the fancy uptown shops and roads leading to adventure. They had wives and children and jobs that turned the world's economy, and they probably never thought about—let alone visited—the mass of humanity that crowded into the Lower East Side, where immigrants fought over tiny tenement rooms with stagnant air, where people lived small, insignificant lives and were forgotten the moment they died.

Lev felt he would disappear completely if Elizaveta didn't appear soon.

At that moment, the sound of the front door opening and closing came from below, then soft, tiny footfalls of someone on the stairs—delicate, as if a lithe ballerina were climbing steps on the flat toe pad of her pointe shoes. But the sounds grew steadily louder and more aggressive as their source drew nearer, until a shadow appeared on the stairs and an imposing figure in an ascot hat rose before Lev and the women.

Lev recognized him immediately—Vitali the Vulture. His immense size and tremendously long beard announced his arrival.

"Ladies," he growled, opening his arms wide, like a bird in flight, "your Vitali is here, your warmth in the winter, your wind in the summer, here again to give you what you have been waiting for this dreary evening."

The women stepped back in unison. Gerta muttered a bit too loud, "Talk about dreary."

Vitali climbed to the landing. "Ah, my fine ladies," he said. "Do I deserve such a poor reception? After all I have given you? And especially you, Gertrude, my flower. I've come for you tonight."

Stolia stepped forward. "You haven't given more than any other man. In fact, a little less."

The women laughed. Vitali's smile vanished.

"You're ungrateful," he said. "We have showered you with money and pleasure. What do we get in return? There are a dozen other buildings on this street dispensing your sad wares. Don't pretend you're anything more than wretched whores like every other. You're as low as it gets. If I want a go, you'll provide it."

"This is an honest business, no matter what anyone says," said Stolia. "We're not doing anyone harm. We're purveyors of love and satisfaction when there is so little in the world. We're in charge of our bodies, and we don't need lessons from anyone, least of all you and your low-life friends. Do you think we *want* to open our beds to you? If we didn't have bills to pay and small mouths to feed, we'd push you down the stairs, and don't think we wouldn't. You think we're afraid of you? We're not. You stink—you and your friends who crawl in here once a month. All of you, take a bath once in a while."

Vitali smiled. "If there was hot water, we would bathe." Then he leaped at Stolia and slapped her hard across the face. She crumpled to the ground.

As the women recoiled, Lev quickly kneeled to help Stolia to her feet. "Are you okay?"

Stolia spat blood, stunned. "Get out," she said, pointing at Vitali. "You're not welcome here. Ever. And the same with all your friends."

"Oh no, what shall we do?" he said. "What a calamity! Thrown out of this house of holy worship. What will befall us? Never to poke your jack-nasty face again? Oh, heavens, the world is ending."

"Lev, make him leave," said Stolia.

Without hesitating, Lev puffed himself up and stood between the women and Vitali.

"This is your savior?" said Vitali. "He's a baby."

"Where I come from, men respect women," said Lev.

"A Russian boy, no less," said Vitali. "Another one who claims to be entitled. I spit on entitlement. But you look familiar. Have we met?"

"Stolia said to leave," said Lev. "I am determined to see that through."

"Are you prepared to fight me, boy?" Vitali slid a hand in his pocket.

"If I must," said Lev. "And everyone here will bear witness to your cowardice if you bring a knife into this situation."

"What knife?" said Vitali. "Who said anything about knives?" He withdrew his hand from his pocket, empty. "You're a smart boy."

"I'm not a boy," said Lev. "If you call me that as an insult or to be superior, then you won't mind if I call you a vulture."

Vitali's face reddened. "I don't like that name. I despise it. I want to break bones when I hear it. It makes me want to thread my fingers around your neck and strangle the life out of you."

"Everyone knows that's your name," said Stolia.

"I don't like it, but I suppose it *is* a sign of respect," said Vitali. "People fear me. That is why they give me that ridiculous name. And when they say it, even when they think it, they are admitting my strength."

"I don't fear you," said Lev. "I have known others like you. When the wise man gets angry, he stops being wise. My father taught me that. It's how to discover who a man truly is. You're not wise or kind. Here, you're only hated. I feel sad for you."

"I'm not a monster," said Vitali.

"No," said Lev. "You're pathetic. These strong women will rise against you with God's fury. Look behind you at the stairs and think how your neck will snap when we push you down. You're strong, yes, but not against our combined might. I'm telling you now, Vitali, these fine women and all the strength I can summon will run at you and throw you down the stairs. Some of us may fall with you. I probably will. But then we'll be rid of you."

Vitali stood motionless. Lev worked to guess how he would respond. Vitali exuded a strength and fearlessness that could easily overwhelm one or two men. Lev believed that Vitali could lunge at them, take several to the ground, and slice with his concealed knives. The resulting chaos and blood would leave no winners.

Vitali put his hand in his pocket, turned, and headed down the stairs. "Keep the lights on," he said. "I won't be long."

2 2

Lev ran the few blocks from Stolia's tenement to Orchard Street in a fevered rush to find Harvey. Although well past midnight, Lev banged on Harvey's apartment door, out of breath and sweating profusely, until it opened to the creased, crimson face of his father, Boris.

"Do you know what time it is?" he asked.

"I'm sorry, sir," said Lev. "I need to see Harvey. It's important."

"It's almost one o'clock."

"I know it's terribly late—"

"Terribly late, is it? And do you know what I say? I say fuck you and Harvey and all the other hoodlums he runs around with. Roaming around at all hours of the night like wild pigs. Have you ever heard of such a thing?"

"I'm sorry, sir, but I wouldn't bother you if it wasn't necessary."

"You talk to me about what's necessary? You're out of luck, my friend. Harvey's not here. He's never here, except for meals. You and everyone in your *fakakta* generation think they own everything. You're all lazy and will never amount to anything. It wouldn't surprise me if he's in a jail somewhere."

"He's your son," said Lev.

"May you be equally cursed," said Boris, slamming the door. Then, muffled, Lev heard, "It's nobody. Go back to bed. Another of his lazy friends. Where did we go wrong with that boy?"

Undeterred, Lev hurried out of the building, across the street, and up the stairs of another tenement to find the door ajar to Uncle Ira's apartment. Without announcing himself, Lev slipped inside to find Bertha hovering over the stove, steam curling up from a pot and circling her head like a halo.

Bertha turned but didn't show surprise. "You helped bring Ira back," she said. "I'm grateful for that. Sit. You'll eat."

"I don't have time," said Lev. "How is he?"

"Grumpy," she said. "The worst patient ever. But he's fine. Crazy in the head, but healthy as an ox. He can't sleep. Neither can I. So I'm cooking. What else is there to do?"

"I'm looking for Harvey and the rest of them."

"I should solve the mysteries of the world, is that it? Do I look like a fortune teller? They were here earlier. Maybe he knows. He's in there." Bertha pointed to the open door of the bedroom, then turned back to the stove.

Lev cautiously stepped to the doorway and saw Ira resting prostate on the bed. He was naked from the waist up, and he looked terrible.

"It's you," said Ira. "How's your jaw?"

"Fine."

"Come here."

When Lev drew closer, he saw that Ira appeared to be older and smaller than the man who had marched through Seward Park with such swagger. His skin looked gray and transparent. A long, thin rubber tube protruded from a bubbling wound on his neck and snaked to the floor, where orange puss dripped into a pan.

"It looks worse than it is," said Ira. "I know these things."

"You don't look so well."

"Thanks for not sugarcoating it, boy," he said. "I know that, of course. There's an infection in my neck that wants to crawl inside my body and take up quarters in my brain, where it's warm and tidy. I need to keep it at bay another day or so. If not, it'll take over my innards and I'll go septic. That doesn't end well."

"I know where Vitali will be soon," said Lev. "He's not a good man."

"A mastery of understatement," said Ira, his voice growing weaker. "But honestly, boy, I don't have time for that now, nor the appetite. That dirty knife took everything out of me. But that vulture bastard? Him I won't give a second thought, or it will hand him another victory. I'm being truthful with you. Stop looking at me with that dejected face. I don't have time for that either."

"I'm not dejected."

"You are. You just don't know it. I'm tired. I'm closing my eyes now."

"Do you know where I can find Harvey and the others?"

"Look, I'm closing my eyes. See? They're closed. Did I mention I'm tired?"

"You're not going to help me?"

Ira squinted one eye open. "I don't want the responsibility," he said. "You'll understand one day. If I expire, tell people I said that. Now go, please. And don't go looking in the alley behind Zivotovsky's on Delancey."

Lev couldn't tell if Ira had purposely mentioned the alley, but he didn't ask. He crept out of Leo's room and almost made it past Bertha, who turned on him and pushed a dripping, wooden soup spoon into his chest.

"I heard everything in there," she said. "I know how sick he is. I'm no dummy."

"Yes, ma'am."

"You go find Harvey and the rest of the boys. They'll do anything for Ira, I know it. You gather them up and do the worst to that animal, that vulture. What he did to my Ira is a sin against the world. I want to see him suffer. Cut his balls open and let the life seep out of him. Kill the bastard, for all I care."

"Yes, ma'am."

Bertha lowered the spoon. Her voice was shaky. "Promise me. He can't go unpunished."

"I promise," said Lev.

Bertha forced a piece of bread into Lev's hand. "Then get on with it," she said. "Don't come back without his scalp."

Without a word, Lev ate the bread and left Bertha standing in the kitchen. He took the stairs two steps at a time and then ran east on Delancey to the alley where he first encountered the boy army. They were crowded together in a corner with voices raised, shouting, "Come on!" and "Are you kidding?" They hadn't noticed Lev, or maybe didn't care.

He joined them to see Aaron kneeling in the center of the group, throwing dice against the brick wall. "Six!" he urged the small, white tumbling cubes, then, "Ah, shit."

Harvey was digging coins from his pocket but stopped when Lev approached him.

"Dumped us for the Allen Street whores, huh?" said Harvey.

"I didn't."

"You're older. I get it," said Harvey. "As soon as I can manage it, I'm gonna spend time there too."

"I work there."

"I heard different."

A roar erupted from the boys as Aaron rolled a seven. Coins were thrown to the ground, and there was a scramble for the dice.

"You can play if you have money," said Harvey.

"I know where Vitali is," said Lev.

"What d'ya mean?"

"He threw the knife at Ira."

"I know who he is."

"He's a bad man," said Lev. "As bad as they come."

"Listen, Lev, my brother. I'm not going near him. None of us will. Uncle Ira told us to stay clear. So you know what? We're staying clear. This is more fun, anyway. Ya got money? It's simple. Only one rule—don't roll seven or eleven."

"It's happening now," said Lev. "The game can wait."

"It's not a game," said Harvey. "If I don't bring a few dollars home, my dad won't be happy. He already thinks I'm no good."

"This is the best chance to get Vitali," said Lev. "The vulture, right? Something bad will happen if we don't act."

Harvey said, "There's always something bad happening. That's life on the Lower East Side."

"We need to do this now," insisted Lev.

"You have good intentions," said Harvey. "I wish I were more like you. But it's over. For now, at least."

Lev pushed Harvey away and leaped into the huddled knot of boys. He scattered them away from the wall and grabbed the dice mid-roll. "I'm serious," he said, holding the dice above his head. "We have to do something. I need your help."

The boys complained. "Get out of the way." "That was my roll." "Woulda been a nine. I saw it!"

"Quiet," said Harvey. "He's upset."

"We have to do something," said Lev. "More people will be hurt. Ira might die. We can't fool around throwing dice."

"We have more dice," said Harvey. "You're on your own."

2 3

No longer in a hurry, Lev slowly walked back to Stolia's tenement, confused and alone, kicking a small rock along the way. *This is not how it's supposed to be*, he thought. *People should stand together.* He wondered what advice his parents would have given him, but he couldn't conjure their faces. What did they look like? *My father had a beard. My mother wore an apron. They loved each other.*

Lev tried to remember the many times he had walked home from shul with his father Saturday mornings. They would talk about the rabbi's sermon and whether it measured up to last week's lesson. His father would say, "The rabbi is a smart man, and I don't mean him any disrespect by pointing out he doesn't live in the real world. Spend one day swinging a hammer with sore muscles, and I think he would see things differently. Don't tell your mother I said that."

Lev told his mother everything and shared his father's critical comments. "He doesn't mean it," she said. "It's his way of saying that life isn't always fair. The rabbi is right. He's always right. Your father knows that, but don't tell him I said so." Lev recalled these conversations, but he still could not see their faces. Was this how it would be from now on? Would time continually rob him of all memories until they vanished entirely?

Yet, he could easily recall the details and vividness of others. The mustache that ringed Smagin's eyes. The sad weariness of Mishal. The curve of Gerta's hips. Everything about Dorete. He thought about Captain Peronard and was instantaneously atop the ship with him. It was cold and dark, and his collar was pulled up to his ears to keep icy gusts from blowing down his back as he strained to spot an iceberg in the black vastness. His words had broader meaning now.

"They hide if you try too hard. They're crafty that way. They want you to overfocus. Misdirection is one of their cruelest tricks. If you listen closely, you can hear them encouraging you to be aggressive." He cupped his hand behind his ear. *"Do you hear that, lad? That's not a whale song; it's the creaking of the 'berg's pitch. That's how they communicate. It's a sound from their bellies as they intimidate everything in the way. Do you know what they're saying? They're encouraging you to look over there. In front of the ship. Behind the ship. Anywhere but where they're hiding. They hypnotize you, is what they do. They'll force you into being complacent and make you drowsy and distracted. That's the way of all dreadful things, Lev. Worse, you can't fight 'em. Best you can do is get out of the way."*

Lev considered this advice as he walked up Allen Street, which was alive only in the shadows. Dark figures clung to buildings and darted inside doorways. Getting out of the way was something that hadn't worked for him very well. He had not sought conflict, but it seemed to come for him. He decided this was what it meant to be a man, to be confronted with an endless stream of challenges—some small, others insurmountable. He had observed this in Komenska as he watched his father overcome lame horses, dyes gone bad, an eye fallen cloudy, and disagreements with customers. Similarly, his mother had pushed away problems every day, from yeast that didn't bubble to the constant darning of socks. She was kind to him, but losing two children before and after him had turned her against happiness. When the pogroms came to Komenska, his parents had faced them without bitterness, until the flames of hatred consumed them.

Fire. All his thoughts followed this path, to a house churning out red and orange ribbons and transforming his parents into thick black ropes that lapped the sky. He saw that everything behind him was burning, falling to ash, settling to the ground on distant acres, and eventually fading away entirely. Nothing was immune, no discrimination, a persistent randomness no matter where you were. A confrontation in a small cabin on a great ship. A glance from a beautiful woman. A body exploding out of a circus tent. An aunt who was as elusive as a moonbeam. If Heaven existed, it manifested inclusion with brutal indifference.

Lonely and fearful, Lev wished he could talk to his parents, the rabbi, teachers, Smagin. Or Dorete. He wished he were back on the ship with her. She would help him see things clearly, wouldn't she?

24

Dorete,

Please don't think badly of me for writing you like this. I'm not feeling well, but I hope you understand. I know you can't help me. By the time you receive this, I will probably already be dead. That's terrible for me to say, but maybe you will respect me for being honest. I need someone to talk to. That's why I'm writing you. I think I owe you the truth.

I am writing from my small room in the New York tenement where I work. I shouldn't say it is a room. I think it used to be a closet. It doesn't have a window and the door touches the cot when it opens. That is how small it is. I said I work here, but that isn't the full truth. I won't talk about that because I think it would be disrespectful. I am a guard and I help protect the workers. I probably should be ashamed of what I do, but I help good people who are trying to get by. I'm performing an important service. I wish I could be prouder of what I do and be comfortable telling you. I suppose that is why I am feeling so bad.

I look at your address often. Your street has a funny name, Dalbygatan. I picture you living in a quiet village on a street that has very large trees and where everyone knows their neighbors.

Don't tell me if that isn't true.

I am a coward, Dorete. I should not have left you when we departed the ship. I feel terrible that you had to walk back to the ship alone, and I hate myself every day for it. I remember everything about the last time I saw you, and I think about you at night and wonder where I would be if I had gone back to the ship with you. I remember the boardwalk in Hoboken and the fog and the sounds of the other ships. I remember everything there and being scared I wouldn't be able to find a place to sleep. All I had was a piece of paper with an address. You gave me yours, and then I had two addresses. I can be brave here on paper and write things I would never have the courage to say to you if you were in front of me.

I won't say that I love you, because that would be unfair, and you might stop reading. But I know I could love you, even though you don't see me that way. You told me so. You think I'm too young. But things change. If I had returned with you to the ship, I wonder if it would have been different between us. I also think about Willem a lot. I wanted to hate him because he was with you. I was jealous at the way you looked at him. I was upset knowing you were sleeping with him.

Trouble follows me. I have stories to tell you from before you knew me, and new ones since arriving in America. This country is not what I thought it would be. I thought the New World would be clean and honest. But so far, everything here seems the same as Russia. There is just as much evil here. I have met good people, yes, but it is confusing.

Now I have to be heroic, and I am not sure I can do it. I'm not a hero. I'm scared. That's why I am in my room, rather than doing hard things.

As I write this, I believe that ugly things are happening upstairs in this building. I have tried to get others to help me, but I failed at that. I feel that I don't have a choice than to go upstairs and face some bad people alone. They have knives and other weapons. They are bigger than me and there may be many of them. I should have tried to do something earlier. I went out to find help but now I am back in my room and have been here almost an hour. When I finish this letter, I will go upstairs. I might be killed.

When I was a small boy, my father took me to town to see the promised argument of three great traveling rabbis. They went from town to town and charged one kopeck to watch them argue about politics. I think they agreed about everything, but they purposely took opposite sides. They stood beneath the great tree in the center of our village and raised their voices and pointed at each other and spit on the ground. They were loud and angry and called each other terrible names. I doubted they were true rabbis, but my father said they came from Kiev and were very learned. I remember them arguing about fate. One said fate was for weak people, and those who believed in it were feeble-minded. Another said fate was the only explanation for everything from marriage to death. He said everything was preordained. The third rabbi argued that a person's life was created by the people around them.

I think about that a lot, Dorete. I wonder if my fate has been set by Hashem. Maybe every choice my ancestors made resulted in me being in this tenement so that I would be forced to act. Do you believe in God?

I want a better life, Dorete. That's what my parents wanted for me. They hoped I would be safe and happy.

I miss you. I think of you often and hope I will see you again. I have to go now. I don't feel like I have a choice.

I am sorry for writing such a long letter, but I feel better. I don't have an envelope, but I will put this on my cot with your address and hope someone will deliver it to you. I wish things could have turned out another way.

Love,
Lev (Leo)

Lev folded the letter, set it gently on the pillow, and took the kinzhal from his backpack. He left his room and paused outside the door, listening to the sounds of the building. There was a low hum coming from above, then a few distant banging noises and something that sounded like scraping. All the sounds were very faint, as if they were from another country.

Lev climbed the stairs, holding tight to the kinzhal and keeping its sharp edges away from his legs.

This is why Smagin gave it to me, thought Lev. Although he was an ocean away, Lev could hear Smagin speaking to him. *"Either you're the one holding the knife, or the one with a dagger in your belly. Which do you prefer? It's a new world, I know. Everyone wants to talk and negotiate, to make compromises and sign treaties. I suppose there's a place for that, my boy. But nothing gets done without a blade by your side. When you're armed, people respect you. They cooperate. They listen and are more agreeable. Even a small sword is a great convincer. You hope you don't need it, but if you don't have one, you'll wish you did. And if it's dirty, even better. Let your enemies see dried blood on it. If it's clean, dip it in red paint."*

Lev wondered if Smagin had ever been afraid. He wished he were with him now.

Lev crept up the stairs, staying close to the wall to minimize the straining of the old wood. He stopped after a few steps to listen. Nothing.

At the first landing, he rested, while the pounding in his chest reminded him he was alive. He tightened his grip on the kinzhal's ivory hilt. He stood motionless and tried to summon the courage to carry on, but he could not find it. He wondered how soldiers could willingly run into battle, knowing they would probably die. He decided it was because they felt committed to a higher purpose—their countries and families back home. But he wondered if they didn't have a choice. Maybe a general stood behind them with threats. But no matter. They moved forward into uncertain darkness to confront their fate. Lev felt similarly drawn to Gerta's room; he knew that was where he would find Vitali.

I'm coming.

Still trying to be as quiet as possible, Lev hurried up to Stolia's floors and where he had stood guard. He wasn't sure what he'd expected, but not this.

The tenement was empty, which was not unusual. When customers stopped coming, usually by 2 a.m., the women would clean their rooms, change the sheets, and head to places they called home. But this was different.

He tried all the doors. Stolia's apartment door was deafening in its emptiness. There was no reason for her to be absent at this hour because she lived there. The other rooms were empty as well, but the beds were disheveled, and incense still burned. *They left in a hurry*, Lev reasoned.

Room after room was unlocked and deserted. He felt as if everyone in the world had vanished except him, and he would be forced to live the rest of his life discovering empty rooms and leftover human relics. The building was eerily quiet, unnerving.

Lev climbed the stairs to the next floor and immediately heard a human sound, perhaps a muffled cry. It was coming from the far room, opposite the landing where he and Gerta had released their clothes and inhibitions, and where she had shown him such unhurried generosity.

Lev stepped softly around the stairwell and toward Gerta's door, listening for more sounds. He extended his free hand and touched the cold doorknob, but did not turn it yet. He held his breath and waited for a signal that he should do anything other than turn back.

If he took a step back, it would be easy to retreat to his small room. No one would know that he had lost his nerve and gave in to fear. He would rip up the letter he'd written to Dorete and go to sleep.

But without further consideration, he turned the knob and pushed open the door.

Vitali and Gerta were naked, except for a white sheet that snaked through their legs. Vitali, his wild beard draped over Gerta's shoulder, was pressed against her, his hand tight over her mouth.

"Ah, the man child," said Vitali. "I thought it might be you. If you were smarter, you would have stayed away."

Lev looked at Gerta's eyes and saw fear. "Let her go," he said.

"I don't take orders from you," said Vitali. "I give the orders."

Gerta squirmed and her muffled moan escaped through Vitali's fingers.

Lev stepped into the room. "A friend gave this me," he said, brandishing the kinzhal. "You don't have any secret pockets with cowardly knives." He walked into the room and kicked Vitali's clothes, which were scattered across the floor. "Where are the women and your men?"

"You are too easily fooled," said Vitali. "There was only me. When you left, so did the sex workers, frightened by my promise to return. So what do you think happened? What was inevitable? I stood in the shadows and watched everyone leave in a hurry. My lovely Gertrude was the last to exit. I had to convince her to come upstairs, but here we are now. We have been enjoying ourselves, haven't we, Gertrude?"

"Release her," said Lev.

"She likes my touch," said Vitali. He kissed her ear. "She's a lovely woman, but I'm thinking you know that already."

"This is the last time I'll say it. Let her go."

Vitali laughed. "Or what? You won't do anything with the blade. You're a baby."

Lev moved close to the bed and touched the point of the kinzhal to the bottom of Vitali's exposed foot. "Last warning."

"That tickles," said Vitali.

Gerta sobbed muffled cries through Vitali's hand.

Lev thought of the promise he'd made to Bertha. He shouted, "Vulture!" then quickly swung the kinzhal over his head and brought it down on Vitali's leg.

The sharp blade clipped the bone and sliced cleanly through the meaty calf muscle. A scarlet fountain bubbled up and splashed blood against Gerta's neck.

• • •

Minsky's Hosiery was one of the two ground-floor businesses in Bertha's tenement at 97 Orchard. It was a Lower East Side tradition, known to stock the latest in fashionable women's garments. The sign in its front window advertised HOSIERY FOR MEN, WOMEN & CHILDREN, but there was only a small section of socks for men and boys, and in truth, only women shopped there for its wide selection of stockings, girdles, suspender belts, and nightgowns. In the back of the shop, behind a green curtain, inventory was stored in an unlit, narrow room lined with shelves that overflowed with opened packages of seamed stockings. It was in this dark space that Bertha arranged to hide Lev in the immediate aftermath of his takedown of Vitali.

Here, Lev had nothing but time to think about the single, brutal blow into Vitali's leg. He knew that Vitali would have bled out if Gerta hadn't quickly fixed a sheet tightly above the knee.

With Vitali delirious in pain and growing limp, Gerta urgently whispered to Lev, "Get out of here, dear boy. Hide."

"I'm not leaving you," said Lev. He looked down at the kinzhal as blood dripped from its blade to the floor.

"If he lives—and even if he doesn't—they'll be after you. Find a place. Don't tell anyone. Hurry." Gerta busied herself attending to Vitali, who was now incoherent. "Even bad men deserve a chance at redemption."

Lev knew Gerta was right, but he stood unmoving, still uncertain if he should abandon her.

"I can handle this," said Gerta. "If you care about me—about any of us—you'll go. Please." She stood and came quickly to Lev, kissing him hard. "You saved me. Saved all of us, probably. There will be more trouble, I don't doubt it. But you need to disappear. Please, just go."

Lev thought he tasted blood in Gerta's kiss, and he saw the future. Vitali's henchmen would come looking for him, and safety would be elusive. He wasn't sure hiding would be only temporary—he wouldn't be safe until he left New York. And even then, who knew how far a vendetta would pursue him. He looked for guidance in the heavens and wondered what his mother would want.

Lev landed on survival. His parents hadn't sacrificed everything to see him rush headlong into a fight with Vitali's men. He thought back to the confrontation at Seward Park and the large group of men flanking Vitali. How could he stand against them and see another sunrise?

"I'll get word to you," said Lev. He took a final look at the blood-soaked bed, where Vitali was splayed out as if already being judged by God. Then he turned and hurried out of the room to the only place where sanctuary was certain.

When he arrived at Bertha's door, kinzhal still in hand, she took one look at him and said, "From the gates of hell, no less. You look like Abaddon's messenger warmed over, straight from the bottomless pit." She pulled him in. "Did anyone see you?"

Lev shuffled into the apartment and sank to the floor. "I'm tired," he said. "I've never been more tired. I want to sleep for a month."

Bertha took the sword from Lev's hand and wiped it clean. "You'll sleep," she said, "but not here."

25

From beneath the green curtain, Lev kept a connection to the outside world by watching the women who came into Minsky's. He could only observe them from the knee down, but he came to associate the curves of their legs with their personalities. Heavy women with thick ankles asked for slimming stockings, usually dark colors. Those with thin, bird-like legs wanted bright colors. And women with long, alluring limbs asked about new synthetics. All complained that their stockings would fall and sag, though they shunned suspender belts that added girth to their hips. They would ask about new styles and what Europeans were wearing. Young women complained they were forced to cover their legs.

The proprietor of the store, Elias Minsky, also lived in the building. He was a stern man with a pronounced Austrian accent. Each day before the store opened, he would check on Lev and wake him from fitful slumbers by jabbing him with a pointed shoe.

"Get up," he said. "I can't have people sleeping in here when customers arrive."

"I'm up," said Lev.

"You're only half up. I can see."

"I'm all the way up."

"I don't want any trouble," said Minsky. "If trouble visits, out you go."

"I won't be any trouble," said Lev.

"I mean it. It's what I told that fine woman, Bertha, your benefactor. She's the only reason you're here. She buys my stockings and makes me that delicious kreplach. But even if you don't disrupt my business, you being here is a disruption. So I am giving you a warning."

"I don't want to be here, either."

"Well, we will see. Now get up."

"I'm as up as you are."

"That I doubt."

Lev had only time. Time to relive his attack on Vitali and to regret what he had done, to ponder if Dorete was still at sea, to wonder how the Kharkov sisters were getting by in Lillehammer and whether they gave him any thought, to think about Natalya and Smagin and how he wished he were with them again, to figure out the puzzle of Mishal and the freedom he coveted more than his life, to think about his parents and how much they'd suffered during their last moments. These thoughts consumed him while listening to the store's customers complain about how their boyfriends and husbands no longer seemed interested.

A few minutes before the shop closed, Bertha arrived, bearing gifts for Minsky. Lev peered under the curtain.

"Ah, my generous neighbor," she said. She carried a large, foil-covered dish and a wrinkled paper bag that had been overused.

"That plate has my name on it, I am thinking," said Minsky. He locked the door and turned the Closed sign to face the street.

"There are a lot of beautiful people in the world, but you are the tops, Mr. Minsky."

"Elias," he said. "It would make me happy if you called me by the name my mother gave me."

"That is too familiar," said Bertha. "It would make me blush."

"A woman like you? A woman with your rare talents and beauty?"

"You are too kind, Mr. Minsky."

"Elias. Please."

"Elias," she consented, surrendering the plate.

Minsky accepted the plate as if it were a delicate artifact. He brought it to his nose and sniffed the foil. "What is it this time? No, don't tell me. Let me guess. There's a hint of vegetable, to be sure. Am I right?"

"So perceptive."

"The aroma is intoxicating," said Minsky. "Whatever it is, I know it will be delicious." He set the still-covered plate on a counter and came closer to Bertha.

"It's cauliflower and mushroom kugel," she said.

"You are the brightness of my day," said Minsky. He motioned to the green curtain. "If he weren't here, I would show you how grateful I am."

"I probably wouldn't be here if you hadn't agreed to hide him," said Bertha.

Minsky sighed. "I suppose that is true."

"Don't be discouraged. I wouldn't bring you kugel if I weren't fond of you . . . Elias."

"You're only saying that so I will continue to let him stay here."

"For tomorrow, I'm thinking chocolate babka," said Bertha, pretending not to hear him. "Would you like that?"

"If I can't have you, that will have to do. I love babka."

She leaned toward Minsky and kissed him on the cheek with measured affection. "Then babka it is. Now go, my sweet man. Leave me with my charge."

Minsky touched his face where Bertha's lips had been. "Tomorrow, then. Babka?"

"Babka."

"I'll be back in a while to finish closing up," said Minsk. He gathered the covered plate and left the shop.

When Minsky's footfalls faded, Bertha hurried to the green curtain and threw it open to reveal Lev facing her. She gasped.

"If you go through life scaring people like that, you won't make many friends."

"I didn't mean to frighten you," said Lev. "I was only standing here."

"I'm easily startled these days, what with all the tumult in the world. It's a madhouse out there. It's a blessing I don't have to leave the building to see you. I'd fear for my life."

Lev had questions, but he remained silent. He studied Bertha and saw in her face that something was wrong. There were many things that might be bothering her, but he was too weary to play a guessing game. If he were more alert, he would consider the possibilities, but his head was heavy.

"You can't stay here any longer," she said, and Lev understood why she appeared so glum. "That Minsky, he's got a big mouth. They're just whispers as of now, but that's how these things start."

"I don't want to hide anymore."

"Everyone's been asking about you. Vitali's men are on the street. The boys. Stolia. The women. There's no such thing as a secret anymore. We need to move you somewhere else."

Lev stepped out of the back room and into the store. He stopped at a display and ran a finger along a pair of red silk stockings. "I'm not going anywhere else," he said. "I shouldn't be hiding, anyway. It's cowardly. Anyway, I have nowhere else to go. If they've discovered I'm here, then they'll figure out the next place."

"I have an acquaintance in Brooklyn with a cozy basement."

"I'm not going to Brooklyn."

"There's nothing wrong with staying alive."

"There are worse things."

Lev moved through the store and looked disapprovingly at the merchandise. "Women did not wear these things in Komenska, except for special occasions. Maybe a wedding."

"It's a new world," said Bertha. She set the paper bag on a corner of a girdle display. "From Stolia."

Lev moved to the store window and edged the sign aside to peer out the window. "America," he said. He pressed his hand against the pane. "When the ship entered the harbor, we were greeted by the tall lady. She looked tired there, holding her hand up forever, raising the torch. I remember thinking that her light cast a spell across the land, and that freedom existed in its purest form here. Only in America. I still feel that way, Bertha. We can do anything we want. That's what freedom is, isn't it? That light and dark, good and bad, are sides of the same coin. We can choose any path."

"Don't be discouraged," said Bertha.

"I'm not. I'm optimistic for the future, even if I'm not in it."

"Let me take you to the train station right now, before it's too late. There's no reason for you to stay."

"Nothing can make me leave."

As he said this, a darkness fell upon the window. A storm, perhaps? He blinked, and there was Vitali's face, pressed against the window.

• • •

Lev, more startled than frightened, took a step back, while Bertha, standing well behind Lev, screamed and hurried to the back of the store.

Vitali smiled through the window and raised a ring of keys to his eyes, jangling them like a mad wind chime. "Minsky's keys," he shouted through the door. "He was very cooperative."

Lev wished he were anywhere else, that he had his kinzhal, that he could turn back time and undo everything. But it was too late. The key was in the lock, and the door opened to frame Vitali and two huge men standing behind him.

Vitali limped into the room on a pair of thick wooden crutches. His left leg was wrapped in gauze and white medical tape. Blood seeped through to form a muted red blotch.

"The doctors at the hospital were very much wondering what could have caused my injury," said Vitali, who winced with each step. "Very curious they were, let me tell you. But did I tell them anything? Vitali?

Do I look like a rat? I told them I was fitting a new window and a pane slipped and did its damage. But where were the slivers, they wanted to know. There were none, I told them. It cut straight through and down so clean you could eat a meal off my leg."

Vitali's men came into the store and flanked him. "Timur and Gizem," said Vitali. "My two most loyal friends. I beg you not to make any questionable moves. You too, Bertha, in the back there. You think I don't see you? Be calm and slow and keep your hands in sight. Timur? He gets spooked when people move faster than his eyes. And Gizem? You don't want to know how strong he is, believe me when I say that. So, we can be friends and no one has an accident. Yes?"

Lev watched Vitali's hands to see if they held small knives. He wondered if there was a hidden pocket behind his beard with dozens of tiny blades. "You look well," he said.

"I am doing fine, yes," said Vitali. "But I tire easily. Mr. Lev, would you mind bringing a chair for the weariness in my bones?"

Lev walked slowly to the side of the store, where a lone wooden chair rested. He watched Timur and tried not to give him cause for concern. He lifted the chair and brought it to Vitali.

"Help me, boy," said Vitali. He passed the crutches to Gizem and put his arm over Lev's shoulder. Lev turned him slowly, and Vitali hopped to stay with him until he was seated. "That's good. Thank you. Slowly. There—very nice." Vitali sighed and straightened his legs. "See what you've done to me? I am an invalid."

Lev thought for a moment. "I regret what I did. But I had no choice. I'm sorry."

"Sorry, he says," said Vitali. "Do you think I came here for an apology?"

"I don't know why you came here."

"We've been looking for you, but you know that already. While I was in the hospital, my men were on the streets to find you. You are very crafty to hide here, but I think you had help, no?" Vitali raised his voice. "Isn't that right, Bertha?"

"Leave the boy alone," she said.

"Do you see me bothering him?" said Vitali. "We're having a pleasant conversation, aren't we, Mr. Lev?"

"We're talking."

"Talking? Yes, of course. God gave us only time, and we are using it now. I see you looking at my leg. I will be fine, so said the American doctors who sewed me up. They said I was lucky, that it was a miracle I was alive. I am still supposed to be in bed, but I made an exception for you."

"Gerta saved you," said Lev. "I would have let you die. I'm ashamed to say it, but I'm sorry."

"Still with the apologies? Gertrude attended to me, it is true, I am told. That is because she cares for me. She needs a man, not a child. But forgive me, you are not a child. You struck a great blow. I give you credit. But look, here we are, alive and well, having a friendly conversation."

"Until your knives come out," said Lev.

"Where would the honor be in that?" said Vitali. "If we were to face each other, I wouldn't do so under unfair circumstances. I wouldn't bring these men with me. Three against one? Is that what you think of me?"

"I don't think of you."

"If I were to exact revenge, it would be me and only me facing you. That is how real men fight. I do not mean to suggest that your attack on a naked and defenseless man was cowardly—perhaps it was. But that is behind us. When I am recovered, then it will be a different story. And then, Mr. Lev, I will crush you like the annoying troublemaker you have become. That day will come soon, my friend, I promise you."

"I'm not your friend," said Lev. "These are good people. Why do you threaten them?"

"Who is doing the threatening?" said Vitali. "I seem to remember a scuffle in a nearby park, led by your uncle Ira. Was he not armed? Was his army of small boys not carrying stones?"

"I suppose," said Lev. "But men against boys doesn't sound fair to me."

"Did we harm a child? We did not. Only the man among you. Only Ira."

Bertha cried, "Don't mention his name. You're not good enough to speak of my Ira. And when he regains his health, it will be you who is squashed."

"I am so frightened I am pissing right here, sitting in a chair," said Vitali.

"Don't be disrespectful to her," said Lev. "She's done nothing to you."

"She is a gossiping pest. But she was helpful in leading us to Minsky, and Minsky to you. So I am grateful to her."

"You haven't suffered enough," said Bertha.

"You have distracted me from the purpose of my visit. You see I have discovered your hiding place, Mr. Lev. If you disappear again, we will find you. And like I said, you and I, my friend, will have a meeting one day to bring this to a resolution."

"I don't want to fight you," said Lev.

"Let us discuss that. Because, my friend, there is another way. Join me. You have shown yourself resourceful and unafraid, and those are gifts that would benefit us."

Lev started to answer, but Vitali raised his hand to stop him.

"Don't talk, Mr. Lev. Listen. I would ask that you think about this, because I can see that you are wise and considerate. Hear me out. You are on the wrong side of justice. The wrong side of history. We want nothing more than what every generation has tried to find. Peace. Security. A place to call home, where we can raise our children. A neighborhood with schools and opportunity. What is the difference between me and you and Ira? We are all Jews. Is it because we come from a different country? Because we have slightly different customs? Because our skin is a little darker, maybe?"

Vitali leaned forward as best he could without bending his leg and pointed at Lev. "This is a sin against God. This is what I am telling you. You have been fooled into thinking I am the enemy. No. Your friend

Ira and his band of boys and the gatekeepers on the Lower East Side here—they, all of them, and for no reason other than ethnic hatred, want to keep us out. But, Mr. Lev, don't you see? We are the persecuted, not the hunters.

"And why? For no good reason, that's why. There are open apartments in many buildings. Why should we be frozen out? And if we have more money, then why can we not offer it? Isn't that the American way? The land of the free? Should we not stand up for ourselves? So please, my friend, consider what I have told you. And then, when you are seeing things clearly, I know you will join us. You can talk to the small boys and tell them all this arguing is silly."

"If this is true, then why didn't you come alone?" said Lev. "Instead, you brought intimidation." He motioned at Timur and Gizem.

"To make you listen," said Vitali, his voice growing softer. "And to protect myself from another attack. And, truth be uttered, I can't get around very well, as you can see. So there—I have said what I wanted to say. I am tired."

Timur and Gizem helped Vitali to his feet and fitted him with his crutches.

As they turned to leave, Vitali whispered hoarsely to Lev, "Hate is easy. Truth is hard."

26

Lev left Bertha with a hug of gratitude, took the crumpled bag Stolia sent him, and walked five minutes to the Eldridge Street Synagogue, the tall, highly ornamented Moorish building that boldly presented a façade of Jewish symbols in wood, brick, stone, terra cotta, and stained glass. Outside, Lev looked up at the large, glass wheel window, intricate arcaded gable, and graceful columned pinnacles that held up globes with Magen David stars, which Lev imagined supported heaven.

As he pulled open the heavy wooden door, a dozen men streamed out after the evening service. Lev stepped aside as they exited down the steps. They were there for *minyan*, Lev knew, for he had joined his father many times at synagogue as the sun went down, a time to pay daily devotion to God. "If you work hard and contribute something meaningful to life, there is no greater reward than spending a few minutes in shul at the end of the day," his father had said. "It is always a burden. You think I don't want to go straight home after working leather all day? My back is sore, my hands ache, even my eyes are tired. But I go anyway. The rabbi expects it. And when I'm there, the weariness melts from my body because I am close to God."

After the last man left the synagogue, Lev bowed his head, stepped inside the vestibule, and marveled at the opulent beauty that seemed like another world. Light flew at him from chandeliers, and he looked up at the impossibly high, barrel-vaulted ceiling of gold stars against a midnight-blue sky. Brass fixtures and high-backed wooden pews reminded him a bit of his synagogue in Komenska, but this was built on such a grand scale that he thought God must have created it himself.

Words from behind startled him. "The minyan is over, but come tomorrow."

One glance told Lev this was an important man. Certainly a rabbi. He was wearing a fur hat, a dark overcoat, and an astonishing, bushy white beard that grew in all directions. He had a bulbous nose and piercing dark eyes. He exuded authority, just standing still.

"I thought I could sit for a minute," said Lev.

"Then sit."

"Anywhere?"

"That's where God is."

Lev sat in the nearest pew. "I didn't know something so beautiful could exist."

"It exists," the man said. "Your accent. Russian. From Novardok, by chance?"

"Komenska."

"That would have been my second guess. Does a troubled young man like you have a name?"

"Lev."

"A good name. To my wife, I'm Avi. To everyone else, Rabbi Yudelovitch."

"This is your synagogue?"

"God's. But I work it for him. Did you come to talk to him alone, or can I sit as well?"

Lev slid over to make room. "Please."

Rabbi Yudelovitch sat with a labored sigh. "They don't tell you this at rabbinical school, but there's a lot of standing on this job."

"I never thought of that."

"There are many more things we don't know than we do know," said Rabbi Yudelovitch. "A lot more."

Lev nodded but remained silent.

"Like you, for example. I know your name and where you are from. I can observe your clothes and see they need a wash. Your shoes, a shine. But what accounts for your sadness, which you show with the slump of your shoulders? What is in that paper bag you clutch so tightly? And what brings a young man into an empty synagogue at night?"

"I should have come here the first day I arrived in New York," said Lev. "Things would have been different."

"Don't be so sure. The more time a person spends in a synagogue, the farther he is from God. Tell me your troubles, and I will tell you mine."

"What worries could you have?"

"Oy, you don't want to be me. Begging for money to keep these hundred lights on. I work too much and shortchange my family. My schedule changes every day. At the drop of a hat, I must go to comfort people and be sincere and preside at a funeral. Not enough time to prepare for Talmud classes. Refereeing among congregants who think the synagogue should do this or it should do that. Minding the repairs to this house of worship. Fighting with the city over matters too many to know. Having to give heady opinions about whether a widow must be forced to marry her brother-in-law. And the burden of knowing that my every word is counted and analyzed. It is true. Troubles to a rabbi are like rust to iron."

"I'm not the person my parents wanted me to be," said Lev. "They would be disappointed."

"What would they not approve?"

"Everything."

"Everything?" said Rabbi Yudelovitch. "That's quite a lot."

"Almost everything, then."

"That's still higher than I can count. I'm thinking that you have found yourself in a predicament. Am I wrong? That you have hurt someone. Physically, I mean. That you feel caught in a war."

Lev sat up straight and locked eyes with the rabbi. "You're reading my mind."

"Mind reader? *Pshaw*! I'm the rabbi. I know everything because people come to me with their problems seeking advice. You think I don't know about Vitali and the Turkish problem? You think I don't know about you and where you've been hiding in Minsky's? As soon as I saw you, I knew who you were. I have been waiting for you."

Lev slumped against the pew. "I don't know what to do."

"And you think God will tell you? Are you one of those fools who look for a sign? Because if you are, you'll be waiting a long time. There are no such things as signs. A car honks a horn. A star shoots across the sky. A book falls from a ledge. Those are not signs of anything, let me be clear. And if you think the clouds will part and a voice trumpet direction, then you are an even bigger fool. God does not work that way. If you're seeking answers, look no further than the feet in your shoes. God gave you a heart and a mind, and that's it. That's all you get. And it's usually enough."

"I only wanted to clear my head."

"Then clear away," said Rabbi Yudelovitch. "Stay for a bit. But I have to get home and face questions about what took me so long. But you? You can stay. A security man will be along in a while to lock up. Be gone by then."

"I will."

The rabbi put his hands on his knees and stood. "Don't worry so much," he said. "Do the best you can. The answers you are looking for may be as close as that paper bag. Who knows? But remember, Lev, the smoothest path is full of stones. *Zei gezunt*."

Lev sat in silence and tried to find a way not to feel miserable. He hung his head and looked at the worn floorboards. He wondered about the many people who had sat here and recited ancient prayers.

Still grasping the small paper bag, he opened it for the first time. Inside was an apple, and he decided he was hungry.

Under the apple was an opened envelope addressed to Stolia with a postmark from an unfamiliar place. It was from Elizaveta.

My dearest Stolia,

Please forgive me for not writing to you sooner. I make no excuses, other than I have not been well enough to lift a pen. But I have felt better the past few days, and I hope to have turned a corner. I am coughing less blood.

There are a lot of sick people here from other places. It is as if we all were advised by the same physician to go to this new state of Arizona because the clean air and dry climate will help our bodies heal. That is what we were told, but people here are still dying. I would prefer to not be one of them.

This part of America is different than other places I have been. I did not think it was beautiful when I arrived, but I have come to love its unique flora and the way each day is no different than the one before. There is untouched desert land as far as you can see, and the sky is wide and blue. The sunsets are orange, red, and purple. Some days, if it is not too warm, I sit outside and watch horses compete with cars for the road. Can you imagine? I am working on my breathing exercises, and I think that is one reason that I am having a good week.

I am not living in luxury. I understand there are some very amazing tuberculosis sanatoriums here, but I am not at one of them. All I could afford is a place south of Phoenix, which is little more than a group of small private tents. But my space is mostly clean, and the people here are very attentive. A physician comes to see me every day and has been encouraging. Many of the people who work here were born in Mexico, and they are pleasant and religious. The sound of their language is beautiful; I am trying to learn it. What else do I have to do with my time? One young woman, who changes my sheets each morning after I have soaked through them, is teaching me something new every day. Today's phrase is "te extraño." It means "I miss you," which is perfect for me to share in this letter. The squiggly mark over the n means that you have to flatten your tongue on the roof of your mouth to make a sound that combines an n and a y.

Stolia, I want to thank you again for all you did to help me earn enough money to come here. And the extra you gave me was unexpected. I will always be grateful, and I am determined to pay you back. When I am well and strong enough, I hope to return to New York. I dream of opening a small flower shop. Maybe I can find an apartment in Brooklyn and meet a nice man who won't hold it against me that I worked with you.

Please give all the girls a big hello from me, by the way. And although I doubt it will happen, if that boy from Russia finds his way to you, tell him I am sorry I am not there. He can write to me here at the Guadalupe Sanatorium.

My very best to you, Stolia. I hope to see you again.

With much gratitude and love,
Elizaveta

27

ike the one in the Eldridge Street Synagogue, the cerulean-blue
ceiling of Grand Central Terminal was full of stars, but this one
was exponentially vast and displayed the Orion, Taurus, Gemini,
and Northern Fly constellations. Lev, alone but content, gazed up
at the wonder and thought how grateful he was not to endure more
wrenching goodbyes.

Only Stolia and Gerta knew he was leaving, and he made them
promise not to tell anyone until he was gone at least three days. "Tell
them I've gone back to Russia."

"But you're not going there," said Gerta. "Is the truth so bad?"

"Elizaveta is from Russia, so it's a piece of the truth," said Lev.
"Besides, it's best if no one looks for me."

"What if I try to find you?" asked Gerta. "What if I finish my work
here and need a change? Then I might want to find a brave young lover
like you."

"He doesn't exist," said Lev.

Before leaving for the train station, Lev circled the neighborhood to say goodbye without saying goodbye. He found Harvey and the boys in the alley, still shooting dice and looking older than he remembered. Harvey was excited to see him.

"We all know what you did to Vitali. You're our hero."

"There's nothing heroic in what I did," said Lev.

"Ah, go on," said Harvey. The boys surrounded Lev and touched him.

"We all want to be like you," said Aaron.

"When I was your age, I was in school," said Lev. "I listened to my parents and gave them respect. I would be proud if you followed that path, not what I did to Vitali."

A few minutes later, Lev felt nostalgic walking up the stairs at 97 Orchard but wasn't sure he would miss it. Predictably, Bertha was hunched over the stove, cooking something that smelled like love. Ira was sitting at the table, looking much better than the last time Lev had seen him. He was still pale and weak, but the wound on his neck was now scabbed over.

"My boy!" said Ira. "The man of the hour. You have represented us with flying colors."

"I came for my knife," said Lev.

"Nothing good comes from men with weapons," said Bertha, but she removed the kinzhal from a crowded shelf and placed it on the table. "You're not going after him, are you?"

"It's mine," said Lev.

"Why so serious?" said Bertha. "You must be hungry. I'm making kreplach, but it won't be ready until dinner. Come, you'll join us."

Ira grabbed Lev's arm. "They'll think twice about messing with us."

"I think that if you and Vitali put your prejudices aside, you would find the things you agree on far outweigh your differences," said Lev.

"Are you going soft on me?" said Ira. "That lot is no good."

"I'm not so sure anymore," said Lev. "I don't think I was ever sure. I went along with it. Talking is always better than fighting."

"You don't know what you're saying, but I forgive you. Believe me, Lev, we tried reasoning with them. But they want too much."

"Even I know the old proverb that a bad peace is better than a good war," said Lev.

"I don't want to argue about it," said Ira. "If I had my strength, then maybe. But come to dinner, and we'll solve all the world's problems over something delicious."

"What time is dinner?" asked Lev.

"When you get here," said Bertha.

"I may be late."

Lev looked up again at the star-filled ceiling of Grand Central Terminal and was brought back to his childhood, when his mother gave him the job as the official family star spotter on Saturday evenings. He would lie on his back outside and stare at the sky. The *Havdalah* ritual, a brief ceremony to mark the end of Shabbat, could not begin until three stars could be seen. Lev took this responsibility seriously and carefully combed the evening sky. The new day could not start without his permission.

•   •   •

Lev could not afford sleeping accommodations on the New York Central Railroad's 20th Century Limited, but he had a fine window seat that paraded the panorama of America in an unending series of fields, farms, bridges, factories, schools, oak trees, mountains, streams, lakes, ponds, rivers, cows, small towns, churches, wildflowers, fences, cafes, motels, and a multitude of hawks flying escort.

For twenty hours, Lev intermittently slept, observed the world beyond the window, studied the delicate way Elizaveta had signed her name in blue ink, and wondered what the future held for everyone else on the steam locomotive bound for Chicago. Across the aisle was an elderly couple who Lev imagined were on the way to celebrate the birth of a grandchild. The woman held a hatbox in her lap, but Lev was sure it was something more precious than that; it was a family heirloom being passed to a younger generation. Two rows up was a man dressed in black head to toe, complete with a black bow tie and a black homburg. He sported a severe mustache that told a story of frugality. He appeared to be on the way to foreclose on a house with three months' rent past due. But Lev's attention was mostly occupied by a young couple—newlyweds, certainly—who were kissing during the journey and whose hands were busy under a blanket all the way to the LaSalle Street Station.

In Chicago, Lev transferred to the Atchison, Topeka & Santa Fe Railway's No. 1, a ten-hour trip to Kansas City Union Station, then to Santa Fe's Navajo No. 9 through Garden City, La Junta, Albuquerque, and finally into the baby state of Arizona. On the way to Ash Fork, a pleasant but overly talkative ancient woman sat next to him and said she was born in Arizona in its early territorial days. "Before the railroad, it was wild, open country," she said. "It was hard living. It still is. Back then, you were at the mercy of the natives who were there before anyone. Rightfully so, if you ask me. But if you were straight and fair with them, they mostly left you alone. Now, that's all vanished. The West is gone, if you ask me. Why? Because progress came, that's why. It was a beautiful, untouched place before the railroads. Now they are stripping the land of minerals. Damming the rivers. Planting cotton like it's nobody's business. It's gone, I tell you. The West, the true West where my parents are buried, is lost to corrupt politicians who have no ties to the land. If you're looking for Arizona the way it was supposed to be, sonny, you missed it. Might as well return to wherever you came from me."

"Then why are you going back?" asked Lev.

"Because it's still the most beautiful place that's ever existed. I can't help it."

At Ash Fork, a small Arizona town founded solely as a railroad siding hub, Lev switched trains a final time for the ride south through the high, shrub-filled plains of central Arizona and into the unforgiving desert.

PART FOUR

ARIZONA

2 8

Lev came to learn that Phoenix proper had grown to five square
miles and had recently erected its first skyscraper, the seven-story
Heard Building. It was an active, ambitious town that did its
best to hide its territorial roots, but just beyond the town's corporate
boundary and the thirty thousand residents of the central valley, its
pretense of being civilized ended as perimeter homes gave way to
cotton fields, ranches, and virgin land, where survival was difficult,
and lawlessness still reigned.

As the train neared the town, Lev absorbed the alien landscape
and was surprised at how both green and desolate the Sonoran Desert
appeared. Creosote, agave, and blue palo verde dotted the landscape,
along with barrel and cholla cactus, all the way to the mountains on the
horizon. It was a serene, lonely place that knew no forests or lakes. *This
is no place for people*, Lev thought. How similar was this unforgiving land
to the one Moses confronted when leading the Israelites out of Egypt?

The train skirted the town and proceeded south to where it met the
Southern Pacific Sunset Route, an easy-to-miss junction that consisted
of little more than a thin wooden boardwalk and a small ticket booth.

When the train came to a stop, Lev stepped from his car and stood on the boardwalk as others left the train, embraced their families, and carted off large trunks. Lev remained standing there as the train pulled away and a stealthy quiet fell upon the junction. There was a whisper of a breeze that did nothing to mute the sun's fury, a heat so bright and fierce that Lev sought out a small rectangle of shade thrown by the ticket booth.

A swirling brown cloud of dust appeared down the dirt road, bringing a rattling, horse-drawn buckboard that stopped only a few yards away from Lev. Holding the reins was a man whose face was shadowed beneath a white, beat-up, open-crowned Western hat.

"Missed her, dang it," he said. He looked at Lev and slid his hat back to reveal a worn, tanned face and a thick, gray horseshoe mustache that covered his upper lip and crawled down the sides of his chin. "You on that train, huh?"

"Yes, sir," said Lev.

"I'm too much of a bastard to be a sir, but I'll take it just the same," the man said. He squinted at the sky. "A scorcher today. Topped a hundred and ten again. I'd guess you'd be regretting getting off that train, seeing how hot it is."

"This is where I was headed," said Lev.

"Meaning you meant to come here, I take it. But you're looking a bit lost, if you don't mind me saying, and that accent of yours tells a story all itself, now, don't it?"

"I have come a long way."

"It don't sound like Chinese, and I know it well because we've got a lot of 'em here. Brought out to build the railroad and stayed. It don't mind me none. Fine people. But your tongue ain't that. Likely from one of those countries we fought in the war—Germany and the like."

"Russia."

"Don't know much about Russia, but I suppose it's as good a place to be from than any other. Now, you know what else I'm thinking?"

"No, sir."

"There you go again with being polite. But don't think that's gonna soften me up. I'm only saying it 'cause of you looking lost and no one else here to take you where you ought to be."

"I didn't know the train station would be in such a remote place."

"Everything here is remote. And I wouldn't much call this a train station. I know, 'cause I've seen 'em elsewhere. Nope. That's why I head here this time of day. I can usually offer a ride to an unlucky traveler thinking they were gonna be in a big city or something. You wouldn't be needing of transportation now, would you?"

"I would," said Lev.

"Don't get the wrong idea about me being a permanent service. I'm a miner. Been forking copper since before you were born, I'd reckon. But there's been some hard times lately, maybe a little work here and there, but usually I can come here and find someone like you who'd be willing to part with some change for a ride. Would that be you?"

"It would," said Lev. "That's very nice of you."

"There's nothing nice about me, but money is money, and if I can coax Baxter—that's my fine animal here—and if I can get him properly watered, then I can go a distance here or there. If you have twenty-five cents, I'm sure I can get you where you're going."

"I don't think it's far," said Lev.

"You drive a hard bargain. Smart boy. Twenty cents, then, if it's in your pocket. Where ya headed?"

"It's a hospital in Guadalupe."

"That's so close, I can spit and hit it." The man removed his hat and swatted a cluster of flies off Baxter's rump. "Bruder. That's my last name. I don't use my first, and don't ask me for it. Any luggage?"

"Only this bag."

"Not much to you, is there?"

• • •

Bruder brought Baxter to a halt on a quiet, narrow dirt road with small, whitewashed adobe homes lined up like toy houses.

"This doesn't look like a hospital," said Lev.

"That's 'cause it ain't," said Bruder. "You won't catch me getting close to that place with all them diseases flying around. Just up the road, then left, and your legs'll get you there. But I'd be holding my breath if I were you. Whether it's the Spanish flu or consumption or whatever else is ailing those unfortunates, you'd best be careful. Keep yer distance if you know what's good for you. Don't be breathing around them is my advice. Take it or leave it, but you best be listening, and I won't charge you extra for it."

Lev gave Bruder twenty cents. "You're an interesting man," he said. "You're honest."

"Truth is truth," said Bruder. "What else does do we have? Are you a drinking man?"

"Not much."

"As far as I'm concerned, we should go back to being a territory, what with this prohibition business. Now go on. Git. I gotta get Baxter to some shade and water. If you get a mind to see me, you're out of luck. But those who know me will find my hide at Pumpkinville. Used to be a bar, only now they don't serve spirits. Officially, I mean. But the water is good, if you catch my drift. I don't think anyone cares about a hole in the wall this far from those sons of bitches in Washington."

"You've been fair with me, and I won't forget it," said Lev.

"Nothing about being fair," said Bruder. "I done what I said I'd do. And you paid me what you agreed to. Let's leave it that."

Lev retrieved his bag and lowered himself to the ground. "Pumpkinville?" he said.

"You heard straight," said Bruder. "It's what this town used to be named before so-called city founders got fancy and named it after that bird of fire. But it's a good bar—I mean, establishment. Now get a move on, young feller."

• • •

Lev walked down the dirt road and wondered if those living inside the houses were watching him. He imagined they knew better than to be outside when the oppressive heat urged ants to stay underground. Beyond the houses, the desert looked infinite beneath a sky unblemished by tall buildings or elevated trains. It was a sky as blue and open and generous as existed nowhere else in the world.

Lev turned the corner and soon stood before a long row of low, slim tents. The front and back flaps of the tents were rolled up and tied. Behind them, set back across a wide swath of cleared land, was Our Lady of Guadalupe, a small Spanish mission Catholic church. The building's adobe looked like fresh snow. Its three crosses stood proudly in defiance of the harsh climate.

Heeding Bruder's warning, Lev approached the tents cautiously. He could see people in most of the tents, some resting on metal beds, others on chairs. A man and a woman were going in and out of the tents from one to the next down the line. They were both dressed in white, and the woman wore a small white cap and carried a tray. Lev stopped a distance away and did not disturb them. He figured they were caregivers, perhaps a doctor and nurse.

When they came from the last tent, Lev called, "Hello."

The man turned to him and gestured sternly. "Stop!" he shouted. The man and woman hurried to Lev. "This area is off limits," said the man. He wore a stethoscope around his neck and looked very tired. "These are sick people. Very contagious."

"My aunt is a patient here," said Lev. "Not my real aunt, but pretty much family. I've come a long way."

"That's different," said the doctor. "They're supposed to tell us when a visitor is expected. But that doesn't happen."

The woman said, "What's your aunt's name?" She touched a pencil to a pad of paper on the tray she held.

Lev looked at the paper and saw a list of names he thought corresponded to the patient in each tent. Then he raised his eyes and met the plain, honest face of the woman who was much younger than he expected. She could not be more than a few years older than him, perhaps less. She smiled warmly and returned her attention to the list.

"Elizaveta Aluşta," he said.

The doctor interjected, "The Russian woman?"

"Yes," said Lev.

"Oh." The doctor stepped closer. He put a hand on Lev's shoulder. "She passed away yesterday. I'm sorry."

Lev looked at the nurse, at her pencil, at the list. Elizaveta's name wasn't on that paper, just as she wasn't in any of the tents. Which one had she occupied? He looked through the tents at the church and tried to guess how much time Elizaveta had spent gazing at it, and if it had brought her comfort.

He lifted his head to the sky and shielded his eyes from the sun. He searched for a cloud but found none.

"I have a letter from her," he said. "She was getting better."

The nurse let the pencil fall to the tray. "She was a nice lady," she said in a voice Lev thought was lovely and musical.

A striped lizard caught Lev's attention. It moved fast, stopped, then scurried away into a low shrub. The ground looked cracked and dry. When had it last rained? A door closed somewhere down the street from where he'd come, and Lev wondered if someone was going in or out.

A cough came from one of the tents. He smelled the fragrance of citrus and smoke from a nearby creosote plant. Lev looked to the three crosses atop the church and decided its god should have kept better watch on the tents. Maybe the sanatorium should have been set closer to the church so that the Catholic saints could better appreciate what was happening.

• • •

She said her name was Adelita, and that she wasn't a nurse. "I'm a volunteer with the church. The patients call me nurse, but I don't correct them."

"Adelita," Lev repeated.

"It sounds like your aunt's name. Maybe that's why she was nice to me."

Lev walked next to her as she skirted the tents and crossed the cleared desert to the church. He listened to Adelita talk and tried to take an interest in her name, but he was distracted. Not about Elizaveta. He was sad for her, yes, but he sent his thoughts to Natalya and wondered how he would get a message to her.

Adelita led him to the back of the church, where they entered a door, walked down a narrow hallway, and into a musty storage room that was stacked high with boxes.

"So many," said Lev.

"Nobody comes for them," said Adelita. "It's heartbreaking. They had mothers and children and lives. They struggled and worked hard. But now their possessions are abandoned."

A box by the door was labeled *E. Alușta*. She removed its top. "I'll give you some privacy."

Lev watched her leave and felt kindness dissipate with her. That she would volunteer to comfort dying people said much about her character. *When have I been so unselfish?*

The box was less than half full. A few articles of clothing. Three smooth stones. Two books—*Chto délat?* by Nikolai Chernyshevsky, and *The Desert* by John C. Van Dyke. An ivory hairpin. A small, badly tarnished silver horse.

Lev stared into the box as if it held a rare animal. He tried to get a sense for Elizaveta but could not find a place in his heart where he could mourn her properly. He wished he had arrived a few days earlier. Maybe then, after meeting her, she would be more than a name and a few sterile objects. But now, as he considered her random possessions, he felt foolish for coming so far to find her. What did he expect? That she would bring him into her life and be a surrogate parent? That she would be living in a comfortable house with an extra bedroom for him? That he would find meaningful work and come home each day to a warm, delicious dinner?

Adelita came into the room. "Do you need more time?"

"No," he said. "Is it permitted for me to take a few of these things?"

"Of course," she said.

Lev slipped the books, hairpin, and silver horse into his bag. "There are rocks in here."

"She enjoyed taking walks in the desert when she was feeling well enough and it wasn't too hot," said Adelita. "She was always in great spirits when she returned. Sometimes she would come back with an unusual rock."

Lev chose one of the smooth stones and placed it in his bag. "It's heavy now," he said, but he could as well have been referring to his head, which now felt full and lethargic.

"I wish you weren't so sad," said Adelita.

"I'm not."

"I know sad," she said. "I see it every day. I saw it last year when my abuela died."

"Abuela?"

"Yes, my grandmother. You seem so sad, Lev. It's fine to admit it."

"I wasn't sad until you said that."

"Sorry."

"I didn't know her."

"You would have liked her."

"I suppose."

"She had a sweet soul. A little noisy. Funny, like you."

"There's nothing sweet about me," said Lev.

"I see you trying to be brave and hold yourself together in front of me. That qualifies."

Lev, tired and overwhelmed, put his bag on the floor and looked into the box at what remained of Elizaveta's meager belongings. He felt his life deflating.

"I have nowhere to go."

"Yes, you do," said Adelita.

29

A delita lived with her parents and grandfather in one of the small adobe homes that Lev had passed earlier. It was identical to the other houses on the street, whitewashed and modest, with a screened sleeping porch and untouched desert landscape.

As they approached the house, Lev said, "Are you sure your parents won't mind? Do you have room?"

"We'll make room," she said.

As they entered the house, Adelita called, "Mamá, we have a guest."

It was a house no bigger than his home in Komenska. It opened into a small living area adjacent to a tiny kitchen with mosaic-tiled counters. Prominently displayed on a shelf was a porcelain statue of Jesus with a crown of thorns and red paint on his head and hands. Beneath was a much larger shelf crammed with dozens of faded photos of dead relatives.

Seated below this altar in a green, thread-worn cushioned chair was a very old man with a great tuft of white hair gathered into a greased curl. He pointed at Lev and grunted.

"My abuelo, Zoilo," said Adelita. "He can't hear well, and he's not very nice. But I love him, of course." Adelita went to him and kissed his forehead. "Abuelo, how was your day?"

"*Mi día fue una mierda*," he said. "Like always. Who is that with you, the painter? I can do it myself. He doesn't know what to do, and he's bothering me. Tell him to go away or I will shove my cane so far up his ass, his eyes will pop out. I am not too old."

"He's not the painter," said Adelita.

"What?"

"He's not the painter. He's a guest."

"I don't care who he is," said Zoilo. "I resent him. I'll take him outside and beat him until he cries for his mother."

"Don't mind him," said Adelita to Lev. "He was like this even before my abuela died."

A woman came into the room from the hall. She looked much like Adelita, though older and a bit heavier. She looked tired.

"My mother, Isadora," said Adelita.

"Another guest?" she said.

"This is Lev," said Adelita. "He came all the way here from Russia to see his aunt in the hospital, but she went to Heaven before he arrived."

"Oh, my dear boy," she said. She opened her arms and hugged Lev. "You are welcome here." She smelled like flour. She held him for a long time and patted the back of his neck. "We'll feed you. You'll feel better."

"I am imposing," said Lev. "I should go."

"Lev, do you know what the Bible says about strangers?" asked Isadora. "Not that you're a stranger, but if you were, I mean."

"Please don't quiz him," said Adelita. "He can't recite chapter and verse by heart like you."

Ignoring her daughter, Isadora said, "Hebrews 13:2. It teaches that we must show hospitality to strangers because they might be angels without us being aware."

"I'm not an angel," said Lev.

"How do you know?" said Isadora.

"I think I'd know."

"Would a true angel tell us who he was? Of course not. We would expect you to deny it. Whether you're a messenger or a guardian, you wouldn't admit it."

"If anyone is an angel, I think it would be your daughter," said Lev to Isadora.

"True," said Isadora. "But if you were the Lord's angel, we would be eternally damned if we sent you away."

"I swear I'm not an angel," said Lev. "Would a real angel lie?"

"If it was a test of our faith, yes."

"She's serious," said Adelita. "You can't reason with her. You're staying."

• • •

A grating racket of gravel and hooves reverberated through the house. Adelita hurried outside.

Her father was sitting with eight other men in an open wagon drawn by two mud-brown horses. Lev and Isadora watched through the window as a tall, fit man climbed from the wagon. Broad shouldered, he wore a wide-brimmed cowboy hat, jeans, and a denim long-sleeve shirt. He moved slowly, clearly fatigued from work, but he smiled lovingly at Adelita.

She said something to him as the wagon pulled away, and his face turned dark. He ripped the hat off his head, flung it to the ground, and kicked it. Adelita retrieved the hat, brushed off the dirt, and gave it back to her father, who shook his head and wagged his finger at his daughter.

"Don't worry," said Isadora. "Gonzalo is tired and hungry."

"He hates me already," said Lev.

"He hates the *idea* of you," she said. "Don't worry. Compliment him on his boots and you'll be fine."

The door opened and Adelita came into the house, rolling her eyes. Behind her, walking slow and with purpose, was her father, Gonzalo, his face weathered and pockmarked. He stopped in the doorway and sighed. "This is how a man finds his castle? With another stranger, a gringo at that, who comes to eat his food and take advantage of his family."

From his chair, Zoilo said, "*No necesitamos un pintor. ¡Escúchame!*"

"We speak English in this house, Papá," said Gonzalo.

"Keep saying it," said Zoilo.

Gonzalo walked straight to Lev, inches away. "You," he said. "What do you want?"

"Nothing," said Lev.

"You desire my daughter, don't you? Admit it and I will respect you. I'll kill you, yes, but at least you'll have my respect."

"Papá," said Adelita. "Stop it. You're embarrassing us."

Gonzalo looked hard into Lev's eyes. "He's a shrewd one, he is. His accent is the giveaway."

"I appreciate your hospitality, and I am sorry if you think I have harmed you," said Lev. "I'll be going now."

Lev turned to leave, but Isadora rushed in front of him and barred the door. "Over my dead body," she said. "Apologize to this young man immediately."

"What have I done that requires an apology?" said Gonzalo, incredulous. "Anyone can see what is going on."

"The only thing that's going on is you being stupid," said Isadora.

Gonzalo took a step back. "Do you see what he has brought into my house? He has already turned my daughter and wife against me. An exhausting day at the mills, and this is my reward."

"Your reward will be sleeping on the floor," said Isadora.

Gonzalo raised his hands above his head and looked up. "Save me, Jesus," he said. He pointed at Lev. "I've got my eye on you." Then he turned and walked away.

"Thank you," said Lev. "You have a beautiful home. I admire your boots."

Gonzalo stopped and turned to face Lev again. "A man who knows fine things must have redeeming qualities," he said. "But tell me, did my conniving wife tell you to say that?"

Lev shook his head. "No." But then he quickly pivoted. "I mean, yes."

Gonzalo nodded and smiled broadly. "In every den of thieves, there is one honest man," he said. "You may stay. You sleep on the porch. My Adelita? Locked in her room."

● ● ●

The soup had been simmering since the afternoon in a huge iron pot. It was filled with onions, bell peppers, corn, tomatoes, mushrooms, chipotle peppers, potatoes, a chicken leg, and an assortment of powders and spices. Adelita helped her mother ladle the soup into bowls and garnish them with chopped avocados and crispy fried tortilla pieces. The first bowl was delivered to Zoilo, who had not moved from the chair where Lev had first encountered him.

The steaming bowls were set on the small kitchen table just as Gonzalo entered the room. He was wearing a fresh white shirt, and his black hair was slicked back. When they were seated, Isadora closed her eyes and bowed her head.

"Jesus," she said. "Thank you for putting food on our table when so many others are hungry. Thank you for nourishing our souls. We are blessed tonight with one of your wayward children and are honoring you and him with shelter and food. Thank you for these gifts. Amen."

"Amen," said Lev.

"You might be an angel, don't forget," said Adelita.

Gonzalo tapped a spoon on the rim of his bowl to get Lev's attention. "Do you believe in God?"

Lev believed it was a trick question, but he answered it anyway. "Yes."

"Which one?" said Gonzalo.

"This is very good soup," said Lev to Isadora.

"Thank you," said Isadora. "Every house on the street is probably having the same thing tonight."

"It's delicious all the same."

"Not if you have it almost every day," said Adelita.

"I would," said Lev.

"You're a very polite young man," said Isadora. "Isn't he, Gonzalo?"

"I suppose." Gonzalo shook his spoon at Lev. "You didn't respond to my question. You purposely didn't answer."

"My father said I should not talk about religion with people I don't know well."

"I see," said Gonzalo. "I welcome you into my house, I put food in your belly, but I'm not good enough to share your beliefs."

Lev, ashamed, said, "I'm sorry. You're right."

Gonzalo straightened and appeared proud. "You see, Izzy? I'm right about something. When was the last time those words were uttered in this house?"

"Men," said Isadora.

"But I'm not unreasonable," said Gonzalo. "If you don't want to talk about your god, that's fine. Tell me about your parents, then. Do they know you're wandering this desert wasteland?"

"They don't know," said Lev.

"I see."

"Leave the boy alone," said Isadora.

"I wouldn't let my children run around the world unsupervised," said Gonzalo. "I'm not judging, only observing. But it's different for young men. My daughter? I've learned not to let her out of my sight. She was born here, and she'll grow old here, watching after us as we age and become feeble. That's what daughters are for. Sons? Not so much, I think. But look at me—I'm taking care of my father. See how content he is over there? He's got his *ofrendas* and everything he needs to bring meaning to his life. If he lives to be a hundred and ten, he will always have a place in our house."

Lev wasn't paying attention to Gonzalo. He was unhappy with his deception by omission. "My parents are dead," he said. "I should have said so."

No one spoke. The only sound was Zoilo's loud chewing. Lev looked into his soup and wished he could shrink and disappear into it, not to drown but to hide behind a potato.

After a long time, Adelita said, "I'm sorry. That's a terrible thing. You have lost so much."

Lev could not bring himself to raise his head. He did not want pity, nor did he want them to see his watery eyes. He brought the spoon into his mouth and let the spicy flavors bring him comfort.

"Some people are forced to grow up faster than others," said Gonzalo. "It is that way for you, eh?"

"Yes." Lev finally lifted his head. Isadora's face was wet, and Adelita touched his forearm without saying anything. Lev turned to Gonzalo and saw a different man. There was warmth in his eyes.

Gonzalo put his spoon down on the table. "What are you doing tomorrow?"

"I haven't thought that far ahead," said Lev. He wondered if he had enough money for the trip back to New York.

"I am thinking that you should join me at work. Some of the mills are in bad shape. You're not afraid of hard work, are you?"

"No, sir," said Lev.

"Good," said Gonzalo. "It's settled. If you do a respectable job, Señor Londos may throw a coin your way."

3 0

The Londos Ranch was an hour from the nearest town. Set in a nearly flat valley between jagged peaks, the cattle ranch's two hundred square miles of scrub and cactus were home to more snakes and gila monsters than people. The ranch's harsh, unspoiled land warned visitors away with its rugged desolation, but a shallow underground water table produced clear, fertile grazing at the heart of the property.

The ride to the ranch was bumpy and uncomfortable. Lev was crammed into the back of the wagon with a dozen men who looked at him suspiciously. They talked mostly in Spanish. Gonzalo translated now and then.

"They don't like you," he said. "But they don't like most people. Don't worry about it. They think you're soft, like all gringos. They're taking bets on whether a mill will slice off your fingers or your head."

The horses pulled the wagon gingerly over a cattle guard, past fences threaded with rusted barbed wire, and to the gated entrance to the ranch. They were met by a huge chestnut Belgian draft that blocked the trail. Atop the horse sat an imposing man who did not look dwarfed by the huge horse. He was entirely bald, except for thick white sideburns, and was dressed all in black but for tan rattlesnake-skin boots and a vermilion bandana around his neck.

Gonzalo nudged Lev and said, "Señor Londos."

"*Buenos dias, amigos,*" said Londos. "Three and seven aren't pulling. Get 'em repaired and up to capacity. Two on each. The rest of you, meet at the feedlot and gathering pens. There will be metal work today. A fair day's work, a fair day's wage." Londos squinted and looked over the men. "Who's the white boy?"

"He's with me," said Gonzalo, raising his hand. "He's a very hard worker, Señor Londos. I vouch for him."

"You vouch for him?" said Londos. "It's a big responsibility when one man vouches for another. A serious thing. I have too many other troubles to worry about him."

"I will watch for him," said Gonzalo.

"You and the boy on seven, then," said Londos. "It needs the most attention. Don't disappoint me." He turned his horse, which lifted its tail and jettisoned six green loafs of manure as it trotted away.

The wagon followed the trail and turned south at a fork. Lev tried to decide if the land was beautiful or ugly. It could be either, he decided. Although there was a wide variety of flora, they were repetitive and formless figures, like a legion of dead warriors sprouting from devastation. This would be a frightening place to be under a new moon. But in its openness and simplicity, the desert was also welcoming. The limitless blue sky met the ground as if to afford every possibility, and the air smelled fresh and full of hope.

Lev tried to rest until Gonzalo tugged at his collar. "We're here."

Lev opened his eyes and was startled by the behemoth above him. It was a massive, forty-foot-tall windmill, all wood and metal and angles that appeared to erupt from the ground like a sentinel keeping watch over the valley. The tower was constructed entirely of chunky eight-by-eight wood boards as thick as trees. A ladder was built into its front, which led to a small platform immediately below the open-gear mechanism that was turned by two dozen curved-sheet steel blades that fanned out twenty feet from its eye. A fat horizontal tail opposite the blades looked like a proud flag. It was emblazoned with STOVER MFG CO., FREEPORT, ILL.

• • •

Lev and Gonzalo hopped from the wagon, which continued down the trail, taking all sound with it except the struggle of the tower's wood as the wind blew through its timbers.

"She's a beauty, wouldn't you say?" said Gonzalo.

"It's big," said Lev.

"Because the wind is up there. More of it. No wind, no pumping, no water. Dead cows. This is everything. It brings life to the desert. Now, Lev, you heard Señor Londos. This is mill number seven. He says it needs attention. This is your first lesson. Tell me what's wrong with it."

Lev looked up at the windmill and tried to discern its problem. It appeared strong and mighty. The wood was in good shape. The blades all seemed evenly spaced. Nothing was hanging, odd, or out of place. "Maybe this is the wrong one."

"Try again."

Lev stepped closer and touched the tower. The wood felt warm. He looked up the central pipe and didn't notice anything that might suggest a problem. He walked around the windmill looking for signs of a leak. Nothing. "I don't know anything about windmills," said Lev. "What am I missing?"

Gonzalo sighed and sat on the ground, his back against the tower. "Sit."

Lev did as he was told. "I've disappointed you."

"Quiet," said Gonzalo. "The secret to pleasing a boss is to look busy, but only when they are watching. Don't try so hard." He reached into his front shirt pocket and withdrew a pack of Lucky Strikes. He shook the pack and offered one to Lev.

"I don't smoke."

"You will," said Gonzalo. He lit a cigarette and enjoyed smoking it for a few minutes. "You are different than the others Adelita has brought home."

"Others?"

"Like stray dogs, she brings them home. She was always that way. Dogs, cats, once an injured rabbit. But people, many of them, total strangers, she invites them to our table. Leeches at heart, all of them. I am not complaining. I am happy to help people. And my wife— well, you know this is true—every person she meets is a sign from Jesus. Adelita knows this. She uses her mother. You think I don't see? Last month, there were three before you—pitiful people, wanderers, vagabonds, all needing a legitimate hand. A warm meal. A place to sleep. She meets them through the church or the hospital."

"Her empathy is a reflection of you," said Lev.

"You are a simpleton," said Gonzalo. "You observe a mill but don't see the obvious. You come to a foreign place without a plan. And you look at Adelita with the same blind eye. People will take advantage of you."

"I can take care of myself," said Lev.

"Time will tell," said Gonzalo.

The two of them sat in silence. A grayish-blue scrub jay landed a few feet in front of them. It pecked at the ground and ran under a gangly bush.

"He's looking for bugs," said Gonzalo. "Maybe a seed, if he's lucky." He twisted his cigarette into the ground to extinguish it. "I was sorry to hear about your parents."

Lev picked up a pebble and tossed it at a cactus. "It feels like a long time ago, only it wasn't."

"Time is like that," said Gonzalo. "It can fool you. How did they die? We don't have to talk about it if you wish."

"Fire."

"Did you see them?"

"No."

"Then how do you know?"

"I saw the house burning."

"Only things seen can be known," said Gonzalo. "I have experience with this. Your parents—if you did not see them perish, then it did not happen. You may believe they died, but it is not for certain. They may have left the house before you saw it on fire. How do you know they were home? What you see is what you can prove. Like Londos. He says he is going to pay me. I work, or pretend to work, and so have earned what is coming. But until the money is in my hand, he hasn't paid me. That is why I don't like banks. If I put my money there, how do I know it is truly in the vault? It isn't. It is only written on a piece of paper that says I have money there. That proves nothing. And if the bank is robbed, where does my money go?"

"You can't go through life without having faith or trusting people," said Lev.

"So far, I have."

"I couldn't live that way."

"Has it always worked out the way you wanted?"

"Not always."

"Two months ago, Adelita brought a man to the house. He seemed nice. Older than you. Was a little sick but did not have consumption. The doctors sent him away. He sat at our table, just as you. He ate the same soup. Told tremendous stories. Had a secret flask with whiskey that he shared with me. I liked him, I must admit. He stayed for three days and was the most entertaining guest we'd ever hosted. But the night before he was to leave, a strange sound woke me from sleep. I caught them in the back fucking like possessed animals. They didn't stop when they saw me. Not him. Not Adelita. I threw a shovel at them, which ended their pleasure. I went back to bed. He was gone in the morning. All he left us was a pregnant daughter."

"Adelita?"

"Who else? The man never came back. Adelita did not come out of her room for weeks. I would not have believed it could be true unless I saw it with my own cursed eyes. Reality, or at least what passes for it, exists only when seen."

"I didn't know," said Lev.

"Of course not. Who was going to tell you? You didn't see it, so it didn't happen. Now, my friend, look up and see with your own eyes that the wind is not turning the mill. That is the problem."

• • •

"There's a dozen reasons that mills won't turn," said Gonzalo. "A broken or slipped gear. A cracked rod. I've seen them freeze up on a cold morning. Once, the wind ripped through here so hard the tail bent nearly in half. These old mills are tough as nails, but everything has its breaking point and nothing lasts forever. Now, up the ladder with you."

Lev wasn't sure the ladder was entirely safe. It was very narrow and went almost straight up with hardly any pitch. He looked at Gonzalo.

"Don't be scared," said Gonzalo. "Up."

"I didn't say I was scared."

"Fearless people make mistakes. The sooner you start, the faster it will be over."

"What do you want me to do when I make it up?"

"Tell me what you see."

Lev put his hands on the rails and looked through the tower's wooden skeleton that framed the still desert at odd angles. Then he stepped on the first rung and began to climb. He should have been thinking about ensuring his feet were planted well, or focused on not looking down. It would have been best if he'd stayed in communication with Gonzalo. But he did none of these things and was not aware of his progress or where he was, because his mind was on Adelita.

He could not reconcile the beautiful and caring person with Gonzalo's description of what happened in the backyard. Her lover must have been strong and persuasive. Had she sought seclusion in her room because she was ashamed, or because she missed him? Lev did not judge her; he had surrendered to the allure of the Kharkov sisters and Gerta's overused bed. Nor did he discount his unrequited desire for Dorete. Every person who ever lived was evidence of a moment of passion. By the time he reached the top of the tower and pulled himself up to the small, precarious platform, he wanted to be with Adelita, to comfort her, to listen to her story, to make sure she knew she wasn't alone.

From below, Gonzalo's voice was a faint echo. "Well?"

Lev turned to the housing and saw that one of the wooden boards covering the gear assembly was hanging by a nail. He peered inside and saw that an animal had found its way inside. Large, egg-shaped droppings were scattered inside, each with small bits of bone showing. Feathers were everywhere. With a deep sense of dread, Lev inspected the mechanism and saw that a colossal owl had been drawn into the gears. Dried blood coated the metal casing. Sickened, Lev sank to his knees, holding tight to the tower.

"What is it?" called Gonzalo.

Lev, eyes closed, said, "Owl."

"What?"

"Owl," he said louder.

"That explains it," said Gonzalo. "Seen it before. Probably a mess up there, but easily solved. Pull it out. All you can. Watch your fingers. You hear me? Careful. Let caution guide your spirit. When you get it out, the wind will start turning the mill and those gears will pull you in if you're not alert."

"With my hands?"

"God gave them to you," said Gonzalo.

Lev stood, leaned inside the open housing, and was met by a terrible odor that made him gag. The owl's large head was hanging limply from the gears, its eyes shut as if dreaming. Lev tugged gently on the bird's head, but it would not come free, so he grabbed it tightly with both hands, his fingers sinking into flesh. He twisted and pulled until it came away with a grotesque snap. He threw it behind him and it bounced off the tower to the ground. The windmill hadn't turned.

"Great horned owl," said Gonzalo. "Beautiful animal. A shame. Get the rest of it."

Where the owl's shaggy head had been, a thick bone protruded from gears like a planted flag. Gonzalo's warning returned to him: *Let caution guide your spirit.* Lev touched the bone. He poked at it. It seemed steady. He put a hand on top and began to push and pull until it gave a little. He worked the bone back and forth until there was an ominous groan and the metal gears began to turn. Lev moved his hands away just as the bone was pulled deep into the gears with a terrible crunch.

"It's moving!" said Gonzalo.

Lev, sweating profusely, rested on the platform as the great windmill came to life and began turning. His hands were covered in blood, and he wiped them on the platform until he could see his skin and dry them enough to be able to climb down the tower.

Londos, astride his horse, came up the trail as Lev touched ground. He brought the horse to a halt a few paces behind the owl head, which had already been swarmed by red ants. "You're a good judge of character, Gonzalo," he said. "Tomorrow morning, check all the wood up there. Replace everything if necessary. Make sure it's strong. Good for the cattle. Good for the owls. After that, both of you, see me at the main house at noon. I may have more work for you."

● ● ●

Lev and Gonzalo returned home that evening, spent but in good spirits. After a modest meal, Lev excused himself so that he could meet Adelita at the tent sanatorium to walk her home. She was working late to clean three tents whose occupants had died that day. Lev saw discouragement on her face when he arrived.

"It was nice of you to come, but I know the way home."

"It's dark," said Lev. "Your mother asked me to do it."

"She thinks I'm still twelve years old."

"Mothers worry about their children, no matter their age," said Lev. They walked by the church that appeared iridescent in the moonlight, the tents like a dilapidated train. "Your father and I will be gone for a few days."

"I know."

"He's been kind to me."

"He's fond of you," said Adelita.

"Is he that way with everyone? Are you?"

"Am I what?" said Adelita.

"Always so nice."

"That's not what you want to know," she said. "Be honest. What are you asking?"

Lev dug his hands in his pockets and kicked a small rock. "Nothing."

"You didn't come here because of my mother."

"No," he admitted.

"My father told you, didn't he?"

"Told me what?"

"You know," she said. "About me. About what's inside of me. Your face tells me that you know."

Lev hesitated, then said, "He told me."

"I don't need you to feel sorry for me."

"I don't."

"You do," she said. "I can hear it in your voice. My father feels the same way, but he is more ashamed than concerned. He won't talk about it. He would rather me disappear to a convent until the baby comes."

"And your mother?" asked Lev.

"She is worried. She thinks I'll be a spinster, that no one will want to be with me. She's probably right."

Lev opened his hand and invited her to take it. "I came here because I wanted to be with you," he said.

"I know so little about you," said Adelita. "You are like a riddle. My mother says you have a pain that eats up everything else. A pain that takes over your voice and doesn't allow you to speak. You are quiet."

"People say that, I know," said Lev. "But the pain you speak about? You know it too, I think."

Adelita turned away. "What do you want?" she said.

"To be with you," said Lev. "I'm sorry for what I said."

Adelita was quiet for a moment, then said, "Don't be sorry."

Lev touched her shoulder and she turned back to him.

"Our pain, they cancel each out each other," he said.

"I look in your eyes and see so many things," said Adelita.

"What?"

"I don't know. But they tell a story."

"What story do they tell?" asked Lev.

She shrugged. "But they are honest eyes."

"I will always be truthful with you," said Lev. "I promise." He again offered his hand.

Adelita looked at his hand, at his face, then at his hand again. She pressed her palm against his, and they walked quietly without talking.

31

ondos was sitting on a padded rocking chair on the porch of his sprawling ranch house when Gonzalo and Lev arrived the next day. He was smoking an ivory pipe. Beside him was a tall, unlabeled bottle of amber whiskey.

"Pretty close to being on time," he said. "That's a good thing."

"The mill is tip-top," said Gonzalo. "You won't have any more problems with it."

"No problems?" said Londos wistfully. He puffed on the pipe. "If that were only true." He picked up the bottle and offered it to Gonzalo, who accepted it and took a generous swig. "My wife has refused to live here during the summer. Says it's too remote and too hot and too much work and too many coyotes crying at night. Too much of everything, she likes to say. So she stays in Tucson with her parents. I'd do the same if I could. But it gets lonely out here, being just me most nights. But the land needs attention. If I didn't have good workers, this place would fall apart like Lee at Appomattox. I've been drinking."

Gonzalo gave the bottle to Lev, who drank as well. It was warm and bitter. "You have a nice place, Mr. Londos," he said.

"Mister?" said Londos. "I haven't been called that since I can remember. Sounds so civilized."

Gonzalo took the bottle from Lev and gave it back to Londos. "You have more work for us, señor?" asked Gonzalo.

"Work, you say?" said Londos. "That's all I've got around here. My father, when he staked the property—got rights for a song from Washington when this was a territory—I hardly saw him until my hands were big enough to be of use to him. He'd be out before dawn and wouldn't come home until dark. I don't know how my mother managed being alone so much. Probably what gave her that tumor. That's why I don't blame my wife for staying Tucson-ways. But I miss the hell out of her. Got a letter yesterday from her and it appears she feels the same. I talk too much."

"I know what it's like to miss someone," said Lev.

Londos looked hard at Lev. "You're different than most others 'round here. You talk funny, but that ain't it. Can't put my finger on it. But you don't seem intimidated. Not sure if I should like or hate you for it. But no matter. There's something about you, though. Saw it in a guy from Philadelphia once. Older than you. Came out here to survey for copper. He had a similar look about him. The same attitude. Not sure of the word—maybe confident. Is that how you'd describe yourself?"

"I wouldn't try to describe myself," said Lev.

"That's what I mean," said Londos. "But I won't hold it against you. I saw something in you when you were climbing down the windmill yesterday. The job you did. I'm a good judge of character if I'm anything. Isn't that right, Gonzalo?"

"Sí, of course," said Gonzalo. "That is what we always say, that you are a very good judge of character. Absolutely."

"Did you hear that?" Londos said to Lev. "Of course, my good friend Gonzalo here would agree with anything I said. What he says is meaningless. But that's fine. He's honest and a hard worker. That's about the most you can expect from anyone these days."

"We can come back tomorrow," said Gonzalo.

"Because I've had a bit too much? Ha! I could drink you so far under the table you wouldn't be able to smell your socks. Follow me."

Londos led them around the house and past the branding pen, barn, and a corral with four horses. They walked east down a narrow, worn path to where a majestic mesquite threw shade over a small private graveyard and its four white crosses. Lev thought it was a beautiful place to rest, with nothing but open desert between them and the mountains far away, where the sun rose each day.

"My parents and sisters," said Londos. "All died too young."

"It's nice here," said Gonzalo.

"I come here nearly every day," said Londos. "I paint their markers once a year."

"It's a blessing to love someone that much," said Lev.

Londos looked at Lev. "You're an old man already, to think like that," he said. "You haven't been out here long enough to be corrupt and hardened."

"My mother used to tell me that it doesn't cost anything to show kindness."

"Where did you find him?" Londos asked Gonzalo.

"He found me, señor."

Londos nodded. "Huh." Then he pointed toward the mountains. "The ranch extends to the hills below the rise. But it's threatened. Everything you see is falling away. The government wants to grab a large part. They say I'm not working enough cattle. And even then, my grazing rights are about to go through the roof. And out that way, at the edge of what's rightfully mine, is a small house my father built. But I can't tend it—haven't been out there since I don't know when. Wouldn't surprise me if the Apache have claimed it. I don't blame them for getting upset at being uprooted and placed on reservations. Some of them are pushing back. They're not aggressive like they once were, but they're smart. I'd probably do the same if I could get away with it. But I can't lay down and let 'em eat at what my father fought for. So if you're up for it, if you're the men I think you are, light out there tomorrow and set about fixing up the place. It'll need a bit of work. I need to demonstrate that I'm working the full property, and I don't want to give the feds an excuse."

• • •

Gonzalo and Lev sat next to each other on the front wooden bench of the wagon Londos prepared for them. The wagon, drawn by two strong quarter horses, was heavily laden with lumber, fasteners, and tools. Gonzalo held the reins and encouraged the horses to keep a steady pace. Lev pulled a bandana over his mouth and nose to keep from breathing the dust kicked up by the horses.

"I am not a superstitious man, but you are good luck to me," said Gonzalo. "If this goes well, Señor Londos might give me a permanent job."

"I'm happy for you," said Lev.

"It would mean stability and more money. Londos takes care of his team. I had mostly given up."

"It doesn't have anything to do with me."

"You are a modest man. He has his eye on you. I can tell. And me, by association. No more piecemeal windmill work. No more weeks of being turned away at the ranch because he doesn't have work. This can change our lives."

"I will try not to disappoint you, I promise."

"I have a feeling that your promises are certain," said Gonzalo.

A gathering monsoon filled the sky with cloud cover, which pushed the temperature down into the low nineties and made the open desert bearable. It also made the country feel more compact and dangerous, as if an oppressive hand from God might break through the clouds and grab an offending traveler.

• • •

As they drew close to the mountains, Gonzalo kept the horses true to the trail that narrowed into a gulley, crossed a dry stream, and climbed a steep incline to a brush-filled plain. There, set back against a gentle hill, was a building that appeared to be nothing more than a storage shed. Even at a distance, it was apparent that it was in bad shape. A person was sitting on a chair on the shaded side of the structure.

"Apache," said Gonzalo. "Be careful."

The full devastation of the building became clear as they grew closer. Decayed wood was strewn about the site, and the windows were void of any panes or covering. The front door was missing, and a portion of the tin roof had fallen inside.

"*Desastre*," muttered Gonzalo.

The person they saw from a distance was revealed to be an ancient woman. Her face bore the wear of years of sun exposure, but her lake-blue eyes were alive with youth. She wore a faded yellow buckskin dress with purple fabric sewn into its neck. The front of her dress was adorned with delicate beading, and her sleeves ended in a dramatic flurry of fringe.

"I've been waiting for you," she said slowly, deliberately, as if each word was only now discovered.

"You didn't know we were coming," said Gonzalo.

"Gazie knows," she said.

Gonzalo said, "Maybe you heard the wagon from a distance, but you didn't know it was us."

"Believe what you wish," said Gazie. "Londos sent you. You're here to make repairs."

"Then he told you!" Gonzalo huffed.

"I've been here since before you were born, before your parents knew each other. I've walked this land back and forth, in and out. I've mastered the wind and rain, the smallest insect and the mountain lion. News reaches me from every corner. And you bring a stranger with you from another world."

Gonzalo climbed down from the wagon and watered the horses. "You can stay for a while," he said. "We have work to do."

Gazie stood and pointed a long, boney finger at Gonzalo. "No one needs your permission," she said. "You talk as if you own this land. You can't own what isn't yours. All that you can see, and all that you can't, once belonged to my people. A piece of paper says it's yours, but that does not make it so. In this world, the unseen has power."

Annoyed, Gonzalo said, "That's none of my business." He stepped inside what was left of the structure.

"You should make it your business," she said, sitting again. "You've made me tired."

"Would you like some water?" said Lev.

"Kindness presents itself," said Gazie. "Yes, please."

Lev retrieved a canteen from the wagon and presented it to Gazie. He knelt beside her. "You shouldn't be out in the heat," he said. "Why are you here?"

"Your friend is intolerant," said Gazie. "But you're different."

"Gonzalo is a good man."

"Perhaps," she said. She closed her eyes as she sipped the water. "I come here sometimes to find memories. It's not what your friend thinks. He's not your father, I can see. He is blind to everything except what others have told him. It's that way with most people; I don't blame him. He thinks a band of our tribe will come rising over the hill, colored in war paint and carrying guns and spears. But those days are over. It's demeaning that he thinks that way."

"I don't believe that's what he thinks. We're here long enough to fix the house, then we'll leave," said Lev. "But others will be coming, I'm sure. Londos doesn't want this place neglected any longer."

"Londos," said Gazie, as if the name were a disease. "He believes the land is his. His family rushed in here and grabbed it, backed up by your government. He's no worse than the others. They come here and throw up a fence, pull water out of the ground, bring cattle that aren't meant for this land. All we have left of this sacred land are these few sticks of wood. Do you know who comes here? Young ones from our tribe. They use it as a plaything, a hideout, a place to have sex beyond their parents' eyes. Me? I come here now and then to sit quietly and think about my parents."

Gonzalo's voice came from the house. "I need your hands."

"I have to go," said Lev. "Will you be okay?"

"You should warn your friend that a rattlesnake makes his home in there, and he likes the place the way it is."

• • •

The rattlesnake wasn't happy being coaxed from the building, but it did not protest. Gonzalo threw water and rocks at it and jabbed it with a long stick while cursing the creature. Uncomfortable and unwanted, the snake slowly crawled outside.

Gonzalo and Lev pulled everything out of the tiny house, including the missing front door, blankets, broken glass, a rusted metal bed frame, and an assortment of bottles and crushed cans. Lev swept out layers of dirt, ants, and scorpions. When everything was out, Lev thought the primitive dwelling could be modestly comfortable, not unlike some of the oldest homes in Komenska. A built-in counter and shelving toward the back appeared to be a place where food could be prepared, and an open area to the right of the door would be enough room for a bed and table.

Uneasy about the rattlesnake, Gonzalo and Lev reattached the door and hammered boards around the inside perimeter to insulate the house and block anything that might seek shelter.

Gazie was interested in what the men were doing. She was in and out of the house while they worked and called attention to bent nails and places where the snake could attempt entry. "This is what happens when people abandon something," she said. "Nature works hard to reclaim it."

In the late afternoon, as the sky grew darker, the men labored to craft farmhouse window shutters that hung outside from top hinges. When down, the wood hung flush against the exterior but could be easily propped open to create shade and ventilation.

Lev checked on Gazie as the day wore on, offering to share water and supplies. She did not accept food, but she sipped from the canteen. "Caring, you are," she said. "Your mother taught you that. Men get strength from their fathers, manners from their mothers."

"My parents would have liked you," said Lev.

"You belong in this place."

"I like the desert," said Lev. "It's peaceful."

"I mean *this* desert. This place. This house."

Later, when the setting sun threw great swaths of bright orange and violet across the sky, Gonzalo lit a lantern and prepared a meal. Lev looked for Gazie but did not find her.

"She should stay away," said Gonzalo.

"I hope she's safe," said Lev.

"People like her live forever. They can't help it. But age and wisdom don't always go together. Don't let her fool you. Look at my father. He was nice, funny, and intelligent until only a few years ago. Now look at him—there's no one as ornery. He's an entirely different person. I'm not saying I don't love him—course I do. But like him? Not so much."

When the rain began, Gonzalo and Lev retreated inside the house, though part of the roof let water in. They made makeshift beds with layered blankets.

As they fell asleep to the sound of harsh rain rattling the tin roof, they were not aware that the rattlesnake returned and tried unsuccessfully to get inside. Thwarted, it slithered away into the darkness, understanding that something had changed.

3 2

They woke to a crisp, quiet desert morning and a blue that had again taken complete possession of the sky. Gonzalo rose first. He opened the door, stepped outside, pushed his hair back, and urinated on a barrel cactus. He walked around the house, then went inside and gently kicked Lev's foot.

"Work is waiting," he said.

Lev was pulled from a dream in which he was pursuing Mishal. They were climbing an infinite ladder, with Mishal many rungs ahead. "Stop trying to catch me," said Mishal. They climbed until the ladder broke through the atmosphere and reached into space and through an orbiting flock of dead owls. Lev slipped from the ladder and fell into the tiny desert house, where flowers had been planted in a window box. He swept out the dirt and removed spiderwebs with a broom.

Fixing the roof was tricky, as they had not brought replacement tin. They worked to straighten what remained of the fallen metal, and then reattached it to a beam that had been compromised from heat and rain. Gonzalo fashioned a temporary truss that reinforced and supported the construction.

"You're good at this," said Lev.

"Either things fit or they don't fit," said Gonzalo.

They brought the bed frame back inside and set it against the wall, swept the house again, and removed the trash pile, discarded items, and remnants of their work. When everything was loaded into the wagon, the men walked a pace away to admire their work.

"It'll do as an outpost," said Gonzalo. "But watch—the moment we leave, Gazie will be back, and within a month it'll fall into shambles again."

They packed and began their journey back. As Gonzalo drove the horses, Lev turned to take a final look at the house and was sure he saw Gazie standing in the doorway. He chose not to say anything to Gonzalo.

"It will be good to get home," said Gonzalo. "Isadora will have something special for our meal, perhaps her most delicious *tres leches* cake. That would make me happy."

A small black speck in the trail ahead became larger and eventually revealed itself to be Londos, seated high in the saddle, his bald head proudly bare, mocking the sun. Gonzalo brought the wagon to a halt as Londos approached.

"I didn't think you would be finished so soon," said Londos. "I was coming to review your work."

"Two hard workers can often do more than four lazy men," said Gonzalo.

"We'll see," said Londos. "You'll be rewarded if the job is well done. Shoddy work? My disappointment will be felt."

"Mr. Londos," said Lev. "My friend Gonzalo has done right by you. He has worked hard, no matter if you approve or not."

"The little bastard has teeth," said Londos.

"He meant nothing by it," said Gonzalo.

"That house needs to be lived in," said Lev.

Londos removed a cigarette from his pocket and lit it with a match he struck on his buckle. His horse swatted flies with its tail. Londos, blocking the trail, smoked the cigarette nonchalantly, blowing rings that floated above his head. "Who do you have in mind?" he said.

• • •

Gonzalo and Isadora did not object to Lev's overture. Surprised, yes, but they would consent if it was Adelita's wish.

"She will never hear a harsh word from my lips," Lev told them.

Gonzalo saw only positives in the arrangement. The small house in the desert wasn't a convent, but it was close. He knew where his daughter would be and was confident she would be respected. A closer tie with Londos was a plus, too. As for Isadora, she had already resigned herself to seeing no suitors for Adelita. And although Lev may not have been an obvious choice—a foreigner, no less—he was kind and resourceful. Zoilo objected, but no one cared.

"We will build a life," said Lev as he made his proposal to Adelita. "It will be hard. It's barely a house. But I promise to expand it. We'll add a bedroom and a separate kitchen. We'll build a courtyard with a great tree that will bear generous shade."

"Do you mind flowers?" asked Adelita.

"I was hoping," said Lev.

"I don't love you," said Adelita, then she added, "yet."

"My parents lived in a world of arranged marriages," said Lev. "Love had to be learned. But maybe we have a head start. It'll be an adventure."

"Perhaps a trial?"

"If you have five seconds of regret, then you'll be back home. No questions."

"All of five seconds?"

"Or less," said Lev. "This is a good place for me to stop. I have been moving too fast for too long."

"Too young," said Adelita.

"I feel old. But for now, this will do." He stepped closer to her and took her hands. "This is what I need. I think it's the same for you. Londos is paying me. We'll have money."

"Don't talk of money," she said. She leaned to kiss him, to see if there was a spark—a connection that would predict compatibility and, with luck, passion.

• • •

There was much to do their first day at the small house at the foot of the mountain. Gonzalo called it an outpost, but Adelita named it La Hacienda, half as a joke and half as aspiration. They emptied the wagon of groceries, supplies, lanterns, clothes, blankets, two folding chairs, and a mattress. More would come. Gonzalo and Isadora promised a table and other necessities. But today, it was only them as they took possession of the house.

"It's small, I know," said Lev.

"What more do we need?" said Adelita.

Later, they set the chairs in front of the house and watched the sun's descent as it painted the sky. They sat, enjoying the dry, warm weather, but said little, each understanding the enormity of what they were doing and afraid to jeopardize it by saying the wrong thing. Instead, they watched the colorful sunset as dusk gave way to night.

Lev took an ivory hairpin from his pocket and gave it to Adelita. "It was Elizaveta's," he said.

"I recognize it," said Adelita. "It's beautiful."

"I thought it would look pretty on you."

"It will," she said. "Thank you."

"I want to give you everything."

"We have time," said Adelita.

They sat in silence as stars appeared. A coyote howled in the distance.

"Have you chosen a name?" asked Lev.

"My father suggests Zoilo, but it's more like a demand."

"What if it's a girl?"

"I don't know yet. What was your mother's name?"

"Vera," said Lev.

"Beautiful," said Adelita. "Tell me something about her."

"She was kind," said Lev. "Determined. Very strong. And pretty. She rarely had cross words with me unless I deserved it."

"Vera," said Adelita.

"If it's a boy—even if it's a girl—don't send it away," said Lev. "Promise me. If you have no choice or if you think it's in the child's best interests, then still don't do it. No matter what."

"I won't," said Adelita. She reached for his hand. "Everything is going to be okay. I won't let anything happen to the child. I promise."

Lev smiled at her and resisted wiping his eyes because he did not want to let go of her hand.

ACKNOWLEDGMENTS

Some of the names used in this novel belonged to real people. Louis F. Peronard was the captain of the SS *Hellig Olav*, a ship of the Scandinavian America Line. Willem Andriessen was a well-known Dutch pianist and composer. Abraham Aaron Yudelovitch was the esteemed rabbi of the Eldridge Street Synagogue (now the Museum at Eldridge Street). But other than adopting these names, their characterization and activities are solely the products of the author's imagination; any resemblance to actual persons, living or dead, or actual events is purely coincidental. Many thanks to Adam Burns of american-rails.com for assisting with the historical accuracy of train schedules that ran between New York and Arizona in the early twentieth century. The author also recognizes Andrew S. Dolkart's excellent book, *Biography of a Tenement House in New York City: An Architectural History of 97 Orchard Street,* published by University of Virginia Press, which helped confirm matters relating to the structure, appearance, and architecture of the Lower East Side where parts of this novel are set.